MW00936204

American Carnage
Tales of Trumpian Dystopia

Edited by

Jennifer King and Paul Brian McCoy

Psycho Drive-In Press

Table of Contents

Introduction: Live to Win 7

What Kind of Monster Are You? 11
by John E. Meredith

The Day the Earth Turned Day-Glo 93
by Rick Shingler

None but the Brave 109
by Dan Lee

Where Eagles Dare 133
by R. Mike Burr

Big Takeover 153
by Paul Brian McCoy

Who We Be 211

Introduction: Live to Win

By Paul Brian McCoy

We bring you UFOs, saucers in the sky
We shoot you full of noise, we aim to kill
We burn like motherfuckers, spit right in your eye
We fight authority, we glorify free will
- Lemmy "We Are Motorhead"

Where were you on November 8, 2016?

Much like the Kennedy Assassination or the Space Shuttle Challenger Disaster, the day real estate mogul and reality TV star Donald Trump was elected President of the United States is a day that will remain anchored in everyone's memories for the rest of their lives. There was much wailing and gnashing of teeth, but many still held out hope that now President-Elect Trump would make a shift to more presidential behavior and rhetoric. Many held out hope that with decent advisors and actual responsibility on the world stage, he might not present himself as a barely-literate lunatic with the codes for nuclear Armageddon and no understanding of international politics.

Then, on January 20, 2017 we got the Inauguration Speech that flatly rejected bipartisanship and served only to ramp up the anger and paranoia of his base; A base already fueled by fear, racism, sexism, and a noticeable lack of self-awareness. Neo-Nazis and White Nationalists lined up to openly declare to the world that Trump was "their president" and that great things were coming for the White race.

This speech became known colloquially as the "American Carnage" speech, as Trump described an America devastated by Islamic terrorists, job-stealing immigrants, and rusted-out factories. Crime was running rampant and he swore to put a stop to this American Carnage. It was an inaugural speech like no other in history. The New York Times put together a list of words from it that had never before been used in an inauguration speech. It included items such as carnage, disrepair, rusted, stealing, ripped, tombstones, and trapped.

Trump seemed to believe, despite all evidence to the contrary, that the Cannon Films *Death Wish 3* and *Invasion U.S.A.* were documentaries about contemporary America rather than ridiculous '80s action/revenge flics.

After hearing the phrase "American Carnage" I knew in an instant what the second PDI Press short story collection needed to be.

In my initial call for stories (in May) I asked for post-Trumpian dystopias in the trash/schlock style of early John Waters films or Lloyd Kaufman's Troma films. To add to the punk rock feel I was looking for, *Repo Man* was also named as an inspiration. Every story was to take its name from a classic punk (or in one case, metal) song, but had to be an original work that spun out from the name without being an adaptation. The plan was to have another line-up of stories as varied and imaginative as *Noirlathotep: Tales of Lovecraftian Crime* (which was published on April 28, 2017) and be ready to publish just before Halloween.

But then life stepped in.

A few writers who had volunteered to contribute stories had to drop out and my own story hit a dead-end that I couldn't get around. It would have been a great screenplay, but as a short story I couldn't figure out a way to make it work. At the same time, I was trying to both write and illustrate a short comic book story about characters from my Damaged Incorporated novel, *The Unraveling*. It turns out that my limitations as an artist are many and after a couple of decent pages, I found myself getting more and more depressed about my shortcomings.

So, hit with the double whammy of choking on my comic and not being able to figure out a way to make my *American Carnage* story work, I became overwhelmed and just gave up on a lot of things.

The problem was, we had four stories already submitted. Three of them didn't really capture the feel I was initially hoping for, but on the plus side, they were *really good stories*. Dan, Mike, and Rick all put together short, dystopian pieces that were better than they had any right to be, so they had to see print. John's story was just as fantastic and really embraced the punk rock splatter horror sci-fi that I was originally hoping to read. I loved all these stories so much it made me feel even worse about my own failings.

And with just the four stories, I didn't really feel like the collection was long enough. We needed at least one more story to really make this an anthology worth paying for. I want to give readers as much bang for their buck as possible, so I pulled my head out of my ass and decided to write a short Damaged Incorporated adventure. As soon I made that choice, my new story appeared in my head practically overnight.

Admittedly, it's not as strong as the other stories, but it is as close to a Troma film as I could come up with and I'm a little in love with it at the moment. I'm sure that'll change, but for right now, I'm happy. And with that fifth story, we have enough solid sci-fi/horror to hopefully make you, dear reader, feel like you haven't wasted your money.

With the stories in place, all that was left was commissioning cover art. We knew that with the punk rock stylings of the stories, we wanted something more like a concert flyer than a traditional book cover, and that's when Psycho Drive-In writer Adam Barraclough suggested his longtime friend, Jimbo Valentine. After a quick look at his website, https://amalgamunlimited.com/, I knew he was the man for the job, and thankfully, he dug the idea of the anthology and hopped on board.

And the rest is future history.

It's a little late. Okay, *a lot* late, but with the help of editor extraordinaire, Jennifer King (who also edited *Noirlathotep*), we are finally ready to release this bad boy into the wild.

We know that a lot of people aren't going to like *American Carnage*, or even give it a fair shake, but to hell with those people. This one's for the people who feel afraid,

9

disenfranchised, and depressed after this traumatizing first year of Trump's term. Every day there's some new controversy, some new low for the office, some new anxiety about our future.

Hopefully, these stories will help alleviate some of that.

Despite being dystopic, there's a lot of heart and most of them have happy endings. Sort of. If you like tentacles, gore, cannibalism, guns, chaos, and punching Nazis in the face.

What Kind of Monster Are You?

By John E. Meredith

"As long as the music's loud enough,
we won't hear the world falling apart."
- Derek Jarman, 1977

The president's head was missing.

When all this shit started, it was the president himself who had disappeared. He was one of those folks who couldn't get enough of his own face and got a boner from hearing his own voice. You'd have imagined him touring the country like he was just so he could leave a little bit of himself everywhere, which is kinda what he did. So, when he suddenly stopped showing up in public a week earlier, it was his absence that made the news. He was still tweeting every morning, the same stupid fuckery as usual, but he'd locked himself in the Oval Office. Not even the vice president or his own kids had seen him.

The news people were saying that he went into hiding because of the strange lights that had shown up over all those cities, or because of the bloody riots that were raging across the country. But he liked that kinda shit too much. He had built his entire presidency, and the billion-dollar empire he had before that, on creating havoc everywhere he went. He was what my sister Lil called *an agent of chaos*, which sounds a hell of a lot cooler than it actually is.

But I knew personally that it was all fucking weirder than anyone had guessed.

Big Mama had the TV blasting all day long, giving us constant updates, whether we wanted them or not. She was always gung-ho for the man and his so-called message about making America great again. But, since he passed through our little shit town over a week ago, she hadn't shut up about him. *He looked right at me*, she said. Meaning from a motorcade going fifty miles an hour. Naturally, she felt some kind of connection as soon as they saw each other.

We were in the middle of supper when they broke in on *The Maury Show*. Mama shushed Pauline and Paw, not that anyone really ever needed to shut him up, and cranked the remote until the newscaster's voice was damn-near shaking the windows.

"*- reports, unconfirmed, that the President has finally been sighted after over a week of virtual seclusion from everyone, including his own family. But the reports are truly bizarre, and White House spokesmen insist that they are just another attempt by the liberal media to impede the progress of a conservative agenda. Democrats have already fired back at the Press Secretary, pointing out that it was the Republican Speaker of the House who made the first claim of having seen the President just a few hours ago.*

"*Speaker:* I was in the Rose Garden when I heard a strange sound, like someone was stumbling about. When I turned to look, I couldn't believe my eyes. It was the President . . . but he . . . *he didn't have a head.* I know how that sounds, but he had no head and yet he was still walking around. I recognized him from the tie he was wearing, because my wife had gotten it for him last Christmas . . . and he had both hands on his phone. By God, he was tweeting. He had no head, but he was still *tweeting . . .*"

"*Both the Press Secretary and the Vice-President have denied the Speaker's candid allegations, citing his recent sessions with a counselor to explore what has been called 'his pathological hatred of the lower class' -*"

"Holy sheep shit," Mama said, "That's the fakest of all fake news. I can't believe how low those liberals will go."

The shit hit the fan before the president lost his head, even before the lights started showing up over all those cities.

When I say shit, I mean the white riots and the government knocking on doors and all the assholes out in the streets with their guns blazing. It was all flag-waving and witchhunts, then folks were punching each other out right there in Congress. Monuments to slavery had gone down all over the country, but then the Nazi flags started coming up. It was like nobody even cared anymore. At first the cops and the Army were trying to keep everything in order, but it all got so fucked-up that even they started turning their weapons on each other. It was American carnage like we'd never seen before. All because of some dumbass president that people were saying wasn't even qualified to run a hotdog stand.

There's only so much you can do when everything goes batshit crazy. So I packed another bowl and pushed the earbuds in a little deeper, cranking the Stooges up as high as they would go. I watched the snow coming down from behind the barn and hoped that Lil got here before the whole goddamn world went up in flames.

We lived in a little town, I shit you not, called Pea Patch. It was named for the veggie, but everybody said it like the thing you do in the shower. That's about all it was worth. There was once some kind of life out here, so they said, but now it was all trailers and scraggly dogs and an hour's drive in any direction to work in one hopeless factory or another.

Paw used to run a pig farm, a long time ago, before the big companies made him close up. *Bankers were the farmer's friend*, he used to say, *but now they all just stab you in the back*. He sold off most of the land and went to work in a slaughterhouse down in Plainwell when I was little. Lil said it was because killing was the only thing that fit his personality, but Paw never seemed that bad to me. He just wasn't big on words. But the house always smelled like pig shit, blood, and broken dreams. Stupid as that sounds, if you'd been there, you'd see I was right.

It was kinda like the farm all over again when they shut down the schools. Something about giving everybody more choices, but there wasn't anything left out where we lived. Everybody here knew bullshit when they smelled it and figured it was rich folks who ended up with those choices. The president himself said *we won with the poorly educated*, and I guess he wanted to make sure he kept on winning.

So I dropped out of tenth grade. It wasn't like a tragedy or anything. If you don't have money to start with, wasn't like going to school would do you any good. Besides, I was too punk for the country kids and too country for the punk kids.

13

Me and the one black guy in the school got along okay, but they pretty much ran his family out of town. That, and the only girl I ever made out with moved away when her dad got a better job in Tennessee. Fuck it, I might as well not waste my time anymore.

I spent a couple weeks getting high with Minor Threat behind the barn. Spent a couple more figuring I'd never get off this big red rocket to nowhere. I didn't even have a damn driver's license, where the hell was I gonna go? Anger burning, I beat on my makeshift drums until my hands were bloody and watched every lousy splatter flick I could find on YouTube. Not much else to do online anymore unless you wanted to meet a bunch of assholes. There was even less to do in the real world . . . not to mention, there were more assholes.

But then I started thinking about when me and Paw used to stay up late to watch those old movies on *Svengoolie*. He still laughed once in a while back then. A couple weeks later, I was pulling old boards off the barn and replacing them with better ones from the wood pile behind the house. Guess I figured I was saving him from having to do it. Not that he ever said shit about school or about the barn.

But then I found something out there.

Something really fucked up.

It was Lil who turned me on to punk. Her name was Lillianna, but she hated that as much as anything else Big Mama ever gave her. So it was just Lil ever since we were kids. She was the coolest fucking person I ever knew. There was this thing she'd always say. I'm pretty sure she got it from a movie or something, but she made it her own. I was still called Jimmy then, so she'd say, *die on your feet, Jimmy, don't live on your knees*. That's about the most punk-rock thing you could ever say to anyone.

She got me high and then got me educated. It was all Ramones and Richard Hell and the Clash for her. *Nobody had ever done anything that bold*, she said, *and those guys just didn't give a fuck*. It was probably those guys who made Lil who she was.

For me it was more about the hardcore scene that came after punk. The Circle Jerks. The Dead Kennedys. Black Flag. They were saying some of the same shit as the bands that got it all started, but they wasted less time getting there. Some folks said it was Reagan that pissed them off so bad, but I figured it was just the new batch of drummers making everything faster. Dudes like Chuck Biscuits and Brooks Wackerman, they were just *maniacs* on the sticks. I didn't know much, but I knew drumming. Call it frustration, or whatever, but pounding on shit always made me feel better. To me, the drums were like the heartbeat of the whole band, and you can't do nothing without a heartbeat.

The one thing me and Lil agreed on was the Stooges.

There was a lot of things that led to punk, but none of it meant shit without the pure anarchy of James Osterberg and his band. Lil thought it was badass how he smeared himself with peanut butter and cut his chest up with broken bottles. For me, though, it was Iggy at King's Cross, packed into those silver pants from the *Raw Power* album cover, dripping sweat, no shirt, and that raccoon eyeliner, climbing all over the audience. They say everybody who was at a Sex Pistols show went out and formed a band. *Maybe.* But Iggy scared Johnny Rotten so bad in '72 that he became the Pistols.

I always figured Lil for that kinda badass.

She was small and didn't look like much, but she wouldn't take shit off no one. She'd call you an asshole right to your face. It became a routine with us before she left for school. She'd look at me and say *don't be such a cunt*, I'd say *no, you are, you're a cunt-shit*, and then she'd laugh and tell me that wasn't even a real thing.

We tried to keep it all away from Big Mama, of course. She'd just go on a rant about how disgraceful we were and *why couldn't we be more like Pauline*, maybe even take a swing at one of us, and then she'd start praying to her Jesus Wall. In the end, it was as much her making Lil go away as it was those scholarships dragging her off the farm. Lil was only about two hundred miles away, but that might as well be the other side of the world from the woods of Allegan County.

The phone she'd given me vibrated in my pocket. Her text said *we've run into a few problems, but should be leaving before morning.* I wondered who was coming with her.

And I wondered if it was gonna be too late.

Iggy was in my head, fast as lightning and kicking like a mule, going on about *I got a right.* I was smashing out some Scott Asheton beats in the air. I could still hear Big Mama in the sitting room yelling at the idiots on *The Maury Show.* Even with the whole world going to hell and the president walking around without a head, people still had time to wonder which Trailer Park Romeo was the father. You gotta love America.

Pauline was in the kitchen with her floppy breasts hanging over a big black pot. She was brewing something for dinner that smelled like it came from the low-end of a hippopotamus. She was my oldest sister, who still hadn't left home, and the one most likely to become the next Big Mama. In her old farmer's-daughter dress, she was looking just like Lil said, *not much more than a breeder cow for the next generation of McNeil dumbasses.*

The Stooges had just given it up to Suicidal Tendencies when Pauline looked out the back window and announced, "Papa's home, and he don't look none too happy. Jimmy, you better get that damn music off your head 'fore you rile him up even worse."

"Told you, it's *Iggy* now, and Paw don't give a shit what I do."

Mama's voice came flying out of the other room, past all the you-are-the-father ruckus of the Maury crowd. "Goddammit, Jimmy, what have I told you about that language? I swear, it's like I'm talkin' to myself in this house. Lord, my nerves are just cracking."

Then, like she often did, she called me and Pauline over to help her up off the couch. She was what Paw, in one of his more descriptive moods, once called *a whole lotta woman.* Lil said she was just a fucking beast. It wasn't that Mama was fat, she said, but that whatever was inside of her had eaten up her heart and soul. I took her arm and braced myself against the edge of

16

the couch, with Pauline on the other side, and we heaved her up on her feet.

I'd seen a movie called *Multiple Maniacs* and there was this woman named Divine in it, except that she wasn't really a woman at all. She wasn't even a good-looking man. She was running around, getting it on in churches and robbing and killing people. Then she'd act like everybody was supposed to feel sorry for her. That was Mama all the way, except that Divine actually made you laugh. There wasn't nothing funny about Mama.

She liked to act all helpless, but we'd seen her in action. She hit me in the back of the head with her fist once for stealing some gum. She did it so hard that I passed out, and then I had a headache for days. Other than that, all I ever really had to put up with was the usual slaps, smacks, punches, and shoves, all of which Lil said weren't usual to begin with.

This one time, when Lil was maybe thirteen, Mama caught her playing that old John Lennon song about *imagine there's no heaven* and just about lost her mind. She wasn't much more than three hundred pounds then and really fast when she was drinking. Before Lil could even think about getting away, Mama reached out and snatched her up by the front of her shirt. She punched Lil dead in the face. Once, twice, then once more for good measure. Ended up breaking her nose.

The worst part, Lil said, wasn't the pain or the blood, but that Mama went right to throwing out every record, tape, or CD that was in her room, pitching it all in a big old garbage bag while Lil was laying there, bleeding all over the floor.

No one fucked with Big Mama's Jesus, not even Lil.

Turns out that Paw lost his job that day. Not that he wasted more than four words letting us know. There was some kinda upgrade at the slaughterhouse and they figured out a cheaper way to kill the cows. Almost fifteen years and he was just done. He took his snowy boots off at the back door. I went to get them, without him needing to ask, and took them over to dry by the old wood-burner.

It was hard to tell if the look on Paw's face was anger or sorrow, or some private mixture that only he knew. He cleaned up in the kitchen sink, all silent rage, then disappeared into the bedroom with Mama for a while. He must have been telling her about it, but all we heard was her big outdoor voice going on and on. Then she waddled out and went right over to her wall, leaving Paw to soak up her words of wisdom.

Let me tell you about Big Mama's Jesus Wall.

One side of the sitting room was almost nothing but the supersized TV, what my sister called *the only luxury left for the poor*. The computer was there too. Paw didn't think we needed one, but Mama insisted. She said she needed to know what was going on in the world. Really, she just wanted to complain to anybody she could think of and fuck with people on Facebook. The other wall was the poor beat-down couch, even though she called it a davenport, and a heap of romance books and potato chip bags and candy wrappers.

Between these walls was what Mama called *the savior's American home*.

Paw had found just about the biggest flag ever. It used to fly above the A&P, but then they closed down and Mama begged them for it. She had nailed it up to the four corners of the wall. I read somewhere that it wasn't patriotic to pound nails into the flag, but Mama had her own ideas about what that meant too.

In the middle of the flag was the creepiest goddamn Jesus ever. The thing was about three-foot tall, stretched out in the crucifixion pose but without a cross, so it looked like he was nailed right to the flag, which he was. His abdomen was pierced with arrows, and there was a slot in the back of his head where you could insert a couple C batteries to make his eyes light up. Most of the time only one of them worked, so it always looked like Creepy Jesus was winking at you. Lil said it wasn't actually Jesus at all, it was Saint Sebastian. But no one was gonna tell Big Mama about that.

If that wasn't fucked-up enough, Mama had been writing down all the stupid shit the president said on little strips of paper and pinning them up on the flag. Like they were

18

scriptures or something. Unless she dragged me over and made me pray with her, I avoided the hell outta that wall. But if you got close enough you could see all this shit about bad hombres and losers and fake news. There were so many quotes on the wall now that the flag was getting hard to see. But she would go on about how Jesus was on the president's side and they were gonna make America great again, and there wasn't a damn thing anybody better say different.

So she was up there whispering to Creepy Jesus soon as she got done talking to Paw. She pushed her mouth right up to his ear, like me or Pauline might be trying to hear the secret, and started stroking his bloody plastic legs. I could make out *Lord* this and *blessing* that and was glad I didn't have to hear the rest. She closed her eyes and her lips trembled and she raised her hands right on up to heaven like she was going to have a vision.

Then she kissed Jesus on his chest and hollered that it was time to eat.

Supper was the worst.

Most of the time I was in my room, checking out some band I'd heard of, or screaming at a wall out behind the barn. Even when I was around the family I still had one ear plugged into the music. It was easier to hear Big Mama's preaching or Paw's silence when somebody else was shouting about anarchy or a teenage lobotomy or safety pins stuck in their heart. But Mama didn't want nothing but a heap of food and her own voice at the table.

Then Paw started bringing a gun to dinner.

None of us was strangers to shooting, not even Pauline. We all learned back when we were little. Paw said you gotta know how to defend yourself in this world. But now he was saying the threat was closer than we thought, and somebody could burst into the house at any time. Sometimes it was a shotgun propped up against the edge of the table, other times it was a pistol right beside his plate like some kinda fancy silverware. Nights like this, it was both.

He was even more quiet than usual. When any of us tried to tell him it would be alright, he just looked away like we weren't even there. I thought about those stories where somebody loses a job or something and snaps, taking out their entire family. They almost always go silent just before it happens. Part of me wanted him to reach over for that gun and put a bullet right in the middle of Mama's face. But I was all please-and-thank-you at the table, more than any other time. I could rage and rebel in quiet, just like I figured he did. And, like Lil taught me, sometimes you gotta play dumb, even if you figured everybody else was the asshole.

So I didn't say a word.

Mama went on about the blacks getting all the jobs now, even though there wasn't a single black person left in Pea Patch anymore.

But I didn't say a word.

She went on about the president and his goddamn missing head.

I didn't say a word.

She went on about the strange lights in the sky, which had just appeared over a couple more cities on the West Coast. All the religious nuts were saying it was God's wrath getting ready to rip. That would've been just fine by her. "California needs to sink to the bottom of the ocean," she said, scooping more of Pauline's hippo shit into her bowl. "Look at all the degenerates in that place. It ain't nothing but Sodom and Gomorrah over there no how. The Lord has told me personally that . . ."

I didn't say a word.

Mama didn't like many things, but there were even more things she hated. She hated to see anybody get something for free, even though she'd never worked a day in her life, and she sure as hell hated liberals. ". . . and I'm still hoping for one good earthquake or flood or Jaws to jump up outta the water and start eating all-a those fruity-tasting fools . . ."

I didn't say a word.

But the day was coming when I'd say plenty.

That night, after I thought everyone was asleep, I went out to the barn to check on the terrible thing I'd found.

Living out in the woods, your eyes get used to the dark. But lately the dark had gotten darker. The moon used to bounce off the yard behind the house, but now it was playing hide-and-seek with a blanket of snow. There were no birds or rabbits or deer since I found that thing either, and it smelled different out there. Like somebody drained a swamp and left a huge pile of fish rotting away somewhere. Some seriously fucked-up shit was going on. I muttered some Dead Kennedys under my breath - *macho insecurity macho insecurity macho insecurity you can't stand yourself* - and tried not to think too much about it.

I stopped at the barn door.

Pauline was in there and she wasn't alone. It took a minute for my eyes to adjust, then I saw them. It was Dwain and Bodean, a couple big-ass dudes who used to run combines for some of the local farmers. One of them had it in Pauline. The other one was trying to get his in the other side, but kept knocking them over. Pauline's monster tits were swinging around and she was laughing every time she hit the mound of blankets on the ground beneath them. I jumped back around the corner and tried to push the sight out of my mind.

Their voices were still coming at me. *Dammit, Dwain, stop lookin' at me . . . I ain't lookin' at you, idjit. And I was here first, so I get the good side . . . You ain't gettin' nothin' but seconds, boy. Nope, make that thirds . . . Bodean, you got a little willie . . . Why you lookin' at my willie, Dwain? You some kinda queer?*

Then came the sound of grunting and scuffling. I imagined those boys shoving at each other even while they were fucking Pauline. Deep down they were probably wishing she wasn't even there. I was about to creep back off to the house when I heard my sister let out a sharp yelp. Ducking down to the ground I peeked back in the barn. She was laying on the ground, holding her stomach, and those dudes were just standing over her with their willies out.

Rubbing her stomach, she said, "Y'all gotta take it easy, you're gonna hurt the baby."

Neither Dwain or Bodean looked like they heard this one before. Sure as hell I hadn't heard it. She said she ain't been to no doctor yet, but she *knows*, a woman just does. It wasn't but a second and those dumbasses were already going back and forth with the *it's mine - no it's mine* dance, shoving each other around the barn. But then Pauline shut them down. "You're *both* stupid," she said, "It don't belong to neither of you. It's from somebody real important, and he's gonna take care-a me and Mama real good . . ."

One of them said, "It better not be no half-breed knee-grow child."

She went on a bit more about somebody taking care of her. It was all maids and four-course meals and the life of leisure. I had to wonder where the hell she'd been because there sure wasn't nobody like that out here. But the guys were just laughing her off anyway, and it was obvious she wasn't saying who knocked her up.

A couple more minutes and the conversation was over. Everybody went back to fucking and fighting. One of them was hooting like he was at a rodeo, which he kinda was.

I turned to sneak back into the house, footsteps crunching in the snow.

I looked up, and out, to the stars. But the stars weren't the only thing there. Way up in the sky, maybe a mile above the house, I saw the lights for the first time. There might have been four or five of them. They were clustered together and just hanging there, turning slowly.

Like they were waiting for something.

Lil showed up the next morning in a cloud of white coming up the road. I'd been in contact with her pretty regular, but none of us had actually seen her for a couple years. We definitely didn't know the old Chevy Malibu that was creeping up to the house through the ice and snow. Pauline called Big Mama out onto the porch, then hollered for me to go get Paw. "He's on the range," she said, "Tell 'im to bring his gun."

The car stopped a few yards away, but I could see my sister in the passenger seat. She was sitting there, looking at the

22

house, talking to a driver who was still in shadows. The Damned was in my ear singing about a *problem child* and I thought that was just about perfect.

"Hold up, I think it's Lil."

"I know damn-well who it is, Jimmy. I *told* you to go get Paw."

Then Lil was getting out of the car. She was dressed different than before, lots of leather, and she had one of those sideways haircuts, but it was her. Sweeping the dark hair from her face, she lit right up to see me there on the porch. She turned to say something to the other person, who was rising up from the driver's seat.

I knew there was gonna be problems right then.

She was about the tallest black girl I'd ever seen. That might have been enough to put Mama in an early grave, but she was rocking even more leather than Lil. Black leather jacket and mini-shirt, studded ankle bracelets, some shit-kicking boots. Not to mention, a bleached-white Mohawk and that Billy Idol snarl on her face. She looked like a total *badass*.

You could just about hear Mama's blood pressure racing.

I was grinning. "See, it *is* her."

Mama's hand was on the back of my neck. "Jimmy, goddammit, your sister told you to do something. You need to do it now."

Even as I was hustling away, I could hear Mama asking Lil what the hell she was doing here. Like she wasn't even her daughter.

Paw called it his shooting range, but it was really just a snowy clearing in the woods where the pigs used to herd. He'd thrown some gravel over the muck years ago and set up a sawhorse with a bunch of old beer cans. I could hear him ping-pinging out there all the time when he was home. Sometimes he would motion me over, and I would go, and he'd hand me whatever he was shooting without saying a word. I'd knock off a few rounds, never as good as him, then hand it back. I could never tell if it was bonding or competition, but it was the only time we ever really spent together since I was little.

It felt wrong to be running up on him without an invite. "*Paw?* Paw, Mama said to come get you." He pulled back from aiming the Remington and squinted at me over his shoulder.

He pushed the old pump-action shotgun at me.

"It's Lil, she's home."

"Oh," he said, but kept holding the gun until I took it.

I chambered a round, cocked it, and took aim at the biggest can. My shooting hand was on the right, but my dominant eye was the left, which meant I always had to lean over the gun more than someone looking through the other side would. Shotguns were the hardest. Paw used to get mad and try to straighten me up, telling me to do it right. Sometimes he smacked me on the back of the head when I missed. But then I'd still look through the left eye anyway because that was just how I was made. Half the time I ended up not hitting a goddamn thing.

From out of nowhere Paw said, "You remember those old movies?"

I nodded. Damn right I remembered, but I was surprised that he did.

The one I thought about most was the last one we ever watched. It was called *The Brain That Wouldn't Die*. This doctor and his girlfriend were in a wreck and he tried to get her out of the car before it blew up, but all he could save was her head. He put the head in a tray in his lab and did all this movie shit to keep it alive until he could find her a new body. Mostly he was trying to find stripper bodies. And the head, it was talking to him and his assistant, telling them she didn't want to go on like that. But nobody was listening because she was just a damn head.

The gun went off, but I missed. I looked at Paw. He looked back until I knew he wanted me to reload and try again. So I did.

"You gotta stay strong, Jim," he said. "Sometimes you gotta take a stand." His breath made shapes in the winter air.

"Uh-huh."

There was this monster the doc kept locked up behind a door in the lab. It was something he'd fucked up really bad, and they were keeping it all mysterious and not letting us see it. Mostly because it was a low-budget movie and the monster actually looked pretty stupid. But I was ten years old and it scared the shit out of me, not knowing what was behind that door. The head was talking to the monster and telling it what to do. Then, when the doctor was out getting another stripper, she told it to kill his assistant.

"Sometimes you might even have to die," Paw said.

I missed again, reloaded.

And I was little again, trying not to cover my eyes when the monster ripped that guys arm clean off. He was screaming and dragging himself up the stairs, smearing black-and-white movie blood all over the walls, while that woman's head just kept laughing and laughing. I was trying not to look away, trying not to cry because Paw was sitting right next to me, and he was laughing too. But I was crying anyway because I wouldn't stop looking.

Then I felt his hand on my back. For just a minute, like *there, there, it'll all be okay*, even though he never said a word. And, for just a minute, I really did feel like it would all be okay. But we never stayed up to watch another movie, so I knew that somehow, I'd fucked up.

The beer can went flying with a loud clang.

Paw looked at me, gave a quick nod. I handed the gun back to him and we were done.

"You little bastard, get your ass over here."

That was Lil, being as affectionate as Lil ever got. But I threw my arms around her anyway and she threw her arms right back around me. She smelled like chocolate and smoke, like she always did, nothing like the backwoods pig-shit palace she managed to escape from. Mama and Pauline had gone back in the house, leaving her standing on the porch.

"You shit-eating liberal," I said, pulling back to check out her leather jacket. Under that she wore a t-shirt with Ted Nugent just smiling away. In the middle of his forehead was a gaping bloody gunshot. "I missed you, sis. Looks like you finally went all the way."

She nodded. "Getting away was good."

"Wish I knew. Who's your badass friend?"

The badass friend stuck out her hand. "Ari. What's up, dude." She shook my hand like she meant it.

"You totally look like Storm from the X-Men."

"Thanks." She just about blushed, which was strange on someone who looked like she could kick anyone's ass.

"Lil, I got some *serious* shit to show you."

"Hi, Dad," she said.

Paw was there all right, holding that shotgun across his chest like he was at a wedding. You could never tell what he was thinking by looking at his face. Wasn't like him to help you out with a couple words either. Him and Lil couldn't have looked more unrelated, especially with her all punked out. She got his scrawniness. Other than that, it was like he was looking at some kinda alien standing in front of the house.

Big Mama came busting back out now that Paw was there. Pauline, naturally, was behind her like a shadow. "Joe, you need to tell these . . . *people* that they are not welcome on my porch. I recognize trouble when I see it, and I'm surely looking at it now."

"Mama," Lil said.

But Mama wasn't having it. "I did not give birth to someone that walks around looking like that. Why, you look like a damn hoodlum, and, even worse, a *Democrat*. I'll bet you even voted for that lying criminal whore, and if there's -"

"Now, Darlene."

It was Paw. That would've shut me right up, but Mama kept on like always. All I could hear was *blah-blah-blah* and all I could see was my sister's face. She had gone past hurt long ago. Now it just looked like she was gonna crack Mama in the skull. I couldn't help but wonder if Paw respected that.

"- and I'm tellin' you, if you think you can just -"

"*Darlene.*"

Swear I heard Paw cock the Remington. That, and the seriousness in his voice, and everyone stopped. Mama just stood there looking at him. Pauline was looking at her and Lil was looking at me. Ari, who didn't know our fucked-up family at all, was looking at her feet. Then Mama threw up her arms like whatever and shoved her way back into the house, leaving the door open behind her.

Lil and Ari got a welcome about as warm as a lake in December. Paw stood around the kitchen holding his gun for a few minutes, then disappeared. Mama was right back at her wall, praying for Jesus to save her from the invasion of black people and punk rock hooligans. Pauline stood in front of her younger sister with a snotty look on her face. She finally said that *no-one-and-she-meant-no-one* could stay in her room, which used to be Lil's room too. There was nowhere for them to go but with me.

Ari said, "Nice town you got here, dude. We passed no less than ten rebel flags on the road in. That shit'll make a girl wanna hide in the trunk."

I shook my head. "This place sucks so bad."

"It sucks *everywhere* right now," Lil replied. "Black versus white, red versus blue, you name it. There were areas on the way over where the fighting is so bad that they've just blocked them off, no one in or out. There were actually Nazi flags and buildings on fire in Battle Creek."

"And those lights just hangin' out up there," Ari said, "Fuckin' *weird*, man."

My room wasn't much. Some posters on the wall, the Stooges and Troma movies and *The Brain That Wouldn't Die*. There were the couple of buckets I beat on like drums sometimes, and a few wooden crates full of CDs. Mostly what I picked up from five-finger discounts in town. A few books were scattered in the clothes all over the floor. The bed had broken a long time ago so there was just a mattress to sleep on, which was totally punk-rock by me.

Lil looked around while Ari went straight to the music.

"Big Mama's getting worse," I said.

"She didn't used to be such a monster. Hard to believe, but she used to comb my hair and sing Motown to me when I was a little girl. Then she found God."

"Yeah, she's like the fuckin' Devil now."

27

Lil shook her head. "And *Pauline* . . ."

"She's pregnant," I said.

"*No* shit."

A whistle from the other side of the room. "I heard you were into Iggy, but *damn*, Iggy." Ari was sitting on one of the buckets while she dug through my crates. It was like someone taking a look inside my heart. "You seen this shit, babe? Misfits. Black Flag. Subhumans. Discharge. The Wipers. Fuckin' Reagan Youth. The Circle Jerks, I used to like these guys too. *Cool* fuckin' kid."

"I told you he was worth saving." Lil said it with a wink.

"Saving?"

Ari nodded her head. "Hardcore was great on the political end, even though it was kinda like a frat party sometimes. You need a little more female rage in here. But otherwise, *yeah*. The Avengers were there at the beginning, but they might sound kinda slow to your ears. Try the Wrecks or Potential Threat -"

"Bikini Kill," I said.

"Yeah, or Sleater-Kinney, Slant 6, maybe a bunch of chicks called G.L.O.S.S."

"L7 kicked some serious ass, too. Are you in a band?"

"I was," she said, "We called ourselves Edith Keeler Must Diet. Pissed-off, femmed-out punk, that kinda thing." She nodded at her leather, like what else would she be playing. "I started on the kit, but figured out I was just as shitty on vocals and guitar. Got myself promoted. At least until everything went batshit. So you're into the drums."

"Aw, drums, man. They're, like, the glue, you know? Holding the bass and the guitar together. Speed, energy, aggression. When I get pissed off around here, I take those buckets into the woods and just start wailing on 'em."

I didn't get to the part where I'd broken at least ten buckets in the past year. Cracked them right apart from hitting them so hard. I was about to launch into my all-purpose Chuck Biscuits speech, but it seemed like something else was about to go down. I looked at Lil, then Ari, then back at Lil again.

"So, um, you guys are like a couple or something?" I wasn't sure, but it made sense.

Lil raised an eyebrow. "You picked up on that, huh? Impressive, you little shit."

"Hey, you taught me to pay attention."

Ari nodded her head, running her hand through that white Mohawk. I looked at her and thought that if my sister had to go for another girl she definitely could do worse.

Lil gave me a look. "You'd better not have a problem with that."

I shrugged. "Why would I? So what's this biz about *saving* me, sis?"

Lil had a speech she wanted to give, I could tell. Like she figured she had to convince me of something. That was just like her. I could've saved her some time.

"Everything is going to shit, baby brother. It was probably *always* shit, but then they elected that incompetent fucking Cheeto. It's like he popped the cork on craziness and now everyone is just doing whatever the fuck they want. He was supposed to be all about law and order, remember that? Well, now the cops and the military are so afraid they can't keep the riots under control that they're just shooting anyone who steps out of line."

She looked at Ari and, I know it sounds stupid, but I swear it's true. It was like I could see a whole world between them. Like they went through shit together that I wouldn't even get. There was the look that Lil got when she was pissed off but trying not to let loose, which I didn't think she got with anybody but me. I figured that was probably love. But there was something else in her face too, something I'd never seen there. It was *fear*.

"I don't know this place anymore," she said, and I knew she meant more than just the house. She hesitated, and I knew they planned to leave. Not just some temporary shit either.

"Where you gonna go?"

"You fucker, you can't let me have even *one* surprise."

Ari got up from the bucket. It looked like she was going to come over, but then stopped. Like she didn't want to interrupt a family moment or something. She said, "Canada. There's a spot up in Wisconsin where they're lettin' people in. No questions asked."

Lil took my hand, like she was gonna propose or something, and said, "We want you to come with us, Iggy. No . . . no, you *are* coming with us, I insist. Unless you're determined to live your entire life on this goddamn farm. So there you have it."

There's probably a lot of stuff I could've thought about. But none of it came to me.

"We could, like, form a band or something," I said.

Hard to say what kinda answer Lil had been expecting, and I didn't really know what the last two years were like for her. But she started crying. *Crying*, man, my sister. This girl didn't even cry over a broken fucking nose. She grabbed me and hugged me for the second time that day, making a lifetime total of maybe three. It was like a fucking Brady Bunch moment.

I had to break it up, so I said, "Alright, but we're gonna barn-blaze one more time. Then I've *really* gotta show you something."

The first time I ever got high was with Lil. I was almost twelve then, so she must've been about sixteen. She knew some older dude from another farm down the road. He would let her take a joint home if he could put his hand down her pants. That one joint became a sandwich bag full of weed, which turned into her own little crop out behind the barn. It'd been years since the farm and she figured no one would ever find it. No one but me, that is.

In our usual spot, I pushed aside the rock that covered a carefully dug hole. It was where I kept the stash. Lil nodded her approval but then produced her own anyway, packing it into a guitar-shaped bowl. Ari looked around like a soldier on the watch for snipers, and said, "Y'all might wanna hold off on that. Plenty of time to get high in the Great White North."

Lil just grinned. She held the lighter over the bowl, killed the flame, then slowly sucked in a breath. Squinting her eyes closed, she passed it to me.

"Alright, bitch," Ari said, "But remember it's always the stoned motherfuckers that die in horror movies." She laughed, but it was like she still meant it.

Up close I could see orange threads running through the weed. That was different. It crackled and gave off a thick earthy scent, even more country than the shit grown here. I sucked it in, coughing a little. My eyes watered, my throat and lungs burned. Then I took another just because I could. But it was already flooding in, a strange citrus glow. I passed it back.

"So you're a lesbian," I said, "That's cool."

This was to Lil, but she was holding in smoke. "*She* is," Ari said, and I laughed. A little too much because the shit was already kicking in. I took another hit in slow motion and looked at her longer than I would have. Snow was coming down like ashes around her.

She was talking and I was watching her mouth move, her lips forming every word, and I know I was staring but I wasn't really hearing anything. Something about someone named Eric and his parents and operations and I was forgetting why we were even here. Then I looked at my sister. She tightened her mouth and smiled, eyes still closed, and started to talk with the smoke sneaking out between her lips. She said something to Ari. I saw her reach for her hand, but everything was kind of hazy and looked like lemon jello.

And I said, or thought I said, "You guys gotta see this. This shit is gonna blow your minds." But it might have been in my head because it took them a minute to start following me into the barn. The barn that still smelled like shit even after years without any pigs. Pig shit, blood, and broken dreams, baby.

And I was floating through the wide-open area with all the old wooden rails and I heard Lil saying that it was where the pigs were herded together all tight and that it was why she could never eat bacon again and I was going to the other room in the back where they used to put a bullet in their brains before they scorched off all the hair and then cut them apart.

And I stopped in front of the barrel full of moldy old black shit that I think used to be pig parts for some reason and this was where I kept the fucking thing since I found it last week. And Lil was laughing because she was crazy high and I knew she sure as hell wasn't expecting to see anything like this as I pulled the top off the barrel and she leaned over to take a look.

The laughter died right there in her throat. Her mouth was hanging open and she looked at me with her eyes all wide, then looked back down into the barrel. She didn't even breathe for a minute, and then said, "*What the fuck is that?*"

It was exactly what it looked like. It was a fucking head.

But it wasn't just any fucking head. Not with that orange-hued hair and that sour look and the son-of-a-bitch's face on the TV and internet every day until last week. "Fuck me with the Washington Monument," Ari said, "That's the *president*."

I laughed, I couldn't help it. "Well, part of him."

There was a round of *holy shits*, and Lil paced around in big circles, then came back to look in the barrel and start all over again. Ari was just staring at it. She reached out, but couldn't quite bring herself to touch it.

Lil asked, "Where the hell did it come from?"

"From the president, I guess."

There it was, like every day since I found it. Eyes closed, like it was sleeping. I'd only touched the thing once, just long enough to pick it up and put it in the barrel. It wasn't very heavy. There wasn't any blood or marks on the neck where somebody, like, chopped it off the president's body or anything. Even though it'd been out in the barn for over a week now, the fucking thing didn't look like it was even starting to rot.

"Someone laced the weed," Lil said, "That's it. We're all standing here, tripping out over some goddamn pumpkin."

Ari pulled a splintered chunk of wood from one of the fences. She said, "Nice try, babe, but I'm not high and I'm still lookin' at this ugly motherfucker. This shit's real." With that she reached in to poke it with the stick.

Once. Twice.

Then the eyes opened.

"I have a great relationship with the blacks," it said, "Really great relationship."

I'm pretty sure we all shit our pants.

Everything was spinning like a son-of-a-bitch. The damn thing definitely had not *talked* before. I was wondering if Lil wasn't right about us tripping. I was looking at her face and at Ari's face and their mouths were big Os and I looked back into the barrel and the head was looking back at me.

It spoke again. It said, "I cherish women. I want to help women. I'm going to be able to do things for women that no other president would be able to do." The eyes blinked.

"No fuckin' way," Ari said. "Absolutely no fuckin' way."

Lil grabbed the stick from her and started to poke at the head herself. It blinked but didn't seem to care that it was getting jabbed in the face. She stuck it in the ear, making it wince a little, and flipped it over. The muffled voice came up out of the muck: "I'm telling you, this is going to get amazing ratings. Just amazing. Believe me."

She flipped the head back over and it was still talking. "A person who is very flat-chested is hard to be a 10," it said. Lil, who fit that description, almost looked offended.

She touched it, reached right into the barrel and put her fingers on its temples. She lifted it up, sort of examined it, then propped it up on an old rusty cart. Wiping her hands on her jeans, she looked at it. I was thinking about the doctor putting his girlfriend's noggin in that tray and watching it speak.

We stood there, all of us looking at the head for a long time.

"A lot of good things are happening," it said, "Really good things. We're very proud of the job we've done." It was fucking weird to see the lips move, to hear a voice coming out of it. Everything was still spinning.

33

Lil looked at her phone. "So the president just tweeted, the usual shit, a bunch of praise for another nefarious character he should condemn." She held the phone in the its face. "He *just* sent this out, so who the hell are you?" She leaned close like she was gonna work some Guantanamo shit on it.

"My Twitter has become so powerful that I can actually make my enemies tell the truth."

Lil was staring the thing down. It said, "Do I look like a president? How handsome am I, right? How handsome?" It blinked, once, twice, then: "Look at that face. Would anyone vote for that? Can you imagine that, the face of our next president. I mean, she's a *woman*, and I'm not s'posed to say bad things, but come on, folks. Are we serious?"

Even soaked in weed, Lil's brain was going into detective mode. "It's the same low-rent New York accent. Some of the same words. It sure as hell *looks* like the president, but . . ."

"I went to Maine four times because it's one vote, and we won. But we won, one vote. I went there because I kept hearing we're at 269. But then, Wisconsin came in. Many, many years . . . Michigan came in."

"There aren't any vocal cords," Lil said, "I mean, there *couldn't* be. How the fuck is it even talking?"

"That head was talking in *The Brain That Wouldn't Die*."

"Come on, Iggy, that was a *movie*."

Ari said, "Maybe there's a slot in the back. You know, for batteries."

"No, there's *not*."

"Maybe we could, like, dissect it," I suggested.

"I think you'd have riots," the head said. "I think you'd have problems like you've never seen before. I wouldn't lead it, but I think bad things would happen."

"*Fuck*," Ari said.

"Bad things would happen."

Lil snarled, "Zip it, prick. No one asked you."

"I'm speaking with myself, number one, because I have a very good brain and I've said a lot of things. " Blink, blink, and then: "I know words. I have the best words. I have the best, but there's no better word than stupid."

She grabbed it by the hair like she was gonna rough it up. I couldn't imagine it'd get much rougher than being separated from your body. "Alright, I *am* asking this: are you really the president's head?"

Maybe it was the weed, but I laughed.

The head replied, "There is none, there is none."

Lil was getting pissed. "How did you get here? How are you still talking?"

"There's no, there's no, there's no word like that."

Ari wasn't looking very happy. "Look," she said, "This shit's *way* outta my league, you feel me? I say we stick to the plan. We get in the car, *right now*, and ponder this motherfucker from about five hundred miles away."

"Look at my African-American over here."

Ari and Lil both glared. In stereo, they told it to fuck off.

"No word like that."

Lil huffed in frustration. "Dammit, I've gotta think. I'm too high for this shit."

Ari: "So we're gonna go, *right*?"

But I saw the look on Lil's face before she even answered. She was that scientist in the horror movies, the one that wants to study the monster instead of torching it. The genius with the stupid-ass notion of *learning something* from the alien species, rather than just hightailing it. She might have been the smartest person in the room, but she was the motherfucker that was gonna get us all killed.

So there we were, all of us having supper together. Goddamn motherfucking supper, when we should have been seven counties away from all this b-movie bullshit. Pauline went about her duties at the stove like it was just a regular day, even though nothing had been regular for a long time and probably wouldn't be ever again. Then we pulled up a couple extra chairs and tried to eat together like a normal family, which we had never been.

The TV was blaring in the other room in case there was any news about the president's head. Lil and Ari and me were looking back and forth because we already knew too much about it. Then I remembered that I was pissed at Lil and frowned. Paw had his guns at the table, the most regular thing of all, but he had an eye on the door more than usual. That is, when he wasn't looking at Lil like he'd missed something. Pauline, she kept her eyes down and kept refilling her plate, which more than half of us knew was because she was eating for two.

No fucking surprise, but I didn't say a word.

Mama was in a particularly shitty mood. Also no fucking surprise. She glared at Lil and stared at Ari, and her face got shittier and shittier, until she finally started in on them like we all knew she would. "It's people like you who're ruining the country," she said. I wasn't sure which one she meant, if she was talking to both of them, or if maybe she had figured out they were together. But none of it really mattered.

Lil smiled and said, "Well, I'm not done yet."

"You're *gonna* be done. You're gonna be good and done when they start rounding up everyone who talks trash about the government."

"They already tried that, Mother. It was called Nazi Germany."

"At least the Nazis knew how to show *respect* for their mothers."

It was Ari who tried to break it up. "This is a lovely soup, Pauline. Earthy, yet delicate." Pauline scowled, then gave her a look that said I don't care what you think. Ari threw back an exaggerated Johnny Rotten scowl, then turned to Paw. "Thank you for having me in your home, sir. So, tell me, were you in the Service?"

Paw glanced at her, almost nodded, then looked back toward the door. "I was in the Army. My father made me join when I turned eighteen."

"Well, then we have something in common."

He looked back at her. Pauline whined, "I don't believe you."

"I was a different person then, but it's true. I could kill you fifteen different ways."

"Mama, are you gonna let her talk to me like that in my own home?"

Ari looked at Mama with an innocence so fake that I almost burst out laughing. "We're actually really good people, Mrs. McNeil," she said, "We've been working on sending bibles to Afghanistan . . ."

We would have left that night. That was the plan, but then something happened.

The bedroom was dark. My sister and her girlfriend were on the floor behind me, hoping for a few hours rest before we all snuck out of the house. I was in my bed, for what I knew would be the last time, but there was no way I was gonna sleep that night.

They probably figured I was passed out. The band X was blasting in my ears. Ari had said her first crush was on the main singer, Exene Cervenka, so I was checking them out. I didn't really get it. But they had this one song that said *my whole fucking life is a wreck*, and that was pretty cool. I paused them the third time through to ask a question.

Lil and Ari were arguing. Quietly, but still.

Their voices sounded the same in whispers, and I only caught some of the words. *Just a damn kid . . . not his revolution . . . being selfish . . . stay and fight, because that's what we know . . . here, like we did . . . Mama and her bullshit . . . for me, please . . . come back when they're not fuckin' shooting people . . . down on the street . . . not running away, we're . . . just do it for me . . .*

That's when I figured out that Lil didn't really want to leave. She wanted to fight, like she always did. Though I wasn't sure how she would fight or even exactly *who* at this point. But Ari was going all Obi Wan on her, telling her that sometimes there are other ways to fight. She even *said* Obi Wan. I thought about how some folks talked up the peaceful way in the movies, even when they could kick more ass than anybody.

I was about to throw them a quote. Probably something like *I have a very bad feeling about this*. But then the words stopped. They started moaning. It was really quiet, but it was definitely moaning. Part of me wanted to look. But I didn't.

One of them whispered, *I wanna be your Joey Ramone*, and that was all I heard.

I pushed play and Exene went back to being desperate. What the hell, I'd be desperate with her, since I wasn't getting any sleep -

But then it hit me.

It was like a wave of something black and tingling. It was fast and it was huge, coming out of nowhere. Like the biggest fucking sleeping pill ever, like green-death flavored Nyquil. I wanted to turn to Lil and Ari, to say something, but I couldn't. I couldn't move. I couldn't speak. And I couldn't hear them anymore, like they were already gone.

It was pulling at me. Pulling me down.

And I could see the lights outside. Bright, so bright, like the biggest truck was parked outside the window, like something landing on the house, like there was nothing but light, light, light, and it was all around and inside of me and -

Darkness.

It was morning when I crawled out from under the dark. Lil and Ari were still tangled in blankets and the alarm was going off on my sister's phone. Everything felt different, something humming, buzzing in the air. It made me feel a little crazy, *kick-out-the-jams-motherfucker* crazy. I thought the sun was up, but it was the lights. There was fog everywhere, and the wind was whipping up a frenzy of snow, but there they were. Maybe a hundred feet above the house now. There was something else hanging there too. Something huge that wasn't moving.

Paw and Mama were in the yard, looking up into the sky. It was cold and they had no jackets. He was holding a sawed-off shotgun but not pointing it at anything. She dropped down to her knees in the snow beside him, started to pray.

I went to get Lil, to tell her that we had to get out of here soon.

Some time back this man from the bank came by the house. We knew he meant business because he was wearing a suit. Paw was a few months behind in house payments. The man told him that this was just a friendly warning. But one more time, he said, and the next visit would be telling us that we had to go.

The visit came that morning.

Paw was bundled up on the porch when the police car crawled through the snow and the fog. I had just walked out to try and talk to him. I saw that he had both the shotgun and the Colt with him now. His eyes were fixed on the man from the bank, who stayed in the car when Sheriff Bud climbed out.

We knew Bud Otto. He'd been here a few times before. Even though Paw was on the porch with his guns, Bud didn't pull his weapon. He was an old man and he's probably seen a lot. He looked calm. But he was shivering at the cold and looking up at those lights. I saw him unfasten the holster on his side, coming up the drive real slow.

"Good mornin', Joe," he said.

"Mornin'," Paw said.

Bud shook his head. "Well, that's the damnedest thing."

Paw nodded.

"I hate to be here like this, Joe, especially when you're about to be abducted and all. But I've got a gentleman from the bank in the car behind me. He's got some official-looking papers that neither you or me can argue with."

"It ain't happenin'," Paw said. He put the Colt down and took a drink from the thermos beside him. The sawed-off was still pointing at the ground but his grip looked firm. "Place is mine, Bud. Been mine since '82. It belonged to my dad 'fore that. It don't belong to no bank."

"I agree with you, pal. But this man has a job to do here this morning and so do I. Please don't make this a bad day for me." He looked up at the lights like it might be inevitable anyway.

"Ain't happenin'," Paw said again. He waved the shotgun in the direction of the police car. "Go on now, Bud."

"You know I can't do that, pardner. And you know I can't ignore people waving guns around. There's just too much crazy these days." He took his hat off, bald head flashing, and

39

wiped away sweat. "Why, I already had a couple good ol' boys shooting buckshot at some passing family on the edge of town, just because they had a Clinton sticker on their car. There's been fights all over. I had a wife beat the hell out of her husband when he said the child she was carrying wasn't his."

He nodded at the sky. "Then there's *this* shit. I'm telling you, Joe, I really don't need all of this so close to retirement. So how about you just lay those weapons down on the porch and get your family together?" He nodded at me, like it was the first time he saw me standing there.

"Hell, I'll put you up in a motel myself until you figure out what you're going to do. It'll probably be safer somewhere else anyway."

"Nope. I ain't movin'." Paw lifted the shotgun up to point it at the sheriff.

"Goddammit, Joe."

Bud was thinking about going for his gun. I could see it in his face and figured that Paw could see it too. Everything was humming. Buzzing. The sheriff's chest rose and fell, faster. Paw was breathing slow and purposeful. His finger was right up on the trigger. A drop of sweat slid down from under Bud's hat. His eyes were all squinty like one of those showdown movies.

The thermos tinged.

The screen door banged open.

All of us jumped, and it's a wonder no guns went off. It was Mama. She was already hollering her damn head off. "Well, this is a loathsome display of justice right here. We ain't nothin' but good people, but here you are at the butt-crack of morning -"

"Ma'am," Bud said.

Paw lowered the gun, just a little.

"- and with God and His angels hoverin' right above our heads -"

Bud looked like he gave up right then.

"- and we're *Americans*, sheriff, born and bred. I'm tellin' you, we have the God-given right to this land and everything on it. That's why you're seeing them divine lights. But you're wastin' your time here, while there's *rapists* and *murderers* sneakin' over our borders -"

"Not in Michigan, ma'am."

"Are you tryin' to smart mouth me, sheriff? Because I've prayed real hard on this, and the Lord has answered, and -"

"Darlene."

She looked at Paw, who still hadn't taken his eyes off the sheriff.

Bud looked at them, then at me too. A big sigh smoked out of his lips. "I'll tell you what," he said, "I've got a lot to take care of this morning. We can let it rest until this evening."

He looked up at the sky again, nodded at Mama, then turned to go. He was talking over his shoulder as he reached for the door of the cop car. "But I'm telling you, Joe, when I come back I'm bringing more guys with me. I've got nothing but sympathy for your situation, but you *will* be leaving the premises by the end of the day."

Paw nestled into a chair on the porch, pulling an old Harvester cap down over his eyes, while the snow whipped and whirled around him. It wasn't long before his breath was making clouds in front of his face. The shotgun was still on his lap and I knew the showdown wasn't over yet. Asleep, he almost looked peaceful. For just a second I didn't want to leave.

But inside it was like Lil had never left at all.

Something smashed into the wall behind me when I walked into the kitchen. There was a splatter like brains all over the wallpaper, dripping raspberry seeds, and chunks of a broken jelly glass at my feet. When I turned back around I could see that it was Mama who'd thrown the preserves. Her and Lil were just a few feet away from each other, but hollering to make up for a much bigger distance.

"I've done everything a mother can do. I suffered and I sacrificed. I have *prayed* for you, Lillianna, and even tried to pound the truth into you, but nothing ever changes. It's so hard being a loving mother."

"Loving mother, my ass."

"The only ass I see here is *you*, child. You're not even half as smart as you think you are."

"*You're* the ass, Mother."

Sarcastically, Mama said, "Then why don't you just get another freaky haircut and start dressing like a dyke. That'll show me." Her hand curled into a fist.

Lil stepped to her. "I'm not a little girl anymore. If you lay one hand on me, I will knock you the fuck out."

Ari was in the corner, watching and not watching, looking at her feet or wherever, looking like what-the-fuck. I stepped around the broken glass and the brain jelly to stand beside her. Even though I'd seen this shit a hundred times, I had no more idea what to do than she did.

"I don't care what your father says, I want you out-a my house."

I figured, like Lil did, that Mama would never just let me leave with her. Not that she gave a shit about me either, but because it'd be like Lil had won. Our best shot was to slip out when Bud showed back up that night. I was about to say so to Ari.

Then Pauline walked out of her bedroom.

Naked as a jaybird and bigger than hell.

Like she had gone from just knocked-up to nine months pregnant since last night. It *couldn't* be. Her belly must have always been that big. But I'd just seen her naked in the barn a couple nights ago. Maybe it was too dark, maybe I hadn't seen right, maybe . . .

She didn't seem to know or care that anybody else was there. "I'm so *hungry*," she said, strolling right between Mama and Lil.

Nobody else said shit.

She opened the fridge and started reaching for anything. Shoving it in her mouth. Last night's leftovers. A chunk of congealed pot roast from last week. She twisted the cap off the ketchup and spurted it between her lips.

Ari put her hand over my eyes, but I pushed it aside.

Pauline dropped the ketchup bottle. The fridge door was open, splashing light across her monstrous stomach. It was

42

shiny and looked like it was moving. Like the food was waking something up. She turned to the sink behind her, flashing the big crack of her ass. When she turned back around she had the old tin can where she drained the grease from dinner.

She stuck her tongue deep inside of it. Making the wettest slurping sound I'd ever heard. Her eyes were closed like she was getting off and grease was splashing up on her face.

"Pauline, my *word*," was all Mama could say.

She squeezed the can like a tube of toothpaste, like it was nothing, squirting the last globs of grease into her sticky open mouth. Then just dropped it on the floor. She walked right through us, toward the sitting room. She let it rip from the top *and* the bottom as she passed. Mama once said that if you could burp and fart at the same time it meant you had no soul.

But Pauline, she took her soulless, naked ass right up to that wall and reached out to touch Creepy Jesus. She was rubbing him like Mama did, but worse. There were weird sounds coming out of her. Almost like words, but not any that I knew. She was crying, laughing, both at the same time, and reached down to touch herself between the legs. Moaning like a horny ghost. "Oh, Jesus," she said.

Lil and I looked at each other. Ari mumbled, "*What the fuck?*"

But Mama was already on the move. She grabbed a blanket off the couch and wrapped it around all that nakedness. She pulled Pauline's hands away from her privates that weren't so private anymore. Took her hands like they were at a prayer meeting, and that's what they started to do. They started to pray together.

While Pauline stood there, head bowed and thumping against the groin of Jesus, Mama looked at us like we were some kind of congregation. She raised her hands up, pulling her daughters hands into the air too. "It's everything I've ever prayed for," she said, "It's a *miracle*."

I propped the president's head up on a fence post, then dropped down to my knees to look it in the eyes. It said, "Not since Harry Truman has anybody done so much. That's a long time ago."

"That's great . . . um, *head*. But I got a couple questions."

"I like thinking big. If you're going to be thinking, you might as well think big."

"Yeah, well, I'm thinking big right now. Like, I'm thinking you *gotta* have something to do with all the crazy shit going on around here. I mean, talking heads don't just show up in barns every day, and -"

"My whole life is about winning. I don't lose often. I almost never lose."

"Happy for you, dude. That's gotta be real nice, but . . . look, my family is about to lose their house, there's something really weird up in the sky, and my sister . . . I don't even *know* what the hell is up with her, and . . ."

"It really doesn't matter what the media writes as long as you've got a young and beautiful piece of ass."

"Well, you can have her if you want, but -"

"She's a lightweight. A total lightweight."

I laughed. "So, it's like, what, you already had her or something? Come on, you're not making any sense. Shit, *none* of this makes sense. Am I really asking if the president's head fucked my sister?" I was having some really messed-up thoughts, like stupid horror movie shit.

"When somebody screws you, screw them back in spades," said the head.

"You *can't* screw anybody, though. You don't even have a dick."

But I thought about the crazy-ass stories that the president was walking around without a head. I mean, we figured all of that was just tabloid bullshit, or another one of the son-of-a-bitch's distraction tricks. But if somebody said they had what I had in the barn, *and it was talking*, I would've called bullshit on that too.

"You could see there was blood coming out of her eyes, out of her whatever."

"So you, like, fucked her somehow, but left your head here to . . . what, *watch over her*?"

"I think the only difference between me and the other candidates is that I'm more honest and my women are more beautiful."

"Women? There's *more*?"

"Women, you have to treat them like shit."

"Dude, this is fucked-up. None of this makes sense."

Then it said, "Something really dangerous is going on. Something bad is happening." And that much made sense for sure. I could feel the crazy rising up and I wanted nothing more than to go in the woods and pound on my drums for about three days.

The head blinked at me as I carried it back to the barrel. I was getting more pissed off by the second. I swear it gave me a cocky smirk. So I dunked the fucker in the barrel like it was a basketball in Playoff season. Sliding the barn door shut, I could still hear its voice, even with the lid on. It laughed and said, "Lock your doors, okay, folks? Lock your doors."

But I figured even that wasn't going to do any good.

I shut the bedroom door and said, "It's snowing like a motherfucker out there. That, and there's all kinds of cars across the street. Like, they're just watching the house and shit. If we're leaving Dodge we might wanna do it soon."

Lil was scrolling something on her phone. "Don't you know, we're *a really big deal* in this town now." She glanced up, threw me a grin, then looked at Ari and said, "When the sheriff comes back, that's our cue."

Ari was going through one of Lil's old scrapbooks. When she left home, Mama went into a frenzy of throwing her stuff out. I might have figured her for at least a little sentimentality, but it was like she was trying to erase all evidence that Lil ever existed. The scrapbook was one of the only things I'd been able to save. Ari looked at something, looked at Lil, then chuckled. Lil was probably wishing I'd saved something else.

I said, "Remember when you believed in unicorns?"

Ari laughed right out loud. "Unicorns? No way. What were you, *three*?"

"No, she was still talking about 'em when she was twelve."

"Was *not*."

"You totally *were*. Remember, you drew a big ol' picture of the sun, with the rays coming out and everything. You put our house down in the corner and then made a little unicorn by the window. You did it all the time, and you always said . . . aw, shit, what'd you say?"

She sighed, loudly. "I *said* . . . that I wanted to be able to look out the window and see both the sunshine and something magical . . ."

". . . because you weren't ever gonna see them here."

"Yep."

"Then you remembered that I lived here too, and *that* was pretty magical."

Lil scowled. "Fuck off, *Jimmy*."

We all laughed, even Lil.

I dropped down in front of her. "Punk me out, sis."

"What? Don't be an asshole. Iggy's your boy and he didn't go for that. Besides, that shit's played out, no one has a legit Mohawk anymore. Present company excluded." Ari stuck her tongue out and Lil returned it.

"Yeah, I know, but I don't wanna be a farm boy no more. Ain't no silver pants around, but we can do this." I handed her scissors, a razor, glue, and some safety pins. "Punk me out."

"Big Mama's going to lose her shit."

"We're leaving anyway, right?"

She chuckled, shook her head. "You're all right."

And she started to cut.

I guess you could call it the last supper.

Paw finally came in from the porch and grabbed a six-pack, but was still facing the door. He never once put the shotgun down. Mama dropped a casserole in the middle of the table, then went at getting Pauline to sit down. She'd been walking around like a mental patient all day, hardly saying a word, looking at everything like she'd never seen it before. The strangest part was that neither Mama or Paw seemed too weirded out about her suddenly being ready to burst. Even Lil didn't have anything to say about it, like she was afraid to admit that we were dead-center in the goddamn Twilight Zone.

And, all day, that humming, buzzing shit from above.

But when I showed up for supper with a Mohawk and a safety pin through my nose, *that* was the fucking end of the world.

Oh yeah, and I brought the music.

"Jimmy, what in the *hell* have you done?"

That was Mama, who stepped away to stop my sister from wandering off again. Pauline looked at me and sniggered. Mama put her in her chair, then got in my face. Her breath was onions and oppression and death. "Exactly *who* do you think you are? Do you think that *this* -" Pointing at Ari and Lil, seated beside me. "- is what you're supposed to look like?"

I shrugged, looked down at my hands.

Mama grabbed my chin, made me look at her big, stupid face. "I wish somebody would stop and think about *me* once in a while. If it wasn't for *me*, none-a you would even be here. If it wasn't for all-a *my* prayers, and the good work of our president, this house would be overrun with murderers and rapists -"

Paw growled. "Can we *eat*??"

"*President*," Pauline whispered.

But Mama was just getting started. "Goddammit, Joe, I'm *gonna* be heard. I have put up with too much-a this blasphemy in my house for too long. It's bad enough that I have to hear it out there in that sinful world, but *here* . . ."

That was in one ear. In the other, Reagan Youth was telling me Jesus was a Communist.

"The president is not God, Mama," I said.

Pauline pushed up from her chair again, but Mama let her go. "*Not God?* I'll tell you what's not God, young man, and that's your *sister*. You always worshipped her like she was, but she ain't no more than just another damn libtard. It's the likes of her and her . . . *friend* here - who I don't even think is really a woman! - that are gonna get us all killed -"

Lil slammed her hands down on the table. "Oh, but we're just fine with some half-senile egomaniac having his finger on the button. Just because he mentioned God once or twice, with a goddamn *smirk* on his face, and gives everyone like you free rein to let all of their prejudices just hang out -"

Mama jabbed her finger in Lil's face, almost poking her in the eye. "Say whatever you want, little girl, but the president's entire *family* is more qualified to run this country than that monkey community organizer we kicked out -"

"Monkey?" Ari said, then added, "*Bitch.*"

"It's people like *you*, computer warriors without an ounce-a backbone, that are gonna tear down the country your ancestors built." Like that wasn't what Mama did every day. She had her finger in Lil's face again. "Have you taken a look in the mirror lately? Honey, you're *white*, and you better start acting like it. Otherwise, you ain't nothin' but the best excuse for the Christian army to start using 30-round mags."

Not only did I jump up from the table, but I sent my chair flying into the wall behind me. "Fuck it, I've had *enough*." I was shouting, something I never did.

"Here's the truth, Mama: *you're full of shit.*"

The anger was boiling through me, not to mention that goddamn humming, humming, and she reached around behind her, feeling for her chair. She had never heard from me like this before. Holding herself up, she snarled at me and said, "You need to sit down, Jimmy. You're starting to sound just like a *liberal.*"

Then I said, "I figured I *was* a liberal . . . because I think everybody's the same. You know, just as good, no matter what parts they got or where they come from. Ain't nobody should be able to tell them otherwise, least of all some fat-ass couch potato housewife who can't even spell proper." I shoved my finger at her face now.

She dropped down in her chair, mouth hanging open.

"I figured I was a liberal because there's always somebody out there wants to hurt you, but, *fuck that*, I'm not gonna be afraid of everybody. If you wanna kill folks that's not

48

like you, it's just because you're scared. In my book, that doesn't make you strong, it makes you a pussy."

Paw was staring at me with a stone face.

"I figured I was a liberal because your religion's a fucking joke. If you got something tellin' you to hate somebody or kill somebody or turn your back on somebody because they don't think the same as you, that shit ain't from God, least not any god I wanna trust. And I figured I was a liberal . . . because I'm not whatever *you* are."

Then I looked at Ari.

"But then I get a bunch of liberals telling me that I'm part of the problem too, because I'm white and I have a dick . . ."

And I turned to Lil, with her eyes so wide and solemn.

"Someone's always going on about *privilege* this - like pointing fingers instead of doing something is gonna fix anything - and about *all men* that, and to me that's just like saying every black guy is a criminal or every Muslim is a terrorist. But sometimes people are just smart enough to think they're the only ones who are ever right."

Lil raised an eyebrow.

"Those people like to turn all that prejudice around and say *I'm* a racist and a rapist because I'm not exactly what *they* are, and I call bullshit on that too. I wouldn't ever be any of those things, because I don't have anything against anybody, and I thought I was on the same side as *they* were, but I guess not . . ."

"So *fuck them too*. I'm just gonna be Iggy."

I was standing there, grinning and proud of myself. Like I just had my big movie-moment. But no one else said a word. I was looking at Lil, and I couldn't tell what she was thinking. I figured she would have smiled, proud that I finally stood up for something like she always did. I figured there was gonna be applause any second now, then the music would start to soar.

Paw threw a beer can at my head.

It dropped me like a rock. Just before the lights went out, I heard him asking again, "Can we *eat*?"

Everything was punk rock after that.

When I came to, there was a full-on ruckus. Lil had jumped up to go after Paw, which ended with Mama getting in her face. Everyone was screaming and hollering at each other. Ari was on the ground beside me, shaking me awake. I could already feel a lump rising up in the middle of my forehead. Somehow, the earbud hadn't fallen from my ear, so there was a Flipper song playing, the one that goes *a-hahahahaha, oh-hohohohoho, eh-hehehehehehe*. It was like even my music was laughing at me.

Then Pauline walked back into the kitchen. She said, "It's time to start."

No one really heard her, not with the chorus of shouting. But she didn't care because she had something in her arms. She was looking down and smiling, cradling it like a baby, even though her stomach was bigger than ever. Her lips were moving. She was making kissy faces, rocking back and forth. There was something pink and foamy oozing down her legs.

And I realized she had the president's head.

"It's time," she cooed, "*Time.*"

It was a chain reaction, Ari looked up to see what I saw, then Lil followed her gaze, until, finally, everyone was silent and looking at Pauline. A whole dining room full of mouths hanging open. And there was Pauline, whispering sweetly to a severed head that was blinking and smiling back up at her.

The head said, "You know, I'm automatically attracted to beautiful. I just start kissing them. It's like a magnet. Just kiss, I don't even wait."

Pauline lifted it up to press it against her lips.

Mama went to her. She held a hand over her own mouth, reached out. Pulled the hand back. Her eyes were huge and full of tears. "Oh," she said. "Oh, oh, oh."

Pauline smiled, some seriously freaky shit, and said, "*My baby.*" Even though it was obvious she hadn't had her baby yet.

Paw was looking around like *what kind of fucking acid trip am I on?*

50

Mama touched the head. Crazy as it was, for just a second it was the picture of a proud new grandmother welcoming the next generation. But it wasn't really anything like that at all. Especially when she closed her eyes and started in with all the praising.

"The Lord is my rock and my fortress and my deliverer, my God, in whom I take refuge, my shield, the horn of my salvation, my stronghold and my refuge, you save me from violence, I call upon the Lord, who is worthy to be praised, and I am saved from my enemies . . ."

She stretched her arms out to Pauline, then said, "Give him to me."

Pauline shook her head violently.

"Pauline, he has been *sent* for me. Give him to me."

Again, shaking her head.

"Pauline . . ."

Then Mama fucked up.

Since Pauline was obviously not giving up the head, Mama figured that she'd just reach over and take it from her. That probably would have worked if everything was normal. But nothing at all was normal anymore. As soon as Mama's hands touched that orange hair, Pauline let out a screech that couldn't have come from human vocal chords.

She hurled Mama across the kitchen.

More than four hundred pounds, flying through the air like a half-full sack of potatoes. Like it was nothing. She smashed into the table, hurling cheese, hamburger, and dishes everywhere, and kept right on going. Only coming to a halt when she crashed into the far wall of the kitchen. The wall cracked out behind her like she was in an old cartoon.

She lay there, moaning.

Paw reacted almost immediately.

I heard the *chuck-chuck* sound of him cocking the Remington. He raised the sawed-off shotgun up at his own daughter, with no hesitation. I thought he was going to say something. Maybe even start shouting. I thought he might turn around and race to his wife's side. I thought a lot of things, but never thought he would pull the trigger.

A shot exploded from the gun.

Pauline's chest and belly erupted in a shower of red and white, bodily fluids splashing all over the dining room. Somehow, she wasn't blown back into the hallway behind her. Instead, she just stood there. She was almost smiling, or maybe it was a grimace of pain. Her eyes rolled right on up toward heaven while her life poured out the gaping red hole in the middle of her.

Then she dropped.

The president's head rolled across the floor.

The moment after the gunshot went off was the quietest moment ever.

It shattered the air, broke our voices too. None of us said a word. We didn't look at each other. I wasn't breathing, my heart had stopped. Gunpowder was thick in the air. Pauline's body was laying there on the linoleum. It looked like she was floating down a widening river that just happened to be red. She didn't move at all.

Someone had turned down the volume.

Then I heard Mama, moaning somewhere behind me. The metallic chatter of Paw's gun, ejecting the spent cartridge, chambering another round. An automatic, mechanical kinda sound. Like he was getting ready to shoot another empty can. Someone, it must have been Ari, let out a tiny gasp.

It was Lil who made the first sound that might have been a cry.

Lil, of all people.

And it was Lil who was the first at Pauline's side. Doc Martens slipping in blood and bodily fluids. Almost falling, catching herself. Then dropping down to her knees in all that red anyway. Reaching for Pauline's hand, touching her blood-spattered face. Looking at those wide-open eyes that didn't blink. Saying her name, like the 12-gauge ammo had just knocked her out and she was going to wake her up.

Pauline wasn't going to wake up.

I got there next. Work boots in the blood, hand on Lil's shoulder. I felt like I was gonna hurl. Lil said, "*What the fuck. What the fuck. Somebody call the fucking ambulance.*"

Mama's voice croaked behind us. "She's not injured, honey, she's *dead.*"

And I looked back to see Mama on all fours, crawling slow across the floor. Coming toward us, it seemed, like a grizzly bear in women's clothes. Her face was all banged up and she had a rabid look in her eyes. I figured she'd start wailing any second now, and I almost felt bad for her. We all knew that Pauline was her favorite.

But she wasn't coming toward us at all.

Oh no, she was after the president's head.

Just then, as she reached for it, I saw something outside. Movement. Some kind of truck pulling right up to the house. It was a dark shape in the swirling snow. I wondered how somebody had already called the paramedics, how they got here so fast. Paw had seen it too and went for the door. He was still holding the Remington.

Mama was on the floor, holding the head in her lap. It had taken some of the shotgun blast. The face was speckled with holes, but it was still blinking. She touched its lips like a lover. It smiled up at her, then scowled, like it was trying to find the right reaction. "We need toughness now," it said, "We need toughness."

She stroked it again, then replied, "I know, my love . . . my lord . . . I already made some plans. Even before I knew you were coming."

Paw threw the door open, brought the gun up to bear. Then lowered it. It wasn't the sheriff and it wasn't the ambulance. I saw the letters on the side of the van. *WMDC.* Saw folks climbing out with cameras, lights, and microphones. Turning them on the house and toward the sky above it.

Mama had called the goddamn news crew.

And here came the sheriff and two more cop cars, late for the party.

Ari was standing beside me and Lil now. She made another gasping sound, then said, "What the fuck is that?"

"Local news," Lil replied.

"No, not that. *That.*"

53

We looked to where she was pointing, down toward Pauline's body. We looked, and we saw it right away. In the bloody hole in the middle of her chest, from her tattered breasts to the middle of her bloated stomach, something was moving.

No, not moving.

It was *squirming*.

It was Big Mama's starring role, the one she'd been waiting for all her life.

Her audience was finally here. So many pickups and rebel flags you'd have figured there was a rodeo in our front yard. Neighbors and strangers were camped out in the snow, like they had been all day. But now it wasn't just across the road. There were people everywhere you could see. There was even some cars parked in the yard, and a few more fools lurking just past the front porch. Almost all of them, cameras and phones pointed up, taking in the lights and the thing above the house. It was a crowd drawn in by the crowd.

The sheriff and his deputies were there, already looking defeated.

And, of course, the news crew.

Mama had never had a more captive audience. Free speech for the dumb, and she wasn't about to waste it. It was like Paw hadn't just blown Pauline away in the dining room, or there wasn't something not-right wriggling around inside her carcass. Mama got back up on her feet, all on her own. Not once letting go of that damn head. She didn't look at us while she shuffled to the door. Didn't pay no heed to Paw, even when he tried to stop her from going outside.

The head was in her arms, but nobody had really seen it yet.

There were some flashbulbs, some minor applause from out in the snow. The reporter pushed forward, two mobile cameras trailing him. "Hello, this is Jeff Starship here with WMDC News, at the McNeil residence in Pea Patch, Michigan, where the strange lights that have been appearing across this nation - and others - have become a reality for one rural family."

The reporter actually yawned on camera. "Someone, who we assume is Mrs. McNeil, has just appeared to speak with the crowd of locals who have apparently gathered in front of her house. Judging by the number of people in the yard, and across the street from the residence, one can only assume that this is a community with a high unemployment rate."

Mama started with a prayer. All that *the-Lord-is-my-salvation-I-will-fear-no-one* shit. Then she said, "Howdy, America. I am one of your true daughters, the Lord is with me, and *I am good people . . .*"

A hoot went up from somewhere in the drifting white horizon.

". . . but my family is under *siege*. Just like the Nazis did to all-a them Jews in Germany, the liberals are doing to the Christians now. It's the *same* thing. The media and the homosexuals are trying to *destroy* God . . ."

Paw shook his head, somehow not looking out of place with his shotgun on the porch.

". . . and they are tryin' to *destroy* our president. But I'm here to tell you, he will *not* be destroyed."

There was some cheering, but not in an overwhelming kinda way. The producer from the news van was talking on a headset, she didn't seem to be listening to Mama. The reporter glanced at his watch.

"The truth is, through God's will, *I* have been chosen to protect our great leader. Through my continued prayer and constant devotion, *I* have been rewarded with being the Lord's messenger here on earth."

She stepped forward all dramatic. "Behold, I give you . . . *proof*."

She lifted the head up for all to see.

A murmur went through the crowd. Somewhere a woman gasped. Another bumpkin made a sound like he was cheering on a stripper. I think it was Bodean, or maybe Dwain, letting out that same hoot he hooted while he was fucking Pauline.

"That's a human head," the sheriff said.

One of the deputies came back with, "Sure is."

Someone else added, "Looks like the president's head."

Even from where I was standing, Mama looked kinda peeved. Like everybody oughta be bowing down or telling her she was the next Jesus or something. "It *is* the president's head, but it's *a sign from the Lord* too." She said it like she was one of them old-timey preachers going on about fire and brimstone, but nobody was falling down in the aisles.

One of the crew peeked out from behind a camera, shaking his head.

Dwain said, "We seen that before."

Bodean, in his best overalls, was like, "*Yup*, sure did."

Mama lowered the head. She looked at it, looked back at the reporter. "But it's *the president's head.*"

The reporter shrugged.

Not even the head had bothered to say anything.

Sheriff Bud remarked, "Haven't you been watching the news, Darlene? The president's head is showing up all over the place."

The reporter lowered his mic. The producer stepped forward, holding her clipboard, looking to console Mama. "Footage has been coming in all day. These . . . *heads* are present almost anywhere one of the ships has appeared. If it isn't, then it's probably just that no one has found it yet."

"Ships?"

"The spacecraft, ma'am."

Dwain said, "Yew eff oh."

Mama leaned out and peered up at the sky. "But . . . *it's one of the Lord's chariots*, come to rain fire down on all the liberals and homosexuals."

"Nope," Bodean said, "It's just aliens."

Mama's shoulders slumped. "But . . . but . . ."

The cameraman said, "We can get a really killer shot of this one, though. Soon as the snow lets up."

Bud adjusted his belt, motioning for the deputies to come forward. "I'm afraid the family's not gonna be here for that. Joe, Darlene . . . I'm sorry that you have to leave your house now, in front of all these people."

But no one was moving, not Paw or Mama, and not the deputies either.

Bodean looked at the reporter. "I heard they saved Hitler's willie. It's in a church in Germany somewhere. They been tryin' to squeeze enough juice from it to make 'em some super-soldiers."

The producer laughed. "One of my colleagues in Portland got a call a few weeks ago. This poor woman was obviously *delusional*. She said that the president showed up in her back yard one night after her husband was passed-out drunk. Supposedly, she had sex with him. Then, after they were done, his head popped off. It just -" She made a popping sound with her finger in her mouth. "- and rolled right across the patio, next to the grill."

Everyone laughed. Everyone but Mama. "The craziest part was when she said, as soon as the head detached itself, another one grew back in its place."

Bodean gave a hee-haw laugh. "That's some crazy shit right there."

Then everybody started laughing.

Even the president's head.

That's what shut them all up. I guess none of the other heads must've made a sound. They sure were surprised when it said, "Do you mind if I sit back a little? Because your breath is very bad."

The eyes of the sheriff got huge. The cameraman jumped back behind his camera, even as the producer was moving aside, going *get this, you've gotta get this*. The reporter shook himself upright and jammed the microphone toward the porch.

No stranger to the press, the head immediately said, "I'm thinking to myself right now, we should cancel the election and just give it to me, right?" And then it said something else. The word was quiet at first, and didn't make any sense, but then it started to get louder. Over and over, it said, "*Covfefe . . . covfefe . . . covfefe . . .*"

As it repeated this dumbass nonsense word, something started happening to Pauline's body. It was shaking all over and looked like it was expanding right in front of us. Lil and Ari backed away real slow. I saw the thing inside her chest, whatever it was, start squirming around even more. It was like an octopus I'd seen on one of those nature shows once. But it was orange and gray, and it looked really pissed off.

Lil pulled me back, just as the first tentacle ripped right out of Pauline's body.

"Sometimes, by losing a battle, you find a new way to win the war."

That was the president's head, and what it said actually made sense. It was some Obi-Wan shit. It was what Ari might have said to convince Lil to leave the country. But the head wasn't talking about leaving. Not unless leaving meant the three of us hauling ass away from the monster in the dining room. We got no further than the opposite wall, squeezing into the corner where the wood-burning stove was flickering.

The thing that rose up from Pauline's chest swayed back and forth. It could have been a snake dancing for a snake charmer, but the colors were all wrong. There was blood, and chunks of something meaty, sliding down the orange-and-gray length of it. *My sister's insides*, I thought. It throbbed like a cock ready to burst, puffing itself up with every pulse. The base of the thing was still inside her body, and it was getting *bigger*.

Then it swung around to look at us. *Look* at us, because *the fucking thing had a face on the end of it*. It was small, and looked even less human, but there was no mistaking. It was the face of the president.

It stopped right in front of Lil. The tiny mouth opened and let out a lizard-like *hiss*.

She punched the son-of-a-bitch.

It blinked hard, recoiled, but twisted back around to make an even nastier kind of whisper. This sound was followed by another, then another, but they weren't coming from the thing in Lil's face. Ari grabbed my arm, pointing past the tentacle-snake thing, where Pauline's body was laying on the floor.

Another slimy limb had oozed its way out of her stomach. It was bobbing around, trying to get the eyes to work, sounding like a pissed-off snake. Like the first one, it was still connected to Pauline's insides.

Then her legs started to move, like she was trying to kick. I had the terrible thought that she wasn't really dead. But that wasn't it. Her legs spread wide, then wider . . . until something *snapped* and they weren't in a position that any human limbs could take. But they had to bend like that to make room for the fucking tentacle, or *whatever* it was, that reached out from between her legs. It was already making a reptilian screech before it even hit the air.

And it was bigger than the other ones.

"*Fuck*," I said.

From the porch I heard the president's head proclaim, "It's gonna be huge! I'm telling you, it's gonna be tremendous!"

For once, I didn't think he was lying.

There was just a glimpse of Pauline's arm reaching up into the air, another little face bursting from the end of it, before my view was blocked by a flash of orange-and-gray. The limb that had us pinned was flailing about, getting bigger, bigger, and hissing louder. It was more like a screech now. And it was still fixated on Lil, the squinty face lolling just inches from hers. It almost looked like it was laughing.

Then it went for her crotch.

She grunted, smacking at it like a pervert on the city bus.

Seeing the way she awkwardly swung at it reminded me of something from childhood. Lil was always the fearless one. She was the first to climb to the top of a rotting old tree, the first to jump in a mucky pond without looking. She never had any problem with spiders and she turned field mice into pets. But she fucking *hated* snakes. The only time I ever heard her scream like a girl was that summer we went camping in the woods and a little garter snake slipped into her sleeping bag . . .

She screamed like that now.

Hissing and coiling, the thing launched itself between her legs again. This time it grabbed hold of her. Her eyes bulged in panic. She pushed at it desperately, slapping the miniature face in vain. It looked like the worst kinda porn I'd ever seen.

Something buzzed past my ear before I could do anything. There was a nasty squelch as a fireplace poker buried itself in the tentacle just below the head. Damn-near chopped it off. It was Ari, who let out some kind of battle cry and yanked the poker free, flecking us with something thick and yellow.

"Get ready to roll," she said. Lil and I nodded.

I rolled and Ari swung again.

This time she nailed it, cleanly separating the head from the tentacle. The snaky limb curved back, twisting around blindly, spurting yellow.

Lil was still freaking, shoving at the head of the thing, its mouth fastened between her legs. Ari gave it a couple solid punches and knocked it to the ground. Sliding around under their feet, the tiny mouth was still snapping away, making a tinier *hiss-hiss-hiss*. Lil shouted and laid her Doc Martens into it a few times. It splattered like a pus-filled pumpkin, then rolled over in the corner, twitching.

Ari put an arm around her. "You alright?"

Lil shook her head, a bit too vigorously, and knocked the hair out of her eyes. "*Yeah . . . yeah*, I'm fine, fine. No, really, I'm good."

She took a deep breath, looked around to find me. She nodded, like *you're okay, right*, and I nodded back. Then she turned back to the growing monstrosity in the McNeil dining room. "But we need to seriously fuck this thing up."

Just in case the president's talking head, alien invaders hovering over the house, and some kind of monster slithering out of my sister's carcass wasn't enough, we quickly figured out that if we cut one of the tentacles off . . . yeah, that's right, *it fucking grew back*. Not only did a new face, even uglier than the first one, push its way out the end of the tentacle, but the head that got lopped off started to grow new limbs of its own.

Like the little bastard that Lil had kicked across the floor.

No more than the smashed-up shell of a thing, the mouth kept moving. Making a weak croaking sound. It got louder, then a bunch of appendages sprouted from underneath it. Something like the legs of a spider if a spider got it on with an octopus. The legs, or whatever, struggled for a second, like Bambi standing up on the ice, then pushed the mashed head right up from the floor.

It looked this way and that, looked like it might have been sniffing the air. Then it started coming after us. Ari swung the poker like she was golfing, knocked it back against the wall. But it wasn't giving up that easy. It started sniffing the air again.

The tentacle it'd been chopped from was flailing behind it with a new face on the end, even tinier and more distorted than the first. It, too, was moving around like a blind man without a cane.

Worst part was, behind that I could see those tentacles had poked out of damn-near every part of Pauline's body. Arms, chest, stomach. There was even one coming out of the middle of her face. They were all swinging around like party decorations from hell, must've been about twenty of them. From what I could tell, every one of them had those little heads attached to them.

We were *so* fucked.

I'm not sure when all of this had gotten attention from outside, but folks were bursting into the house now. Deputies were moving up against the wall, about as far away as they could get. Sheriff Bud was in the doorway. His gun was out, but he looked too stunned to remember how it worked. Behind him were some good ol' boys who'd figured out that bulls might not be the wildest ride that ever was.

And Paw was there. Just standing in front of the thing, shotgun hanging down at his side. His eyes were all big and frozen. Like he could blast the fuck out of his child with no problem, but *now* he was gonna freeze up.

Someone said, "What in the hell *is* it?"

From the porch: "If you see somebody getting ready to throw a tomato, knock the crap out of 'em, would you? Seriously, okay? Just knock the hell - I promise you, I will pay for the legal fees."

So, just like that, someone tackled the sheriff.

One of those big-ass country boys leaped on him from behind. Knocked him right down to the ground. He grunted, his service revolver skittering across the floor. This must have spooked one of the deputies because all of a sudden there were gunshots. *Bang, bang, bang,* in the direction of the doorway.

Paw flinched, but finally raised the shotgun.

One of the monster arms snapped across the room.

The deputy fumbled his gun, but it was too late. The thing had attached itself to the middle of his face. He tried to scream. The sound was muffled under the force of the tentacle, which started to push. Not quick, but just enough to make the most pain. Turns out, Pauline had given birth to a five hundred-pound asshole. At first blood was seeping from around the tentacle arm, but then it was spraying all over the place. He stopped trying to scream.

Paw continued to watch. Frozen, I guess.

The head of the deputy caved in with the sound of a rotten pumpkin. It left a nasty-looking red and gray flower shape on the wall behind him. The arm flung him carelessly to the side, where he thumped into the upside-down dinner table.

The other arms started rising up.

"Iggy, *here.*"

It was Lil, shoving the hatchet from beside the fireplace into my hands. "Don't get in the way. But if one of those things tries creeping up on us, *castrate the fuck out of it.*"

Then she reached into her leather jacket and pulled out a gun. It was a Sig, which I didn't know she had. I didn't know she had a gun at *all.* I looked at Ari, who already had her Glock out and ready. There must have been some surprise on my face. Lil said, "You didn't think we'd show up in this town unarmed, did you?"

"Damn straight," Ari said.

"*Hey, Dad*," Lil shouted, taking aim at the mess of tentacles that used to be our sister, "Are you gonna use that thing on something other than us?" Paw looked at her, puzzled, then picked up what she was laying down. He raised the shotgun up toward the monster.

I cranked the music, hoping the gunshots wouldn't leave me deaf.

GG Allin screamed *bite it, you scum, here I come*, and the bullets started flying.

Bullets were flying all over the dining room, smoke was everywhere. Ari loaded at least one more clip. Lil took her time with each shot, calling the monster a motherfucker every time. Paw kept throwing more shells into the Remington. The sheriff joined in, until it was nothing but chaos and gunfire. Big orange chunks of the thing were flying through the air, splatting against the walls, the ceiling, and the floor.

But the monster was still standing when the smoke cleared.

Every piece of it, all of those nasty bits, here and there, were squirming. Every one of them was sprouting tendrils and heads and mouths.

"Fuck me," the sheriff said.

Ari must have seen it before I did.

Scurrying movement in the kitchen. Pots and pans rattled in the sink, then a partial, misshapen head with spider legs was in the air. Flying right at Paw, who was staring into the squirming pile on the floor.

There was a single pop to my right.

Ari was still looking down the barrel when the thing hit the ground at Paw's feet. He glanced at her, at the pus-covered jawbone connected to a leg, and then stomped it.

He looked up and gave her a nod.

She lowered the gun.

I said, "Guess you weren't kidding about that military shit."

"Wasn't kiddin' about the rest of it either." Which kinda confused me. She grinned, shook her head. "Oh yeah, you were high. That shit'll melt your brain, kid. *Well . . .*" She reached into her jacket for another clip, jammed it into the gun.

"My name used to be Eric," she said.

Before I could say anything, the monster started screeching.

Then, I shit you not, it started to walk.

The tentacles that had been flinging around in the air leapt toward the floor. Pushing all the little faces into the ground like feet, they lifted the whole squirming mess of things up. Pauline's body, which barely looked like anything human, was suddenly a big, nasty-looking thorax. Damn thing twisted around, moving a few feet this way, then a few feet that way, looking like the worst fucking spider nightmare ever.

The biggest tentacle, the one that had wriggled out from between Pauline's legs, was the one making the most noise. It sounded less like a snake and more like something that should have been extinct.

Lil said, "Fuck it, *that's* our cue."

She grabbed me by the sleeve, reached over for Ari. Pointed to the window a few feet past the fireplace. She was already halfway there when I said, "So we're just gonna *leave* like this? What about Paw? What about dying on our feet?"

She stopped. "You're fucking kidding me, right? Not like this, little brother."

"You guys go, I got this."

We looked at Ari, who was creeping back toward the fireplace. "For real, get the fuck outta here. I'll be just *fine*." She snatched up a fireproof glove and kicked the grate aside. "But it might get hot in here."

"Babe," Lil said.

With the glove, Ari reached over to grab her, pulling her close. "Don't give me that babe shit, babe. I'm about to be your Joey Ramone." She pulled Lil's face up to her own and gave her the biggest, hardest kiss I'd ever seen outside of the movies. Tears burst from the corners of Lil's closed eyes, but Ari was solid, wiping them away with a gentle flick.

She winked at me, holding out the Glock. "Get her outta here."

I took the gun. "Ari, *I* . . ."

"Yup. Now, *come on*, this ain't that scene."

It was hella hard dragging Lil away from the house, but I made it happen. She finally shrugged herself free of me, pissed off, but nonetheless determined. Looking back at the open window and our tracks in the snow, she muttered something I couldn't hear. "Lil, she *knows* what she's doing," I said, turning the whole gender thing over in my head, "You gotta trust her."

"I *do*, it's just . . . come on, Iggy."

"What are we doing, Lil? *Lil?*"

"Getting the car. But we're *not* leaving her here."

Some of the cars had already cleared out as we rounded the side of the old homestead. Whether they had left out of boredom or fear, I couldn't tell. Most of the folks that remained were alternately clamoring to get in the front door, then hauling ass right back out again. The news crew was hanging back a little but still relentless. I guess they'd be assholes to miss out on something like this. Dwain and Bodean were in their monster truck, with the big-ass tires and the rebel flag flying, making circles in the snow in the front yard. Who the fuck even knew why.

I didn't see Mama or the president's head anywhere.

Oh, and the thing above the house . . . yeah, that was *definitely* some spaceship shit.

We crept up behind the *WMDC* news van. The producer chick was in the back, headset pressed up against her ear. The reporter, Jeff Starship, was huddled under a blanket beside her, shivering and drinking from a thermos. One of the cameramen was still in front of the house, getting footage of the ship, while the other was attempting to get on the porch.

Lil rapped on the back of the van. "You might want to get the motor running."

The producer lowered her headset. "Hey, were you guys in the house? We're trying to get confirmation on what some of these cowboys are saying."

"It's all true," Lil said, "Someone got knocked up a week ago, gave birth today, and it was a bouncing baby boy . . . weighing five hundred pounds, with twenty heads that grow back when you cut them off."

Jeff Starship stopped sipping his coffee. "Shit," he said.

The producer asked, "Do you know the family who lives here?"

"I wish I didn't."

Into the headset, she said, "*Hold on* . . . no, we lost the McNeil woman. She climbed off the porch when the gunshots started. Bystander said she went behind the house - yes, she had the head with her . . . but we've got someone here who was inside." She hollered for one of the cameramen, then, to Lil, "What's your relation to the McNeils?"

Lil was scanning the yard, looking for the car. "I'm their daughter." It pained her, bad, to admit it. "Hey," she said, "When the . . . uh, *head* started in with that strange word -"

"*Covfefe?*"

"Yeah, that. It seemed to be what triggered some seriously weird shit in the house. Have you heard if any of the, um, *other* heads said anything like that?"

There were gunshots in the house, a murmur of voices.

"No, they've all been silent. This is the only one that's spoken, at least from what I've been getting." She motioned for the camera guy, who started filming us. "*However* . . . I was hooked up to another station in Chicago when this thing started chanting. As soon as it did, a hot mess broke out on the other end. Details are sketchy, but some teenager gave birth to some kind of octopus or something. Then there was all kinds of chaos and we lost contact."

"Huh. Well, that was *no* octopus." Looking back at the house, "But I'm serious about getting out of here. Something is about to happen."

Jeff Starship winked at me. "What's your take on this, kid?"

"Well, when I was talking to that thing, it didn't make a lotta sense, but -"

The producer, "Talking to what, the *head?*"

"Yeah. It was kinda bragging about gettin' it on with these different chicks. Like, all over the place, and then it leaves a head there to . . . I dunno, *watch over 'em*, maybe."

"So, wait a minute, this head said that it had been with women in *all* of these places?" I shrugged, then nodded. "Because in every place where there's been one of these . . . *ships*, there's been a . . . *head*. We've also gotten rumors of strange pregnancies in each case, and a live birth in at least three. Nothing's been confirmed, but the speculation is that they're all related."

I shook my head. "Fuckin' *duh*, dude."

"How does a head, *without a body*, make love to a woman?"

Another shrug. "Didn't the president visit all these places?" Like that explained it.

The reporter pointed up above the house. "But what's with the *War of the Worlds*?"

Well, since he asked, "It's obviously their *ride*, man. Don't you guys ever watch old sci-fi movies? All of the crazy shit this dude's been doing is just to distract us from the *real* mission. They came here to mate with human women, so they can repopulate their world. It's probably dying off from, like, years of inbreeding or something."

The producer and the reporter looked at each other.

Lil had an idea. "What I'm *wondering* is -"

Then the house exploded.

It happened fast.

The sheriff was the first one out, shoving the cameraman off the porch even as he was diving into the snow. A bunch of random dudes were next, hightailing it like something out of a cartoon. One of them just kept running, past the news van, down the driveway and beyond. I figured him for two counties away by the time he finally passed out from exhaustion.

Paw stepped out onto the porch, staring back into the house. He wasn't even hurrying. He was just standing there, looking inside, when it went. There was a flash of red and orange, reflecting across his face.

Then, *KABOOM*.

Paw went flying off the porch, while the porch went flying off the house. It was all chunks of wood and fireballs hurling everywhere. People hitting the ground in a hurry. Lil pulled me behind the van. The van moved with the blast. It was a wave of heat and sound, with fiery bits raining down over everything. So loud that you felt it more than heard it. So loud that I was laying face first in the snow and someone was singing really quiet in my ear, like there was a concert about a mile up the road. It was Iggy, and he had a lust for life.

I mean, *everybody's* seen explosions in the movies, don't care who you are. It was just like that, but I was *in* that shit.

Lil was a few feet to my left, sideways in the snow. She rolled over, looked at me, looked back at the house. Her eyes were huge.

I said, "*Whoa, this is intense.*"

Sat up in the snow. There were tentacles squirming right by my hand. I flinched, but not fast enough. A little head chomped down on my finger. It was like getting bit by a kitten. Didn't hurt so much, but it made me jump, and pissed me off even more. I didn't even know I still had the hatchet, but there it was. I hacked that fucker into bits.

Then watched.

Beside me, Lil was saying Ari's name.

The hacked bits immediately started growing new heads and limbs. But now they looked more like acorns than pumpkins. They hissed, but it was weak, really weak. A couple of them rose up, no more than six inches tall now. They half-hissed again, then went after each other. Tentacles writhing and flopping, pinning other tentacles to the ground, heads smashing into other heads, biting, chomping, then slowing down.

"Hey Lil, you gotta see this."

"Ari," she said, "*Oh, Ari.*"

I didn't want to, but I turned to look. "It's alright, sis. I'm sure that -"

The house was fucking toast.

Like the kind of toast that didn't have a kitchen or dining room anymore. The kind that was pretty much missing a bunch of walls. Nothing but pieces and piles of smoking wood, charred chunks of bed, bath, and burning beyond.

Fire was flickering over everything that was left, mostly the walls toward the back. The ones that used to be bedrooms. Creepy Jesus was still hanging on the burning flag and both eyes were lit up. Smoke was rising like a mushroom cloud over the house, raining down chunky ashes of gray with the falling snow. Raining down on the blackened mass in the center of everything. The smoking mound with all the scorched limbs reaching out in every direction.

The shit was unreal and totally felt like a scene out of a movie.

And it was the place I'd spent my entire life.

Under a nearby tree, something moved, and I saw that it was Paw.

There were voices freaking out somewhere. *Holy shit are you getting this you gotta get this are we still live start hooking up to our sister stations get this national this is fucking unbelievable . . .*

The Ramones in my ear, no joke, started blitzkrieg bopping.

The burnt-up monster was still moving.

And where the furthest end of the dining room used to be, rubble shifting. Something big and round, rising and turning. It was the supper table. Ragged and torn, imbedded with pieces of debris, but intact. The table rolled aside, then fell into the burning embers, and Ari was standing behind it. Over by the wood-burning stove, also untouched by the blast. She must have jumped behind them when everything went up. She was tattered, scuffed, and one of her legs was cut from the knee right up into her leather mini-skirt.

But mostly she just looked pissed off.

Ferocious.

Jeff Starship said aloud, on live national TV, "Fucking *badass*."

The monster was pushing itself back up from the burning wreckage. Sluggish, missing limbs, it stumbled, once, twice, but then bucked up. Like it was shrugging off the explosion. Some of the tentacles started raising up and looking around, sniffing the air. The faces were all scowling, like thirty angry little presidents.

Then I started seeing pieces of the beast. They were *everywhere*. Strewn across the debris of our house. Hanging from scorched tree branches. Stuck against the side of the news van. Scattered across the yard and all around us. All of them, wriggling around, twitching, and sprouting new parts. The president's face, popping up wherever I looked, twisted, small, and full of mindless fury. Somewhere in my mind, I was like, *just wait until I can finally vote, you fucker*, but immediately figured I'd never make it that far.

What had been only a few nasty faces were hundreds now.

They were everywhere, creeping up on us.

They went after the country boys first.

The monster truck was in the middle of the yard, just covered with the things. Dwain or Bodean, whichever one it was, had jumped out to start shooting at them. Big-ass rifle blasting, like he was popping squirrels in his back yard. Hooting all the way.

But they were already squirming across the hood, the roof, and through the open door. Covering the other guy inside, who was thrashing and screaming like a girl. The dude with the gun took aim, maybe figuring to shoot them off his friend. The gun exploded, the window shattered, and Bodean or Dwain slumped over, a bloody mess, on the seat of the pickup.

"You sumbitch! And here I voted for ya!"

Paw was still propped up against the tree, his old Colt in his hand, swatting at the little bastard that had dropped out of the branches above. Sheriff Bud was kicking madly at a trio of little monsters near his feet, trying to reload. Panic rising up on his face, it was definitely a bad day for him. Jeff Starship was in the middle of bitch-slapping a tiny president's head while the cameraman pulled in for a close-up. The producer, headset still intact, brought the edge of her clipboard down on a tentacled arm like a guillotine. Split in half, it started sprouting two new lives right in front of her.

"Lil," I said. But she was watching Ari in the debris.

Ari, who was going up against a couple blackened serpent arms. She had the fireplace poker in one hand and a burning chunk of wood from the house in the other. Swinging and spearing at the arms, they flailed and ducked. A third slipped around from the side. It went for her legs, then higher, like the one that attacked Lil. But this time it recoiled.

Ari backhanded one of the arms with the poker, burying it in the things face, immediately following through with the makeshift torch. I could hear the thing screeching its reptilian screech from across the yard.

"Lil, *you gotta see this.*"

She glanced back, and I swung the hatchet at her.

Even as she was hollering, *Iggy what the fuck*, the squirming thing by her arm turned into two. She looked at me, looked at the wriggling parts, then saw what I'd been seeing. Mashed-up faces squinting, blind and dumb, just before they started going after each other. It looked like a couple little presidents face-fucking each other. They went at it for almost thirty seconds but quickly slowed down. Both of them burst into yellow pus, stopped throbbing, and were still.

I nodded at her. "You thinking what I'm thinking?"

She totally was.

It was absolute punk rock fury.

Lil said that she sent me some music files, just before she gave me the Mohawk, and gave me a wink. Then she started hollering for everyone who was still in the yard. "Listen up, folks, my brother figured out how to stop this shit. Pick up anything you can find - it doesn't matter if it's an axe, saw, gun, pocket knife, or a big fucking rock - and just start bashing these bastards to pieces."

71

Someone tried to argue, but she pushed on, like she always did. "I know, it doesn't make sense, just making more of them, but the stupid sons-of-bitches will start cannibalizing each other. Then we can stomp them into the ground!" She looked at me, pulled a switchblade out of her jacket - yet another surprise - and shouted at the top of her lungs, "*Kick out the jams, motherfuckers!!*"

I pressed play.

And it was on.

The soundtrack for fighting monsters goes like this.

I raised the hatchet in the air. The Clash unleashed a battle cry, *this is a public service announcement . . . with guitar!* And I started swinging. Someone blew a whistle and David Peel was chanting *up against the wall motherfucker.* I slammed a tentacle against the van and chop, chop, chopped it in half.

The Stooges were having no fun, and the Dolls were having a personality crisis. A band called Death revved up and said *you're a rock and roll victim and I know this is true because I'm a rock and roll victim too.* But I didn't plan on being anyone's victim.

Jesus died for somebody's sins, but not mine, Patti Smith said, and Creepy Jesus wanted to make America great, *my sins are my own, they belong to me.* There was Pere Ubu, pounding in my head, *don't need a cure, don't need a cure, don't need a cure, I need a final solution*, and the Ramones with a snotty fake accent, *I don't care, I don't care, I don't care.* It was anger, apathy, and attitude, and it was all truth.

Beat on the brat, beat on the brat with a baseball bat, oh yeah, oh yeah, oh, oh . . .

The Saints were there in no time. The Alan Milman Sect, with stitches in their head, chorus kicking in while I stomped a bunch of heads, *I wanna kill somebody, I wanna kill someone, I wanna kill somebody, just for fun.* The Avengers, a strong female voice that just screamed Lil, was also screaming *I believe in me, I believe in me.* Devo had an uncontrollable urge. Eater had an outside view. The Dils just hated the rich, like the greedy fucks who took away the farm and the school and all the safety in the streets.

Insane society, Menace snarled, *they don't care if I live or I die . . .*

While around me, folks I'd never even met were hacking, chopping, stomping, and shooting, turning bigger monsters into smaller monsters.

Some people think little girls should be seen and not heard, but I think - oh, bondage! up yours!

Song after song poured into my head while daylight left the sky. What Lil had given me was like the history of rebellion told through music. But it was more than just that. It was the story of her life. And it was becoming mine too.

Whatever happened to the heroes, the Stranglers asked, *no more heroes anymore.*

Paw, under the tree, reloading the Colt. In my head, *animal world, screaming fist, pumping ugly muscle.* Dwain, with a shiny hunting knife raised high. *Small wonder, sick of you, see no evil.* The sheriff, spraying the thing on top of him with mace. *Wild weekend, better off dead, I love livin' in the city.*

I pulled the Glock, but suddenly lost my balls. What if I missed, and then it was too late?

The monsters were on me as soon as the Buzzcocks said *oh shit! oh shit! oh shit!*, but some lady from the store up the street pulled them off. I remembered her having posters up for the president before he won the election. We whacked and hacked and cut the little monsters up together, kicked them aside, and got back into the battle.

The Jermz jumped in with cheap & nasty guitars, chopping away with a powercut. Armed Force left bloodstains across the U.K. with a cry of *attack! attack! attack! attack!* It was the end of civilization for the Molesters, but the Pagans argued that it was just a dead-end America. *State of emergency*, cried Stiff Little Fingers. But the Skids' drummer and guitarist insisted *the saints are coming, the saints are coming.* Bohemia was waiting in the wings, just to say that American life was *no more fun for the rest of your life.* The Fun Things came back with *I'm a rock 'n roll kamikaze and you know that I'd die for you . . .*

The snow was coming down but I was burning up. My hands were bloody, sore, and drenched in the crusted yellow of chopped-up monster parts. The handle of the hatchet was chipped and worn, the blade no longer sharp. It wouldn't hold out forever and neither would I.

And that fucking ship was still up there.

Watching everything below.

Watching as . . .

S.O.A. tells me *you're gonna have to fight*, and I do.

The Teen Idles say *get up and go*, and I'm going berserk.

Bad Brains are wailing about *the big takeover*, but I'm not having it.

Bad Religion says *we're only gonna die from our own arrogance*, but not me.

Black Flag says *I see my place in American waste*, and I'm wasting the fuckers.

Disorder is clanging away with *civilization*, but I'm not gonna be civilized.

Saccharine Trust, *we don't need freedom*, and I'm disagreeing with every blow.

Potential Threat insists that I *take no shit*, but I'm already all done with that.

The Effigies, *I live in a body bag*, and that's where I'm putting them.

Iron Cross says *live for now, don't tell me about tomorrow*, but I'm killing tonight.

The Seize, warning me that *everybody dies*, but it's not gonna be me.

The Subhumans insisting *it's gonna get worse*, but not yet, goddammit.

United Mutation, *D.C. screws the world*, as I stomp the president's head again and again.

Angst, chant *die fighting, die fighting*, but that's not the plan.

Scream screaming *what the fuck you gonna do*, and now I knew what I could do.

And I knew what I had done.

Slant 6 asked *what kind of monster are you, why should I be scared of you?* But no one was really that scared anymore.

The music was slowing down.

By the time Sonic Youth showed up, we had torn the monster apart. There were pieces everywhere. The unearthly limbs that had sprouted from Pauline's body were in a hundred harmless, squirming bits all over the yard and in the burning wreckage of our house. Someone had taken an axe and made her remains too small for anything to regenerate. I tried not to look at the ripped up, bloody parts that were once something human, that were once my sister.

I tried not to think about the inhuman things we had done to stay human.

Kim Gordon snarled *support the power of women, use the power of man, support the flower of women, use the word fuck . . . the word is love.*

But it was fucking hate that had given me power.

I reached up to touch the lump in the middle of my forehead, and all the scratches and bites across my face, neck, and arms. I touched the naked sides of my skull, felt the Mohawk that was still standing firm, crusted now with my own blood and that of the beast. Suddenly, it was cold standing out in the swirling snow.

Bonsai Kitten was in my ear. *Don't mess with me, don't mess with me, don't mess with me.*

And then Ari was there, drenched and dirty, bloody and torn, holding an axe that still dripped a bunch of darkness. She had a kinda crazy look in her eyes, like I figured we all did right about then, but she was grinning.

I grinned back at her.

Sheriff Bud came over, and some of the other folks too, crowding together like sports teams do when they win a game. There were rounds of high-fives and fist bumps. Even though I was feeling shitty, it was like everyone was kind of united for a minute.

Then Ari asked, "Where's Lil?"

"I told her that it wasn't done yet," the producer said.

She was splashed with crusted yellow blood, her hair all crazy and her suit jacket ripped up. Otherwise, it looked like

75

she'd just won the raffle at a moonshine party. One of the cameramen was nowhere to be found, but the other was with the reporter, busily recording everything.

"No, we got this," Ari said, "We kicked its ass. These things can't hurt anyone now."

She nodded toward the few little monsters still wriggling around, none bigger than a bird. An old man yee-hawed. Dwain let out a hoot and stomped one of the mini-things. It made the sound of a tomato being squished.

"Maybe *we* did, but they're not having as much luck everywhere else. There's been *new* reports of women giving birth to these things. Like I said, it's not done yet."

"Where'd she *go*?"

The producer shrugged. No one else said shit.

"It's like in the movie," I said.

It was all coming to me, and I was wondering how none of these grown-ass adults were putting the shit together any faster. "The doctor puts her head in the tray, but she's not just a head anymore, know what I mean? I mean, it was like she had *powers* now. Maybe she always did, but - well, now she was controlling the thing in the closet, like the president's head was controlling . . ."

Blank looks. Jesus, these people were fucking stupid.

"There's all these heads, but *this* is the only one that matters, and Lil *knows* that. See what I'm saying? She probably figures she's gotta stop it, or *none* of it's gonna stop."

Ari was on it.

Searching the horizon, past the smoking house and the unearthly remains, she said, "Dammit, you're right, I'm with you now. We've gotta find the president's head."

Dwain said, "What fer?" The son-of-a-bitch actually said *fer*.

"So we can destroy it."

More blank looks.

The sheriff raised his hands. "Now, wait a minute. This has been a crazy day, no doubt about that, and putting this . . . *thing* down was nothing but good. But we don't really *know* what's going on here, and I can't allow anything to happen to . . ."

"The president's head?"

"Um, yeah."

"The president's head, that's not attached to his body, but is still *talking*?"

"Yeah, that. I can't allow it."

"You don't think it might have something to do with all of this craziness?"

He shrugged. "Look, I don't care who you voted for, but -"

"*Voted* for? Holy fuckin' shit, dude. You're kidding me with this, right? It's got *nothin'* to do with voting this or voting that."

Cue up the national anthem: "It's got to do with billionaires wanting to shut down the schools. It's got to do with insurance companies and stockholders mattering more than people. It's got to do with the goddamn government *encouraging* everyone to distrust their neighbors. It's got to do with riots everywhere and the fuckin' cops not even *knowing* who to shoot anymore. It's got to do with making enemies of every other country in the world - shit, maybe even the universe! - while they just let fuckin' *Nazis* march through the streets of America. And it's got plenty to do with *fuckin' women getting fuckin' knocked up so fuckin' tentacles can rip outta their fuckin' bodies!*"

Someone said, "You must be one-a them *liberals*."

Ari sighed.

I threw my hands in the air. "The hell with this. I've gotta find my sister."

But, as I turned to leave the scene, Dwain walked right in front of me. I tried to sidestep him, but he dodged and put his arms out to catch me. "Hold on now, Billy Idol." His breath was a thousand miles of tobacco and ass.

"Get off me, man. I'm *serious*, we're wasting time. We gotta get Lil."

But he wasn't letting me go.

Not until I heard the metallic click of a gun. Ari said, "I don't think so, tractor pull."

The arms dropped. Ari had the axe up against Sheriff Bud's throat, the Glock about three inches from the middle of Dwain's face. I felt around my waistband, not sure when she'd even snatched it back from me. The sheriff was shaking his head, almost sadly. Dwain looked like he didn't have anything against hitting women or children.

That's when the lights came on.

I don't mean the *eureka* kinda lights either. Nope, we were still in Pea Patch. I mean the lights of the *ship*. You know, that big-ass son-of-a-bitch the size of a city block, still hovering above the burning crater that used to be our house. It was like somebody just flipped a switch. Boom, instant *Close Encounters* moment. Night into fucking day, those kinda lights. And there was a sound, a really deep one, like somebody revving the biggest son-of-a-bitching engine you've ever seen.

Everybody was freaking. Looking up like, hey, where'd that come from?

"The barn," Ari said.

"Gotta be." I mean, how far could Big Mama have gotten anyway?

There wasn't anything holding them back, but nobody was in hot pursuit when we took our leave. They probably figured we wouldn't get that far. It was true, we didn't have that far to go before we found my sister. The spaceship lights made it easy to see the entire back yard, even with the snow whipping around, blurring everything. What always seemed like such a big place had suddenly shrunk down to nothing.

They were just outside the barn. The tracks leading to the open door said that a scuffle had happened. It looked like Lil had dragged Mama out into the yard. Mama was on her knees, maybe in prayer, and the president's head was still in her arms. Lil was a few feet away from her, looking like a cat ready to pounce.

No surprise, but they were shouting at each other. In the wind, the words weren't clear, just the tone. Mama, holierthan-thou, and Lil, pissed off. It was the way they had looked forever. A vicious gust of white made them disappear for a minute, but they hadn't changed when I could see them again.

We crept slowly closer, Ari and me.

Then closer.

A voice came out of the angry snow. It was the head. "We don't win anymore," it said, "It will change. We will have so much winning that you may get bored with winning. I don't think I'm going to lose, but if I do I don't think you're ever going to see me again, folks."

Lil looked up, saw us approaching. She held out a hand, telling us to stop.

We stopped.

Ari shouted over the wind and the sound of the ship. "It's good to see you and your mom have patched things up." Her voice cracked, sucked up into the storm. "But it's time to go, babe. So let's just put a fork in this fucker and get a room somewhere."

Mama looked at us, looked at Ari, and laughed. "I knew it. The Lord spoke to me and told me all about it. You're dirty clam-kissers, both of you."

The head, meanwhile, was back on the campaign trail. "They have been doing this to our country for a long time, for many years. They're pouring in. They are bringing drugs. They are bringing crime. I would bring back waterboarding, and I'd bring back a hell of a lot worse."

Mama pointed at Lil. "You think you finally done it, huh? Embarrassed me on my night of fame. But it's not over yet."

The wind was howling again, and so was Lil. "No one cares about that, Mother, and no one cares what you think. Especially not this *thing* you're holding."

"That's what you think."

Then, for the second time that day, Mama grunted and slowly stood up on her own. She wobbled, but stayed on her feet. Her face was burning red in the blowing snow. Her eyes were huge and reflecting crazy light. She raised an arm into the sky, like an old-time gospel show, still clutching the president's head with the other.

Lil was about to dive for it when another light hit Mama. An orange beam pouring down on her from above.

It went up and up, into the swirling column of white, all the way up to the ship. Snow and ice pelted my eyes. It must have still been over fifty feet above us, even more, but nothing was clear. There might have been other lights, spinning around the spot where the orange light started, but I was getting dizzy trying to see it. My teeth were chattering, my face frozen.

Ari was stuck in place beside me too, and Lil was looking lost.

Big Mama was cackling like a madwoman. It looked like her and the head were taking a bath in orange paint. "My chariot has come," she said, shutting her eyes in ecstasy. "Tomorrow will be a great gettin-up mornin' for me. But for the rest-a you sinners . . . may God have mercy on your pitiful and pathetic souls."

And she started to rise into the air, straight up to heaven.

The sound of a band tuning up whispered in my ear. Then a guitar began strumming gently. It made a couple short rounds and a female voice started singing. *My baby loves me, I'm so happy . . . happy makes me a modern girl.* I knew it was Sleater-Kinney.

Big Mama was being lifted off the ground. The orange beam was calling her home, just like she said, with the head held firmly in her arms. Her feet left the ground. One inch, two, three, and more. Ari and I were too far away to do anything. It took me a while to figure that out, but I know it now.

But Lil was right there.

She looked back at us like she knew. Her face said *I don't have a choice*, and it said *I'm sorry*. It said a lot of things. But then she was running to get Mama. I don't know if she wanted to save her, or if she knew that letting the head escape would be disaster. She just acted, doing what she thought she had to do. Just like she always did.

Mama was already a few feet off the ground when she got there. But Lil didn't hesitate. She hurled herself into the air, throwing her arms around Mama. It was like the first time they had hugged in years, even though it wasn't that at all.

The beam dragged her right into the air too.

Took my money and bought a TV, TV brings me closer to the world . . .

She was six feet above ground, then seven, eight, nine, and I was screaming *let it go, Lil, let it go.* I don't know if it was in my head or out loud, but it kept on, over and over, until letting go wouldn't have been a good idea anymore. She was at least fifteen feet high and rising when we got there. Ari crouched and jumped with everything she had, but it wasn't even close.

She crashed into the snow, while I dropped down to the ground too. This time I know I said it out loud, *let go, Lil, please . . . just let go*, because she was still only about twenty feet above us. Anybody could survive twenty feet.

But then twenty was twenty-five, then thirty, and forty.

And the voice in my head sang *my whole life was like a picture of a sunny day, my whole life is like a picture of a sunny day.*

"*Goddammit,*" Ari cried, yanking the gun out at the sky. But what was she gonna shoot?

The guitar plucked along while my sister grew further and further away. She must have been fifty feet in the air, I could barely see her.

I might have been crying, maybe I was screaming, I don't even know. But Ari was there, grabbing me, like we just got bad news at the hospital, and her face was wet. The gun accidentally smacked me in the head. She was crying, but kept it quiet, not like me. I was bawling like a fucking baby, and I was pissed off as hell.

I was screaming at the sky.

My baby loves me, I'm so hungry . . . hunger makes me a modern girl.

Higher and higher they went, but something was grinding above our heads.

Like some kinda motor.

Took my money and bought a donut, the hole's the size of this entire world.

It definitely sounded like something was wrong.

My whole life is like a picture of a sunny day . . .

Maybe it was the combined weight of Mama and Lil together. Maybe alien tractor beams have to be calibrated for every new load. Maybe something happened way up in the darkened sky that we couldn't see. Maybe this was the plan all along.

.   Or maybe it was just a really shitty day.

. . . my whole life was like a picture of a sunny day.

We were looking into the sky and the lights and the falling down snow, hanging on to each other for dear life. They looked like nothing more than part of the blizzard at first. Like part of the snowfall that for some reason was bigger than the rest. But it wasn't snow that was falling that fast. It wasn't snow at all.

They didn't make any sound as they fell.

But it sounded like a meteor hitting the ground.

It sounded like the end of the world.

Baby loves me, I'm so angry . . . anger makes me a modern girl . .

.

Mama hit first. She didn't have a word to say about it, and she'd never say another word about anything. Her head was twisted almost completely around. The snow covered most of her face, except for the one eye that was staring out at me, unblinking. The immense bulk of her was still.

Lil was stretched out across her, almost like a baby in her arms.

My first thought was that she was okay. It sounds stupid, but that's what I thought. Because she landed on Mama, it cushioned her fall. I'd seen it happen in movies, so maybe it happened here. Before I got there, I saw her move, I saw her breathe. So maybe, maybe, maybe.

Took my money, I couldn't buy nothin', I'm sick of this brave new world.

But she was twisted up all wrong.

82

She was bent, and her eyes were already filling up with death. Nothing was moving now, nothing but her lips. Her mouth, curling just a little, just enough. I fell on top of her, trying to hear. Her eyes flickered, not much more than light passing, a reflection. And I was crying and I pushed my face up to hers, and pressed my ear against her mouth.

And it was quiet, it was so quiet, but I heard.

"Die on your feet . . . don't live on your knees."

And that was it.

She was gone.

Ari was beside me, her face a wreck, putting her hands on Lil. Trying to shake her, wrapping her arms around her. Then screaming, but not with sound. Her mouth was wide open and nothing was coming out.

My whole life was like a picture of a sunny day . . .

And the rest of them were there.

The reporter with his microphone, and the man with the camera. The producer with her face all slack in shock. The sheriff was crunching forward in the snow. Somewhere he must have lost his hat. Behind him were country boys and old men and the women who worked in the shops in town, where Lil or Mama would never go again, and no one was saying a word.

No one said shit, and I was glad.

My whole life is like a picture of a sunny day . . .
My whole life was like a picture of a sunny day.

I was destroyed when my sister died.

It's hard to say what I figured life would be when I got older. Most of the time it was just like the Sex Pistols predicted, that there *was* no future. When I looked around at all the stupid shit that everyone was doing, especially our so-called leaders, it pissed me the fuck off. Because they were all a bunch of fat old white men with piles of money, and they'd already had their chance. What they were doing, in all of their greed and selfishness and stupidity, was taking that same chance away from everyone else. I didn't really want to hurt anyone, but by the time I was sixteen I already wanted to burn this fucking world down to the ground.

I always figured, however it went, that Lil would be right there beside me.

But no matter how bad it fucked me up to see her laying dead in the snow, no matter how destroyed, or full of rage I thought I was, Ari was a thousand times more.

She was absolute silence.

She was total fury.

When she finally let go of Lil, there were no tears left on her face. There was hardly any expression at all. She stood up, really slow, and stared into the sky. If she could have reached that ship, still hovering above us, she would have torn it apart with her bare hands. No one dared to utter a word. If anyone said the wrong thing at that moment, maybe *anything* at all, you can bet your sweet ass they would have died in place of the unreachable alien invaders.

She turned to leave, to just walk away from everything. That's what she was going to do, and no one was going to stop her.

She was walking away when the president's head spoke.

It said, "Do you remember that date? Was that a beautiful date? What a date."

Probably like her, I hadn't thought about it for a few minutes. I figured the thing had been snatched up by the ship. Maybe it had been destroyed in the fall. I didn't know and I didn't care. More than that, I don't think anyone there would have gone looking for it. But that stupid son-of-a-bitch just couldn't keep his mouth shut.

Ari stopped in her tracks.

It spoke again. "I'm good at war. I've had a lot of wars of my own. I'm really good at war. I love war in a certain way, but only when we win."

It was somewhere in the snow just beyond Lil and Mama. Ari turned in that direction, her face a mask of rage. Her body, taut and feline, following the scent of vengeance in the wind. Her eyes were pure murder.

"It is better to live one day as a lion than a hundred years as a sheep."

She stopped, then dropped.

With her bare knees in the snow, she sat there. Her head was bowed. It almost seemed like she was praying, and maybe she was. Until she lifted her arm up in the air. Something glinted in the light from the ship, and I saw that it was the switchblade. The knife that Lil had been fighting with, still crusted with creature blood.

No sound other than a grunt, she drove the knife down into the snow.

She lifted it back up. The president's head came up with it, the blade having been plunged deep into the socket of his eye. She stood up. Holding the head in front of her, she spat in his face. The eye not filled up with the knife blinked, trying to clear itself of saliva.

Even then, it didn't have enough sense to keep quiet. "It's extremely unfair, and that's a mild word, to the president."

Still, no one else said a word, no one tried to stop her.

"I was going to hit one guy in particular," it said, "A very little guy. I was gonna hit this guy so hard his head would spin and he wouldn't know what the hell happened."

But Ari was already setting him up to spin. She dropped him down to the ground, put one of her Doc Martens in his face, and yanked the knife out. She took a few steps backward, like the biggest, baddest, blackest soccer player ever, and took a run at him. She must have smeared his face all over her boot, she kicked him so hard. Then she went back for more.

"I think if this country gets any kinder or gentler, it's literally going to cease to exist."

She held the battered face deep in the snow. So deep that you couldn't hear the son-of-a-bitch speak, even though he kept on. She held it down, but it would not be frozen or drowned. She flipped it over and looked it in the eyes.

When she pulled out the Glock, I thought someone might try to stop her. Dwain got restless, like he might make a move. I guess shooting this thing was too much for him, even if the rest of it wasn't. But the sheriff put a hand on his chest.

Stopping him cold. I realized then that the camera was still rolling, that everyone in the world might be watching this.

Ari put the barrel of the gun against its forehead.

"We have to be much smarter or -"

BANG.

For a moment she just breathed. In, out. In, out. I'm not sure *I* was even breathing.

"- it's never ever going to end."

Then she screamed.

She picked the head up, with the gaping hole in the middle of it, oozing brains and blood that were rotting, yellow, and inhuman, and she wailed in its face at the top of her lungs. It wasn't just a scream of rage, but a scream of frustration and grief that would probably never end. She tightened up her fist and punched it in the face. Again and again and again, all the while unleashing a cry that grew ever more guttural. When she reached the end of what her voice could do, she took a breath and screamed some more.

She screamed like no one has ever screamed before.

Then she screamed again.

Finally, when she could find no more screams, when her voice had all but died, when her hands were bloodied, scraped, and broken from pounding him in the face, she snarled her most animal snarl and spread her legs wide open. She spread her legs and mashed his face between them, pushing it as deep as it could possibly go. There were tears falling down her face, but they had gone miles past anger or grief for just her dead lover. They were for so much more that it would be impossible to name them all.

He struggled.

For the first time, he *really* struggled. If it was because she had not been born the woman she was now, or because her rage was that much stronger than he was, no one could say. If she knew that this would work when nothing else had, she's never really told me. But the son-of-a-bitch struggled, for the first time in his long and pampered life.

The camera was on, and the entire world *was* watching.

He tried to bully her.

86

I'll beat the crap out of you, he told her. Then, when that didn't work, because she wasn't listening to him anymore, and she was not afraid, he threatened her with *I don't know if I'll do the fighting myself, or if other people will.* But there were no other people to be found then.

He tried to buy himself a savior. *I promise you, I will pay your legal fees*, and all that bullshit. There were a few who looked like they might step up to the challenge, but they did not. The folks who wouldn't put up with it still outnumbered them, and the woman's rage was far too strong. *Our allies are safe*, he promised, but no one was going to side with him here.

He whined that *part of the problem is nobody wants to hurt each other anymore*, then cried that *it's a national emergency.* Because it wasn't a national emergency when the Nazis started marching in American streets. *Why don't we use nuclear weapons*, he asked, but none of his generals were there, and they wouldn't have dropped the bomb for him now anyway.

Finally, he had nothing other than excuses. *I'm just a fucking businessman.*

But Ari wasn't much for excuses.

She squeezed her legs tighter.

She rode his face like a total warrior, clenching so tight that she started to cave in his skull. It was his turn to scream now, and it was his turn to cry. He did both very well, some might say better than anyone. After a few minutes, alien blood was seeping from under her mini-skirt. A minute more and red had joined the yellow, because the thing had started biting her. It was the only defense left for it now.

But she didn't cry out, and she sure as hell didn't stop.

The rage hadn't left her face yet.

"We've got to be nice and cool," it said, "Nice and calm. Alright, stay on point, stay on point. No sidetracks, nice and easy."

But it was obvious that the fascist fucker wasn't gonna win. Somebody had started clapping, and then a great cheer rose up from the spectators. It was fucking weird. Not just because nobody bothered to step up and help, but that it was still like a bunch of folks watching to find out who the father was on *The Maury Show*.

There were some who didn't join in. Big Mama would have been with them. I guess they figured an alien that put tentacled monsters in the people could still make America great again. But none of them tried to fight the crowd.

The president's head didn't die immediately.

It still had bribes to offer, deals it tried to make, and insults when none of that worked. But when everything that got it here had failed, it ended up where the rest of us spend our fucking lives: in fear and desperation, with no hope to be found from the government.

"Nothing changes," it said, slowing down, "Nothing changes."

I held Lil's hand, still, though it was colder than cold. More than anything, I wanted the son-of-a-bitch to tell us why he had come here and what he was trying to do. I wanted him to tell me personally why she had to die. But it wasn't gonna happen. Maybe I was right. They had come to mate with human women so they could repopulate their world, which was dying from generations of inbreeding. Yeah, we'll just go with that.

Ari closed her eyes, threw back her head, and delivered the same kind of compassion that she would have gotten from him.

"I think I've made a lot of sacrifices. I work very, very -"
Splat.

Apparently, that was it.

The moment the spaceship had been waiting for.

The president's head, whatever the fuck it might have been, was nothing but a crushed pumpkin now. Mission has failed. E.T. phone home and tell your friends, this is how we do it down here. If you know what's good for you, you'll send the smarter aliens next time.

The ship hovered a few more minutes, blowing up another blizzard within the blizzard. There were more strange sounds, different lights than before, then it started to move. I shaded my eyes with my hand and stared up into those lights. We all did. It's not every day you see something like that.

Then it was lifting, up and up.

Getting further and further away, until, finally, it was gone.

Ari wiped her thighs off with handfuls of snow.

Even though there had been cheering, and applause, I'd *heard* it, now there was nothing but silence. Nobody bothered to come forward, not even to offer her a goddamn coat or something. If I was wearing one, I would have walked over to her and wrapped it around her shoulders, that's what I would have done. Because, to be honest, I didn't know what the fuck to say either.

She stood up, kinda wobbly, and her legs were a mess. But it wasn't like anybody was gonna question her strength. Not here anyway, and definitely not right now. She was a total badass. It was no wonder that my sister fell in love with her.

The snow crunched under her feet as she approached.

She looked at me, looked down at Lil.

Then she knelt down, pulled my sister into her arms, and tried to stand. She wavered, but I reached out. Helped to steady her. My hands lingered on them for a moment, Ari and Lil, and I felt like I would cry. When she looked at me again, it was like she might cry too.

She started to shuffle off, carrying Lil. Then stopped, looking back at me.

"It might be tough now, getting into Canada. But you should still come with me."

Wasn't like I had fuck else to do.

The crowd parted for us like some Moses shit, except for the sheriff and news crew. I was waiting for Bud to try and stop us. Maybe give us some bullshit about the law or assassinating the president or something. But he just nodded his head, looked down at Lil, then stepped aside.

The camera was still rolling. Jeff Starship stood, microphone in hand, though he didn't say anything either. He just held the mic, in case we wanted to talk. Neither of us did.

The producer was back on her headset. "You guys are either heroes or outlaws," she said, "I'm not sure yet. But all of the ships are leaving now, and no one else is giving birth to any monsters."

"Just the human kind," Ari said.

And we walked away.

Paw was still propped up against the tree, watching the house burn. I found his old Remington in the yard, picked it up. Funny, but I didn't have that much to say to him. I guess that's what he'd taught me. But I would give him the gun, like all the times he handed it to me out on the range. That, at least, felt right.

Ari had gone ahead, carrying my sister's body. I could see her fumbling with the door of the Malibu, bundling Lil into the back seat.

"I'm leaving now, Paw."

He nodded his head, slow, considering things. He held the shotgun a minute more, just looking at it. Then he handed it back to me.

I figured that was it.

I nodded my head at him, at a loss for anything more, and turned away. He made a sound, almost like a croak. I thought it was my name, so I turned back. Leaned down so he could impart the last family wisdom I'd ever get.

"You gotta stay strong, Jim, and sometimes you gotta take a stand."

I kinda figured I'd done that, but I gave him another nod anyway.

"Good advice, Paw. Thanks."

He reached up, grabbed my shirt, pulled me close. Like he was about to give me a secret. "The first chance you get, you take that gun . . . and you put a bullet in that nigger dyke's skull. You keep on doing that, Jim, because this world is full of roaches that need to be stepped on and exterminated. You got me, son?"

I just looked at him, pulling his hand off my shirt.

Now the tears came.

"Yeah, I got you," I said, and I started to walk.

Ahead of me, the car was running. Ari finished brushing the snow away and started to get in. She paused, looking back at me. I could hear the Stooges, already cranked up inside, going on about being the world's forgotten boy.

I stopped, turned. It was about fifty feet now from the tree where Paw was sitting. The gun still didn't feel right in my hands, but I lifted it up just the same. With my left eye, the one he had always told me was wrong, I found Paw in the sights.

"Sometimes you might even have to die," I said.

And this time I hit the bull's eye.

The Day the Earth Turned Day-Glo

By Rick Shingler

As everyone knows, there was pandemonium on the day the sun came back. People left their workspaces to rush to the windows. Many who were outside at that moment ran for shelter. Young children screamed and clung to their parents, even as the parents paused to bask in the flood of warmth. The media was swamped with exclamations, accusations, and trepidations. In all the chaos, it should come as little surprise that a lone video transmission could have gone unnoticed, even if it did come from Earth orbit. In fact, it was nearly a month before someone officially noticed it.

Unofficially, a lone data processor named Frederick discovered it that afternoon and had surreptitiously watched it more than a dozen times over the past three and a half weeks. In that time, Frederick had yet to set foot into the sunlight. The winter days were short enough that he could enter the Federal building before sunrise and didn't have to leave until the sun was little more than a colorful hint along the western horizon. His days were spent in a basement office, with only a window of opaque block glass to remind him of the outside world. It was barely an office. It was an old storage closet full of dusty, outdated audio/visual equipment. One entire corner of the room was a museum of slide projectors, overhead projectors, amplifiers, and outdated sound equipment. Across from that corner was a bank of the most up-to-date computer servers. All incoming information passed through and was stored on these servers. The rest of the room was divided into grey cubicles.

Admittedly, at first he thought the video was an elaborate prank, like the old footage of the moon landing in the 1960s. But the more of it he watched, the more he came to realize that he had been unwittingly christened as confidant and confessor. True, he may not have exactly recognized it in this way at the time, but the significance of the transmission he was watching was going to impact his entire life. The thrill of discovery was slowly overshadowed by an inexplicable sense of anxiety. The mere act of watching this woman, of hearing her words and basking in her glow, made him feel complicit in her actions. Despite that, he was transfixed. He could not help but be drawn into her eyes. He often had to rewind the transmission to refocus his concentration away from her exquisite cheekbones or her perfect halo of curly, knotted hair. Her lips parted and closed as she spoke, and Frederick convinced himself he could feel gentle pulsations of air leaving them as she formed her words.

"My name is Thea," the recording began, "and I am a moon baby. In fact, it could be said that I am The Moon Baby. I have been alone here for the last twenty months. My mother died when I was a toddler, due to an airlock malfunction. Since that time, all of the other people working on this base who didn't die in similar accidents have committed suicide. Eventually, it was just my father and me, until he was caught in an explosion outside of the base while trying to repair a faulty backup generator."

Thea grew quiet for a moment and looked away from the camera. The screen jumped and she was instantly looking back. It was impossible to tell how much time away from the camera was contained in that tiny digital jump. Her eyes looked red, but there was no sadness left in them. Frederick could only see a steely resolve.

"I can't know who's going to see this, but I can only hope that it's someone who needs to hear it. Thanks largely to the giant construct blocking the Earth's signals from me, the satellite feed here is shitty on the best of days. With the increased solar flare activity the last few months, it's been fucking shitty on a scale where "shitty" is a normal day and "goddamn fucking shit for shit" is the worst imaginable. Even so, I've been able to see enough of the news feeds and political coverage in the last decade to tell you one simple truth: Those people who fellate you for votes are a bunch of assholes. It would be easier if I could say they're all lying assholes, but I can't even say that. It's actually pretty unusual for these people you insist on putting in charge of things to tell an actual lie.

Typically it's nothing but manipulative half-truths that can't be disproven, even though everyone with the tiniest shred of intelligence must know that they are only being told the half of the story they want to hear. And it's always – ALWAYS – the half of the truth that will instill the maximum amount of fear. But in the case of the moon people, I can say without hesitation that you all fell victim to a flat out lie. How do I know? Because I have heard the news programs tell the lies about me, my life, and the people I love. The moon colony? Not one of us ever came home. The people you saw on the news shows were fakes, probably placed by those with an interest in continuing the narrative of our heroic return.

"Here's what's true: When President Buffoon couldn't wring any more approval rating points out of rattling his sabre at whatever piss-pot despot he thought might get riled up, someone suggested the Moon Base. Trust me when I say that there was never anything more to this project than that. Someone on the White House staff was inexplicably possessed to blow enough dust off of a history book to find Nixon's approval bump during the moon landing. Never underestimate the ingenuity of an unpopular narcissist. Within a year, the first wave launched. My parents were in the third wave. Mom was a biologist; Dad was a mechanical engineer.

"Then President Ryan decommissioned the Trump Moon Base program during his first hundred days in office. Only he didn't arrange a shuttle to come get us like he said he had in the news conference. Instead, he neatly cut off our communication channels to Earth and forgot about us. Six months later, those fake Moon Base scientists made the rounds of the talk shows, were given their Medals of Freedom or Honor or whatever, and quietly faded into obscurity. I'd love to know how much those posers were all paid for their silence.

"Meanwhile, up here, things began to decline. Sure, the systems of the base are largely self-sufficient, with the solar cells providing most of the power, aided only in emergency situations by power leeched from the miniature nuclear reactor installed half a mile from the southern end of the base. The sewage reclamation system serves to provide potable water as

95

well as fertilizer for the greenhouse wing. The air filtration system works alongside the chlorophyll-enriched ferns in the greenhouse, which have been engineered to maximize their oxygen output through photosynthesis. What's really cool is how the first Basers were able to terraform a small patch of the moon's surface by oxygenating the soil with…

"Sorry. Dad always said it reminded him of my mom when I would get excited and start talking science. The technology that kept the Moon Base project operational isn't what this message is all about. Let's just say that this base could conceivably remain fully operational for decades, if not longer, without any support from the outside.

"Nevertheless, I remember the fear and sense of abandonment everyone felt when that chimp-eared walking genital wart's final direct transmission faded to black. At least the president found the balls to make the call himself. If you ask me, he seemed to almost enjoy delivering the news that sealed all of our fates.

"Some switch got flipped somewhere on Earth, and from that day on we could only receive sporadic satellite feeds and stray radio signals. If our outgoing messages were getting back to Earth, there were no replies to acknowledge them. Eventually, the rest of the scientists gave up trying to contact the rest of humanity and returned listlessly to the monotony of maintaining the base. My father did his best to rally their spirits and build a sense of community, but as we lost people to accidents and carelessness, even his indefatigable spirit began to lose its luster. The first suicide came as a surprise. When the next one followed a couple of weeks later, it was less shocking. I'm ashamed to say that by the time the fifth body was found hanging in her quarters, it became more of a morbid curiosity, with many speculating how long it must have taken for the noose to tighten in the moon's diminished gravity. Here's a sad thought: I'm not yet twenty years old, and I've buried the rest of my kind.

"I say that, recognizing the fact that I am the only human being in history to not be born on Earth. It sounds like some old sci-fi movie from the twentieth century, doesn't it? 'I

96

Was a Teenaged Extraterrestrial!' Hell, even if someone did come to rescue me, I don't know if my body could acclimate to the extra gravity of Earth. It would be like instantly gaining a hundred pounds, and I don't know that my bone structure would be able to withstand the pressure. I was born here on this base. But if everything goes according to plan, I won't die here. I won't be on Earth, either, but still...

"Stop getting ahead of yourself, Thea," she chided herself. She drew a deep breath, exhaled, and began to get up from her seat. The audio crackled as white horizontal lines jumped across the screen and she reappeared in her chair, her eyes leveled at the camera.

"One might say I have a perspective on the rest of humanity that is somewhat unique from anyone else. My father made an effort to let me be a normal little girl. He used the color printers without authorization, just to print images from Earth for me to hang in my quarters. They were mostly landscapes. I was always fascinated by the vividness of the colors of the world where you live. In contrast to the aggressive grayness of the only world I've ever known, those colors became the stuff of fantasy. He tried to let me be a kid and experience wide-eyed wonder, even during the times when what he really needed was a jaded colleague with whom to share the work of running the station.

"I went through a phase when I was five or six years old where all I wanted to do was draw rainbows – which I had only seen in pictures on monitor screens and color printouts. One of the other crew members had an antique personal computer that she let me use sometimes. It had a file folder loaded with stock images of places all over the planet Earth. There were shots of deserts covered in red sand, lying motionless under a sky of incomprehensible blue. There were yellow banners hanging over a crowded shopping mall that I would stare at for hours, trying unsuccessfully to wrap my head around what it must feel like to be surrounded by that many strangers. One picture had a flat horizon at the very bottom of the frame. The rest of the image showed the pulsing striations of colors in a sunset over a body of water. It started near the horizon with orange, pink, and red, before fading imperceptibly upward to purple and blue and eventually a star-dappled black.

"But of all the pictures in this digital file, my favorite was the bridge. It was a simple construction of wooden planks and rope that stretched across a chasm. Over both sides of the bridge, and rising up to tower over the far end of the bridge, were trees and bushes. All of the plants could be considered green, but I painstakingly and agonizingly catalogued *all* of the various shades of green to be found in that single frame. In the end I stopped at two hundred and forty-seven, but I'm still sure there were more.

"I cannot imagine living among such gorgeous day-glo colors every day and ever reaching the point that I would take them for granted. But then, I'm probably not the only one who feels that way these days, am I? Who could have ever imagined humanity allowing someone to take all of those colors away?"

At this point on the video, she paused. It seemed to Frederick as if a thought had just entered her mind.

"But I guess it wasn't humanity, as a unit, who allowed this to happen. Most of mankind was just going about its daily business when a small handful of villains took control of the sunlight.

"I know it might seem petty to refer to these wretched scum as 'villains,' but when one of them is an opportunistic narcissist whose actions serve only to fulfill his own delusions of power and fatten his profits at the expense of every living thing on the planet, he has to surrender any chances at ever being handed the Nobel Peace Prize. Incidentally, he also has to develop a thick enough skin to withstand being referred to as a 'villain,' or even 'wretched scum,' for that matter.

"As I said earlier, my reception of Earth transmissions was spotty on the best of days. Despite their ongoing attempts to defy the rest of the world, the leaders of a single political party of a single nation were forced to face a harsh reality. Namely, their financial interest in fossil fuels was growing extinct. More and more nations had moved forward with innovative technological achievements in renewable energy, while those with influence over this one godforsaken, wanton nation had maintained a stranglehold on the industry's standards. But eventually, even these pigs were forced to awaken to the harsh reality of their situation. Backed into a corner, they were forced to grapple with the necessity for an alternative form of energy.

"I read an article about a failed attempt on the part of a group of college students to build an automotive combustion engine that ran on methane and hydrogen collected from the flatulence of the driver and passengers, through filters built into the cabin's seating. The design was staunchly supported by a leading Tex-Mex fast food chain, but was never fully embraced by the public. Everyone loves a fart joke, but no one will ever admit to laughing at a fart joke. It's one of the fundamental rules of humanity.

"My very favorite thing about humanity has always been its capacity for invention and problem-solving. There are so very many examples of it right here around me, and I have never once taken a single one of them for granted. There isn't one more responsible for my continued existence than any other. My very least favorite thing about humanity is its pathological need to own and control its inventions in order to turn a profit. While I was able to marvel at the ingenuity behind it, my heart sunk the day I watched the installation of E:CLIPS.

"There is a powerful telescope in the observatory, and I like to use it when I know something is being launched into Earth orbit. I've gotten pretty good at finding objects as they leave the atmosphere and refocusing on them for a closer look. I was watching the day E:CLIPS was launched. The full name was 'Energy: Collected Lumen Integrated Power Source,' which seemed pretty damned forced, if you ask me.

"But then, I guess no one ever will.

"Ask me, that is.

"Because, you know" - she pointed a slender finger at her mouth -"alone on the moon."

She sat quietly in front of the camera for nearly a full minute before continuing.

"I'll happily admit that I found the installation of E:CLIPS to be a fascinating show. The satellite was massive. One of the biggest I had ever seen launched. I've spent a little time studying rocket science, and the amount of fuel it must have taken to launch that payload into a geostationary orbit had to have been, well, *astronomical*. Once it reached its position, that was when the real show began.

"If you've never watched slow-motion video of a ladybug unfolding its wings from under its red and black carapace, you should really look it up. Because that was what E:CLIPS' installation looked like. The dome split in the center, and four thick panels swung outward from underneath them. There were two on each side. Each of those panels produced two more, which then unfolded to double in size. Each of those unlocked two more, and so on, until this single man-made object was large enough to cover a sizable portion of the North American continent from twenty-six thousand miles away.

"It *was* fascinating to observe the technology in action and to wonder at the sheer scale of the manufacturing facility that could have produced such a thing. (I later learned it had been assembled in an underground facility built beneath what had been previously called Arizona, before climate change rendered it unlivable).

"But I felt a part of my soul wither as I witnessed the effect this device was having on Earth. The vivid blue and green planet became shrouded in a shadowy approximation of color. It was as if a thin wash of brackish grey paint had been applied over the colors I had always seen through the window of my observatory. That glowing iridescence had gone dull and lifeless. I can only imagine what it must have been like for the rest of humanity.

"My father was born in Ohio, and he used to tell me of his childhood summers, spent out on what was left of his grandfather's farm. He would talk about getting lost in the corn field and getting bellyaches from eating under-ripe cherries plucked directly from the tree. For as long as I can remember, I've had this dream where I'm lying on my back on a grassy hillside in the dappled shade of a lone maple tree. There's a breeze moving the leaves over me, so that the sunlight teases my closed eyelids. As I open my eyes, I sit up to find all of these vivid fantasy colors surrounding me, like when that girl and her dog stepped out of the house in some bizarre and terrifying movie my dad made me watch with him once.

"I may be a scientifically-inclined extraterrestrial, but I'm still a teenaged girl. So I don't think anyone could blame me when I find myself wiping tears from my cheeks as I imagine this scenario. It just feels hopeless now, you know? Even if I could somehow conduct myself to Earth's surface safely, there's no guarantee that my body would survive for long. And besides, who would choose to live in a grey, sunless place? I suppose the threshold between innocence and experience is demarcated by the shedding of such tears, as someone's personal reality crashes into her carefully-cultivated fantasy.

"Sure, E:CLIPS was pushed through as an extension of the first lady's sunscreen initiative, but how could anyone have doubted that it would just be a new way for greedy dickholes to make money? They told you it would be used as a protective screen during the hottest months of the summer. They told you it would eliminate the incidence of skin cancer. They told you that the panels could be turned to allow for enough direct sunlight every day to charge everyone's solar cells. And everything they told you was absolutely true. Well, half-true.

"See what I'm saying about the half-truths?

"What was truly vile was the stuff they chose not to tell you. They didn't tell you the precision with which they were able to control those panels, down to a square of approximately two by two meters. They didn't tell you how much they planned to charge consumers for turning those panels enough to provide daily power to a house's lithium cells. If you couldn't afford to pay, you didn't get sun; it was as simple as that. *Assholes.* That's some Bond villain shit. But that's the way it's always been. As soon as mankind finds a new way to prove its usefulness, some smirking shithead finds a way to use it to take other people's money. Man makes fire, then some asshole starts selling engraved silver lighters. One

101

guy invents the wheel only so someone else can jack up the prices at the tire shop three weeks before Labor Day, to support the 'buy three get one free' sale. Someone sharpens a stick, then the other guy opens an overpriced hunting supply shop out on County Road 60. And, I mean, *fine*. I'm sitting up here on top of the world, literally looking down on creation (Dad played goofy, sappy music sometimes between the punk and garage rock that he loved), and I'm bewildered at the silly people with their silly money and silly wars and silly need for power, and it all looks so damned silly that it's sort of funny. And it could be funny, if not for those people dying and starving and freezing while just a few of them stockpile more than they could reasonably need in ten lifetimes. Because that takes the silliness out of the comedy pile and puts it smack on top of the tragedy pile. Silly, completely avoidable tragedy. Then they even find some way to take away the damn sun from the non-paying customers? And have the audacity to call those now living in perpetual twilight "lazy" and "sponges on society?" I've spent a lot of time studying the history of the people of planet Earth, and every time it looks like they had reached the utter nadir of self-destruction, they amaze me by finding a new depth to slide merrily down into."

"Shit. I'm -"

Frederick stopped the video and looked at the rectangular casement window at the top of the south wall of his basement cubicle. The window was made of thick tinted glass, but even through the diffused material, he could see the glare of direct sunlight and shadows passing along the walkway outside. Despite his developing resolve, he was still reluctant to step outside. For the past several years, the constant barrage of warnings about the health risks of direct sunlight had merely assuaged a deep concern that had lingered inside him since his first childhood sunburn. He had learned to be thankful for "The Sunscreen" (as most of the world had taken to calling it). He had heard all the insistent proclamations about how it protected the Earth, even as it provided life-sustaining power to the Grids. And of course it was necessary to pay for access to the solar power it provided. How else would the Sunscreen be able to be maintained?

This girl, this "Thea" – she had never lived on Earth. She couldn't possibly have been expected to understand the good being done by those who provided E:CLIPS. There are commercials during every nightly news cast that talk about the statistical decrease in skin cancer diagnoses. It's even said to have lowered the average global temperature by nearly half a degree within months of its installation, garnering criticism of the climate change people for their reluctance to acknowledge the positive impact that Phaethon, Inc. has had on the world.

"Yo, Freddie!"

It was Mike, who worked three cubicles over. He was the only person who had ever called Frederick by the diminutive, and he always emphasized the second syllable. Reflexively setting his lower jaw forward, Frederick pressed a button on his keyboard, darkening the screen. Thea's frozen face winked from view. Frederick took a silent, deep breath and spun around in his desk chair to face the corridor.

"Lunchtime, dude! Some of us are going over to the Trump Library for taco bowls. I mean, it's gotta be Chinko de May-o somewhere, am I right?"

Frederick barely resisted the urge to respond sarcastically to Mike's blatant slur. Inwardly, Frederick was unsure whether he was cringing at the slur or the fact that his pronunciation of 'Mayo' sounded like he was talking about the sandwich condiment. Somehow he maintained a friendly smile. Mike was a buffoon, but he was a well-liked buffoon. Frederick didn't need him as an enemy in this office.

"Nah, not today," he said, shuffling papers on his desk. "I brought lunch today. I'm just going to stay here and catch up on some emails."

"Yeah, suit yourself. What were you watching?" he asked, his eyes flicking to the black monitor screen. "Porn?"

Thinking fast, Frederick glanced at the monitor. He rocked forward in his seat toward Mike.

"I'm a couple weeks behind on Celebrity Apprentice."

103

Mike rocked back on one foot and stabbed an exuberant finger toward him.

"I knew you were up to something, dawg. So who do you pick to win? My money's on Sean Spicer."

"I haven't really made a pick yet. Is there an office pool I should be aware of?"

Mike hesitated for several seconds before a vacant grin broke across his face.

"Hilarious! Freddie, I can always count on you for a laugh! Welp, I'll let you get back to catching up on your work."

With Mike gone and the rest of the building hollowing out for lunch, Frederick put his earbuds back in and returned to Thea's recording.

"--ranting. I didn't want to get ranty. I should probably go back and delete that last section. But I'm not going to. I would like it if this message reached someone who would spread it to the rest of the world. But in all likelihood, it will be intercepted by some government henchman who will pass it on to his superiors, who will in turn cut and edit the whole thing to paint me as some sort of terrorist. The best I can really hope is that the henchman won't automatically dismiss me as some "ignorant Socialist libtard," and will spend the rest of his day thinking about the ways he's sold out his own humanity for the sake of a poverty-level minimum wage and the occasional favorable review from some puppet controlled by the few people rich enough to pull the strings. You know who I'm talking about: the ones who shout the loudest the instant someone begins to suggest a better way. If I can offer an outsider's observation, those guys (and let's face it, it's mostly men) will shout down anything that looks remotely like Socialism, because they believe that even in an environment where everyone has access to what they need, some people will hoard *more* than they need and not leave enough for the rest. But I call bullshit. I see the majority of humanity as kind and generous and unlikely to take much more than they find necessary, so long as they feel secure that there will be more when they need it. Those bloviated types, however, lack the imagination to see beyond their own avarice, thinking that everyone is a self-centered, greedy jackass just like them.

"Rant. Rant. Rant.

"I'm cutting myself off soon. I know I'm probably wasting my breath anyway.

"So. On to the technical part of our program. As it turns out, I have sort of a knack for rocket science, and have managed to salvage enough bits and pieces from the base and the old moon landing site to build a serviceable transport for myself. It won't get me all the way to Earth, but it won't need to. I've equipped my ship with a homemade nuclear device. I couldn't figure out a way to navigate it to the right position along the central spine of E:CLIPS and then trigger it remotely, so I'm going to need to do it manually. I wish I could survive long enough to see that glorious day-glo green and blue of Earth, but I know I won't. Before I do the deed, I'm hoping to jimmy some kind of radio relay, using some equipment from here at the base and the receiver relays on E:CLIPS, so that I can transmit this message.

"To be honest, I won't mind that much if I can't get it through. I have a little inner anarchist who thinks it would be hilarious for everyone to spend the next couple of decades scratching their heads and wondering what happened to the thing that turned sunlight into a profit industry.

"But if it does get through, I'll have you know that this has been Thea, Redeemer of the Sun, Defender of Earth, and Goddess of the Motherfuckin' Moon, telling you to get over yourselves and stop being such dicks to each other."

Frederick sat at his desk, staring at the frozen image at the end of the recording. Thea's face filled the screen. Her mouth was opened wide in a confrontational laugh. Her nostrils were flared, causing a barely-noticeable wrinkle on one side of her nose. Her right eye was opened a bit wider than her left, but both were wild and sparkling with fiery liberation. And all of these features were dramatically framed between her two extended middle fingers.

He had studied every line and curve of that face for the past twenty-four days, but he knew he was pressing his luck.

105

He spent the rest of his lunch hour working on another project before his colleagues came back. They all returned slightly drunk and plenty gassy from their noon-time indulgences. At the sound of footsteps outside his cubicle, he tapped at the keys on his keyboard. Dante, his supervisor, leaned into the cubicle's entrance.

"Yeah, the whole system rebooted while everybody was at lunch. I put in a call to tech support to come check the servers," Dante said, nodding slightly toward Frederick's keyboard. "Listen, I printed a report this morning that said you accessed some sort of transmission from the day of the E:CLIPS bombing and then isolated it onto your hard drive."

Frederick spun in his desk chair to face his boss.

"Oh, yeah," he replied.

Dante raised his eyebrows and tilted one side of his face toward him.

"…And?"

"Nothing. Random static. Probably something to do with solar flares that day. I listened to almost a half hour of it. At one point, I thought I heard an old punk tune playing, but it was just my imagination. I'm sorry I forgot to log it."

Dante drew a deep breath through his nose.

"Well, remember this is government work. You gotta cross your I's and dot your T's, know what I'm saying?"

Frederick nodded to indicate that he understood, but didn't acknowledge the poor attempt at humorous camaraderie.

Dante deflated somewhat at the lack of a response to his joke.

"You feeling okay, Fred?"

"Actually," Frederick said, "I think I might be getting a little touch of something. Can I take the rest of the day off?"

He stopped short at the door leading out into the street. The gray-white sidewalks beyond shone blindingly under the afternoon sun. Across the street, a pile of melting snow reflected a brilliant whiteness. He took a deep breath and stepped out into the sunlight. He closed his eyes and tilted his face up toward the yellow ball.

He walked three blocks, until he found a bench looking out over the Potomac. Pulling his coat tighter against the brisk chill of the February afternoon, he managed to corral a burgeoning anxiety attack. How long would it take for someone to notice that his hard drive had been wiped? Would it be obvious that he had taken apart one of the speaker cores from the dusty sound equipment and used the magnet to erase it? How long until someone remembered that he had stayed at the office while everyone else left for lunch? If he had to bet, he would put his money on Mike. Mike will be all too happy to sell "Freddie" down the river and garner points with upper management. And then what? There would be a lot of questions, he would likely lose his job, and he could even end up in prison. And for what? Thea was gone, likely vaporized instantly in a home-made nuclear blast in the vacuum of space. So why did he feel like he needed to protect her? Especially at such a risk to himself? He was eligible for a review in a month; what was he thinking? After all, he was counting on that extra half-percentage.

The swirl of work-related neuroses was threatening to overtake him when the light changed. It was late in the afternoon, and the wintry clouds had swept away in time for the lowering sun to paint an orange hue over everything. Except rather than tinting everything orange like he would expect, this wash somehow intensified the colors all around him. The green grass and bushes along the walking path glowed green. A fluttering flag along the bank resonated with the intensity of its red stripes. The few wisps of clouds were pink, purple, orange, and yellow.

Frederick realized how much he had missed seeing colors. The perpetual twilight of the last few years had altered his perception of the world around him, and he was diminished because of it. His eyes were drawn to the sleeve of his coat. He lifted his arm wonderingly. This black coat he'd worn for the past three winters wasn't black at all. In the sunlight, he realized for the first time that his coat was blue. Something about this struck him and he began to laugh.

His laugh cut short at the sound of his phone ringing. With a shaking hand, he pulled it out of his pocket and looked at the screen. Dante's desk number scrolled across the screen. Frederick bit his lower lip at the effort to resist the reflex of tapping the green "ANSWER CALL" button on the screen. The fifth ring bumped it to voicemail, but Dante didn't take the time for that. Immediately the phone began to ring again. Frederick cast his eyes up to the slowly darkening blue of the sky. With a rustle of his navy blue coat, he threw the ringing device as far into the middle of the Potomac River as he possibly could.

As the last light of day glowed all around him and falling fragments of E:CLIPS continued to form golden streaks across the sky, as they had for the past few weeks, Frederick sat on the bench and laughed to himself.

None but the Brave

By Dan Lee

Thunder rumbled through the night, drowning out the repetitive voice of the loud speakers outside, peddling their useless wares and impulse buy items. It was a deep, steady growl that rolled through the night sky and gently rattled the glass of my bedroom window as I lay awake, staring at the ceiling fan spinning lazily overhead. It was two in the morning and the sky was bright orange in the false dawn of neon lights and LED screens lighting up entire walls outside. Shades drawn and all the lights off, the perpetual twilight was enough to make out all the intricate details of my spartan home. From the bare desk in the far corner to the neatly made gray linens I had sprawled across without ever feeling drowsy, I could see the bare walls and beige carpet as clearly as my own hands in front of my face. It was always a struggle to sleep without the darkness of an actual night, but I didn't want to be *that guy*, the one you heard stories about, with his bottle of pills and his hopeless addiction. A tranquilizer junkie.

Of course, I was at the opposite end of the spectrum, with a half empty bottle of stimulants beside my phone on the nightstand.

Another rumble, less gentle than before, cracked across the sky and shook the windows with more force. This time the entire building trembled as a bright yellow streak flashed across the shades and brought the full glory of a faux sunrise into my room. I could hear the crunch as the thick glass spiderwebbed into a mosaic of distant flames, while a chorus of panicked noises joined the symphony of the storm raging outside. Frantic shouts, the wailing of sirens, and the unmistakable hum of the emergency broadcast system replaced the usual cacophony of advertisements blaring from the speakers beneath their lighted billboards.

My phone began to buzz, dancing and vibrating across the top of the nightstand, adding to the crescendo of chaos. Blue light glowed from the screen and filtered into the otherwise drab orange haze filling the room. I waited patiently, letting it dance along the smooth fiberboard top and ring over to voicemail. Almost immediately it started again. I continued to ignore it. It wasn't logical, wasn't realistic at all to hope that maybe this had been a dream. I tried to convince myself that I was asleep, snoring, with the covers pulled up tight around my neck. But I knew better. The phone chirped once to let me know that I had a new message, then began to buzz again.

"Dover." I groaned my last name as if it were a proper greeting.

"Thank god you're alive," said the overly concerned voice on the other end of the line. Her name was Nancy Coulton. She was a thirty-eight-year-old career investigator, my handler, and probably the closest thing to a friend I would ever have. She was the sympathetic, needlessly protective sort, prone to outbursts of emotion and worry. "We're getting reports of a massive attack near your block."

"Yeah," I told her, sitting up in my bed. "Shook the whole damn building."

"How soon can you make it to the scene?"

I sighed and looked at the orange glow flickering though my broken bedroom window.

"Five minutes to dress. Another ten to grab my gear and get downstairs."

"Okay. I'll see you there."

The call ended.

I grabbed my pills, popped a fistful and put the bottle back. It was going to be a long night.

*

Seeing the smoke and debris, the powdery mixture of concrete, glass and plastic puffing into a thick dust, had never shocked me. The attacks had become so commonplace, so routine in urban life, that they were just accepted by most of us as the price you paid for living in the civilized world. Outside the safety of the walls were lawless, brutal things that had managed to survive the horrors of the atomic wasteland.

110

They'd traded their humanity for an animalistic barbarism, a sort of violent faith that they hoped to share with all humanity. A bit of bone crunched under my boot as I crossed the cordon into the scene. I knew it was bone, likely a bit of skull, from the way that it felt under my heel. Gravel and glass had a different texture, a sort of give that bone never offered. The gray and black of the exploded walls gave way to splatters of red, deep pools of burgundy congealing in the broken, dusty tiles and clumps of textured orange-yellow that had been fatty tissues before they were forced away by the indiscriminate blast. It was a grotesque Rorschach dripping into the scorched cement.

There were two uniformed officers standing guard at the entrance to the blast site. Both were rookies, in their loose fitting blue polyester jumpsuits with sparkling new badges over their chests, and had that untested air of freshness about them. Baby-faced looks of innocence that would slowly be chipped away from their features as they fought their own quivering revulsion at the horror laid out for them in the high definition spectrum of real life. They wanted to retch, to curl up and cry and forget the nightmare they had found themselves presiding over. I showed them my credentials and walked into the building without ever speaking a word to either. If they needed a shoulder to cry on, they could find a counselor or my more-than-sympathetic cohort, wherever she might be. I wasn't there for *them*. I had been trained to exist outside the banal and reassuring platitudes that most people craved in the midst of a trauma. All emotion was compartmentalized, locked safely away where drugs and theta wave therapy could properly mitigate it later on. For me, this was just another day at the office, and I was prepared to work.

The room smelled like cat piss and burnt hair, ammonia and sizzling flesh, as I approached the bulk of a torso with a tattered vest still clinging desperately to the now unidentifiable mass that had been the second bomber. I'd seen enough of these suicides to have the scene laid out in my mind. The chunk of torso was as close to the epicenter of the blast as anything left in the room. More techs and cops were gathered around the charred remains and scattered bits of people and possessions tossed about carelessly by the force of the attack.

"EOD cleared that thing yet?" I called from a safe distance. The last thing I wanted was to walk up to a corpse that still had a bit of bang left in it.

"Yeah," some nameless tech snapping pictures answered absentmindedly.

I walked up and sat my briefcase down on the least bloody patch of tile that I could find. Again, I showed my credentials, then handed my jacket to the tech with the camera.

"I'm going to need a few minutes here."

And with that, I went to work.

Opening the silver briefcase I'd brought from my apartment, I immediately removed the metal probe from inside and started looking for an opening. The probe itself was a silver spike about a foot long and two inches around, with a razor-sharp tip that could pierce bone if it had to. Rolling the trunk of the corpse over, I jerked it up as hard as I could by the remaining strap of the suicide vest and looked at the stump where his head had been. The spinal column was mostly intact and, having little hope of finding the head, I chose to drive the spike directly into the marrow. It crunched and locked in place. I dropped the body unceremoniously and connected the wires to the reader. It had to be a direct connection, nothing wireless or digital that could be disrupted or remotely interfered with. I locked one end of the cable into the spike, the other into the tablet in the case. Using a second cable, I connected it to the other side of the tablet and then into a smaller, less intrusive spike. The second spike fit on a pad the size of a bandage and was barely as big as a sewing needle. Running my fingers along my neck, I found the dip at the base of my skull and pressed the small pad to my flesh until the adhesive held the metal flush against my skin.

The tablet chirped and flickered to life. I logged in with my password, programmed the level of information I was seeking, and waited for the device to calibrate. A small orange circle began to spin around in the center of the screen as an orange bar below it began to stretch horizontally. The screen flashed once then became a field of blue with a single red button in the center. I pressed the button.

Electricity sparked inside the device, whipping into the large spike in the dead man's spine before feeding back into the device and directly into my brain. In a jolt of shocking ozone, a fragmented sort of memory came to mind. It was hazy, like trying to piece together a dream after waking up. Sifting through the genetic memory imprinted in the cerebrospinal fluid, broken and incomplete thanks to the obliteration of the brain and nervous system itself, I began to experience the otherwise intangible aspects of another man's thoughts. I could see through his eyes, this dead man lying in pieces on the floor beside me. I could hear and smell and feel everything he had felt. I watched him build the bomb; sew every stitch as he modified an old waist coat into a suicide vest. I watched as he knelt in prayer by an unsettling but familiar altar, and felt the concussion, the searing pain, as he carried out his final act of violence. Every emotion he'd ever known washed over me at once -- everything from his birth into this world until the very instant his life suddenly stopped.

I yanked the cable from the back of my neck and collapsed into the fetal position, sobbing as my body shivered off the last lingering bits of this stranger's emotions. Trying to fight the trembling urges lurching up from my guts, I managed to get to my feet only to vomit where the bomber's head should have been. Wiping my mouth on my sleeve, I sat back down in the rubble, disconnected the tablet, and immediately sent the data back to headquarters. Within minutes, the entire federal police force inside the city would know everything that I knew.

Everything except for the pain.

*

We were bred from the hellfire and ash of the last World War, the one that had taught all mankind just how truly depraved and wicked we really were at our collective core. We were men and women trained to lack empathy or emotion in

113

the name of peace. Some called us sociopaths, but they were the sort of small minded creatures who had caused the last Great War – frightened children clinging to their dogma and their rhetoric because they weren't able to see the bigger picture. People like me could move through the death and carnage, could seek out the truth unencumbered by the crippling pain of the human experience. I'd seen people collapse at crime scenes, men who were otherwise unshakable, because they'd seen or felt something that so ruined them that they could never hope to find a rational explanation. I didn't share that weakness.

Using the spike, the neurological interface between the specialized machine and two minds, I could see and experience and feel everything that the other person had. Unhindered by my own personal feelings and emotions, I could live another's life in seconds and begin looking for answers to questions that might otherwise have remained a mystery. I'd been selected as a child, pulled from hundreds of thousands of students to become part of an elite group that could be raised up to serve. Nancy Coulton was my handler, a specialized mix of police investigator and psychotherapist whose only real job was to make sure that the constant influx of emotional stimuli and memory didn't result in a full on psychotic break. We'd been partnered for five years now and she was arguably as skilled and resilient as I was.

Nancy was a short, frail looking woman in her late thirties who always wore a uniformed set of blouses and skirts covered by a dark trench coat and fedora, like some gender swapped noir detective from the Golden Age of Hollywood. With her short, mousy brown hair pulled into a bun and tucked under her hat, she looked at me quizzically over the steam in her cup of coffee as we sat in a café near the crime scenes.

"How are you feeling?" she asked in her matronly way.

"I'm fine," I replied. I always was.

"Jim," she said. "I just need to make sure you're actually okay. The things you have to do and experience would be difficult for anyone to go through, even once. But you've spiked at least a dozen times in the last eight months. I need to know what's going on inside of your head."

I sighed. It was a tiresome routine to have to go through every time we had a bombing or a homicide or some other violent crime in the heart of the city. I understood the need to make sure I wasn't on the verge of a break, but it was barely eight in the morning now and I was too tired to be psychoanalyzed.

"Everything was fragmented." I told her. "One minute I was shivering and apprehensive. The next I was certain, with this sort of *righteous positivity* that what I was about to do was absolutely the right thing."

"And how does that make you feel?" she asked.

"Nancy, it doesn't make me feel anything. Once the effects of the spike wear off, I go back to normal. There's no emotion that lingers on in me, if that's what you're wanting to know. I don't feel anything more about that terrorist now than I did when you called me this morning. That's how this works. You should know that as well as I do."

She sighed.

"I know, Jim. It's just, well, part of me always hopes that we'll break through this barrier."

"*Barrier*? It's not a barrier, Nancy. It's what I am. If I was like you, full of all those emotions and feelings you keep wishing on me, I'd never be able to do my job. It isn't a barrier to me. If there were ever an emotion in my heart or mind, it'd be the death of me. Let's just enjoy things as they are, okay?"

I lifted my cup for a toast. "Here's to the status quo."

She nodded and looked absently at her coffee.

"Look, I'm no different than those old bomb sniffing dogs they used in the war," I told her. "Teach an animal a task, reward it properly, and it'll step into danger for you whenever you ask. Put a competent handler in charge and you can save a lot of lives. That's what we do, Nancy."

"I wish you understood why that's so unsettling…" she muttered under her breath, "…comparing yourself to a bomb dog."

"You feel that it dehumanizes me. Well, it doesn't. If anything, I'm more aware of myself and my surroundings than anyone else in this room. Look at them. They're all buried in their devices, listening to the speakers outside peddling all the drugs and entertainment they could ever need to stay blind to the world around them. As long as they're not stuck in the blast radius, they're content to be kept up as pets. At least I serve a purpose."

Nancy stared into her coffee cup.

"So, what'd they learn over at the other scene?" I asked, changing the subject.

"Not as much as we'd hoped," she answered. "The site closest to your apartment, the metro station, seems to have been a diversionary tactic. The bomber remotely detonated the first charge, which caused a stampede for the exit. Then he jumped into the crowd and detonated his vest. The main attack, though, seems to have been a club a few blocks over. Three separate charges went off around the building before the bomber detonated himself in the fleeing crowd."

"Eh, I don't go out much anyway." I took a sip of my coffee. "Our guy didn't know anything about the secondary attack. He thought that the location he hit was the intended goal; it was a blow against the imperialist infrastructure. They used him as a patsy without him ever knowing."

"You sound disappointed," she said.

"I suppose I am, a bit," I told her. "If he'd known the intricacies of their overall plan, I might finally have a name or a face for their leader. Better luck next time."

"You say that with so much confidence."

"As long as there are still those few who won't conform, we'll always have to deal with these kinds of assaults."

I finished my coffee and put the cup in the center of the table.

"Why do you do this, Nancy?"

"Because I like to think I'm making the world a bit better."

"But you're too sensitive," I told her. "You've got all these emotions bursting out of you in a world designed to crush people with your affliction. I mean, look at us. You've been trying to find some spark of feeling in me that was never there to begin with, that's never going to be there. You go home and cry and feel sorry for these people after every attack as if your tears and personal grief are going to bring them back from the dead. I don't understand you."

"That's because I'm human," she argued.

"And I'm not?"

We were silent for a moment, neither of us speaking or even making eye contact with each other.

"Maybe that's why we work so well together?" She laughed. "We're always trying to find what it is that makes us the same."

The phone in her coat pocket began to buzz and chirp. She pulled it out, read the message, and slid it back into her pocket.

"They need us over at the morgue. They're trying to identify who a head belongs to."

"Sounds like fun."

*

The room was pristine and clinical, its tiled floors and walls bathed in the bright white glow of florescent lights. Metal tables lined each wall, with sink basins, scales, and computer terminals beside each one. People in lab coats and scrubs, face shields and paper smocks fluttered back and forth between naked bodies in various stages of disassembly and decomposition. To the left of the door an autopsy was finishing up. The removed and dissected organs had all been placed in a clear plastic bag and stuffed inside the thoracic cavity, the way giblets are packed inside a turkey sitting in the freezer at the grocery store. The body was that of a middle-aged man with burns along the front of his arms and face; he'd likely been a victim from one of the blasts. Further down, there was a group of medical students gathered at a steel table

117

looking at the charred remnants of a head. It had been torn away from the body by the force of the blast and deposited gracelessly a dozen yards away.

Without a word I lay my briefcase in the ample open space between the head and the edge of the table and went to work. Inserting the spikes, setting the tablet, and activating it once it had calibrated, I felt myself immediately dropped into the man's final moments. It was like a waking dream, a lucidity that allowed me only the slightest differentiation between the man whose head lay on the table and my own mind. He was a father of two boys. I felt the overwhelming love and pride, the boundless joy that he had found in their births and their lives. He watched the news in anger every night, feeling that his rights, his freedoms, and those of his sons were being robbed by the Federation that had formed from the ashes of North America. He sympathized with the terrorists, with the subhuman rabble outside the protection of the wall. He had lived a life of complacency and comfort. He prayed to his gods for solutions and found only frustration in the silence.

I dove deeper into his mind. I found the man in the trench coat who had met him the week before. He was tall, slender, and oddly familiar, as if I'd seen him before. His face and voice were obscured somehow in the memory, almost as if they had been purposefully blocked. There was an uneasiness, a trepidation that had grown into outright fear as their meeting continued. They spoke of making a new world, a *better* world in their opinion, where men's thoughts and actions were their own, answerable to no greater collective authority or societal standard. Rhetoric. Propaganda. Dangerous thinking that could lead us back to the era of the Great War. A heavy cost to pay for such freedom. Hatred, anxiety – feelings fueled by a growing certainty that the only solution was to…

Suddenly, calmness. Utter, total acceptance of his fate.

It was a chilling sort of switch, marked by an eerie swiftness as he formulated the plans, built the device, and embraced his destiny.

He cried out in the middle of the terminal, felt the palpable panic as the device stuttered around his body. He pressed the button once as they all looked on. Then again.

The last sensation was of a crushing pressure through his body before the lights went out, and I found myself clutching the morgue table once again. His calm had allowed a more gentle return for me than the last one had offered. Without the stress, the aggressive pain stabbing into my body, I was able to exhale a deep breath, and in a quiet, dignified manner I removed the spikes and transmitted the data. I looked at Nancy standing in the back of the small crowd. She was biting her lip. She looked so concerned, so conflicted. Maybe it was the residual effect of the link, but I almost felt the need to hold her. It passed. I quickly sterilized my tools, enclosed them again, and started for the door.

"I'm going to send the request in for a warrant," I told her as we went into the lobby. "I know where to find their leader."

*

The spike doesn't lie.

I'd done it over two hundred times in my career, and the accuracy of my information was in the upper nineties every time. I could see the minute details, capture the mindset and the visual image, while the computer coded everything into data points that could be translated into any medium. I'd go back to the precinct at the end of my day and connect with every other investigator like myself, downloading the physical memory from my mind to be shared with the thousands of others like me around the nation. But first, I'd have to go and catch a terrorist. We had a visual depiction of the leader of our local cell, knew his voice and the persuasion tactics he used to recruit new martyrs for his cause.

"Look at all of this. So many reference points. So much data…" I thought aloud as I scrolled through the tablet. "Factors for radicalization. Recruitment tactics. We could eliminate so many threats through education and medication.

A whole army of counselors and pharmacists could put an end to years of uncertainty and fear. The war against society would finally be over before another terrorist could even think about building a bomb."

"It's a violation," Nancy said from the driver's seat, as I continued to read over the data.

"What is?" I asked absently.

"You're talking about rounding up hundreds if not thousands of people and subjecting them to some kind of reeducation. And all of this based on feelings and thoughts you ripped out of a dead man's brain. A man has a right to his own thoughts, even if they aren't socially acceptable. It isn't right for us to just *intrude* and take them."

"I've never met a person who cared what we did with their corpse after they were dead," I offered. "Never had one bit of protest on the matter, in fact."

"It's an invasion, though. Is nothing sacred to us anymore? Hell, all of this intrusion is what's breeding half the radicals we've dealt with in the last year."

"Privacy or security…" I said, "You can have one or the other, but never both."

"There were people before the war who disagreed with that sentiment," she said bluntly. "People who thought that you had to fight for your security and value your privacy, and that trading one for the other meant losing both entirely."

"They're probably the same sort of short-sighted, reactionary people who caused the war in the first place," I answered, ambivalent to the discussion she was trying to have.

"You've got no problem with what we do?" she continued. "You're completely fine with invading people's privacy, with raping their minds, as long as you get what you need?"

"You're getting awfully defensive over what we do to mass murderers. It's not like we're killing random people and stealing their thoughts. These are bad guys and killers. They're animals. This is how we keep people safe."

We rode in silence for a few minutes. Then: "What are you working on?" she asked.

"I'm going over some of this data we collected. If I'm right, we'll be able to create an algorithm that calculates the most likely candidates for radicalization. We can stop them before they ever build a single bomb."

"How will that work?"

"I mean, I'm not a policymaker or anything, but all we'd have to do is plug in known details about citizens: economic factors, political activism, religious involvement, social media content. It's for their own good. Besides, it's nothing that they aren't already making public record on a daily basis."

"You just want to snatch people off the streets because they aren't in agreement with the way we think?"

"That's a bit glib, but *yes*, it would certainly make it harder for these animals to slaughter people by the dozens."

The car came to a stop in a small garage near headquarters. Without a word, Nancy reached into the rear seat and opened up the small metal case with my equipment in it.

"What are you doing?" I asked.

"Something I should have done a long time ago," she answered, jabbing me in the thigh with a needle. Before I could react, before I could speak, the tranquilizer had taken hold. As the last moments of lucid awareness slipped into the encroaching darkness, I felt her lips softly on my forehead. "I'm sorry it had to end like this, Jim."

*

Everything felt odd, a warbling back and forth that distorted sound and vision, that bent reality sideways and backwards as I struggled to stand up in the stark white emptiness. My hands were soot black, shadow clouded, and felt detached from me by miles. Focusing for a moment, I made them a part of myself once more, made them tangible in a universe of intangible things. Up ahead the world was taking shape: a narrow, cobbled street with towering obsidian buildings at either side. Each was a shimmering black megalith that reflected everything with the same fun house mirror effect up into the starless stratosphere. An immense nightscape spread out in shades of red and purple across the black felt of the sky.

"None but the brave!" a voice roared in the distant, amorphous haze.

"What?" I asked.

"None but the brave may pass." A shape was forming. Loose, shredded flesh draped over a body piecemeal made and woven together by dark red seams. Horns growing from his forehead and skull formed a black crown, while snaking appendages from his groin, chest, and back seemed to move independently of the rest of his body, waving towards me. Each of his arms was massive, with bits of metal and machine woven in and out of the bare flesh. His fingers were familiar looking shivs of glinting metal that I'd become all too familiar with in my life. Each digit was a spike ready to pierce the veil between life and death, conscious and unconscious thought, and open two minds to one another. "Why do you stay?"

"I don't understand. Where am I? What's happening?"

"It's a very simple question," Nancy said softly from over my shoulder. I tried to turn, to look at her, but my eyes were frozen on the blood-soaked monster in front of me. "Why do you stay?"

"Stay where? I don't understand."

"On the brink of emotion," she answered. "You feel it every time you spike, and it leaves you a bit more empathetic every time, whether you'll admit it or not."

She was right. There was always a lingering thread of emotion that lasted long after the memory was gone.

"I'm afraid," I told her.

The creature ahead of me snorted. Taking two great steps to the side, he disappeared into the onyx walls of a towering building and was gone, leaving me alone with Nancy.

"Why are you afraid, Jim?"

"Because I don't understand," I said as I struggled to look at her. "How could you be here? Where is here?"

"We're inside a sort of false memory," she answered sweetly. "One of many that have been seeded and cultivated for decades in the wake of the new world order. This is the revolution you've been fighting against, the entire army of reprobates and terrorists are all living inside my mind, and now, yours."

"No. That's not possible. Right now, our strike teams are raiding their headquarters and taking out the cell here in the city."

"False memories, Jim," she said matter of factly. "Deep plants into the subconscious of every freedom fighter and volunteer. Right now, the strike teams are actually launching an assault on an abandoned hospital on the far side of town. It's all about misdirection, Jim. Sleight of hand. Send the dogs upwind while you make a break for it."

"But why?"

"Because they are inhuman. They steal children away from their parents, brainwash and drug them into submission, then use them to strip away the last inch of freedom we have left to us: our thoughts."

"But we are free."

"Freedom isn't living in a city on the brink of radiation poisoning, behind high walls that protect only the chosen few, while millions of others suffer in the wastes. Freedom isn't being told how to think and how to feel by propaganda machines outside our bedroom windows. It isn't about giving in to authority. You think the feds care about you? You're a tool, another replaceable piece in their machine. As long as they placate the ignorant with impulse desires and tawdry entertainment, no one will care about being subjugated."

"You're wrong, Nancy."

"Am I? Tell them what I'm showing you. Watch how fast they decommission you, shove you into a state home and drug you into lunacy. You're a federally owned sociopath. As soon as you've served your purpose they'll put you out of sight for that 'greater good' they try to sell us."

The world around me began to dissolve, replaced by scenes of carnage and devastation. Around me, shelves grew up from the blackened ground, each level filled with old paper books with broken spines. Some glowed in faint shades of luminous blue. I reached for them. Opening the first book I read aloud the words printed inside.

"It was a bright, cold day in April, and the clocks were striking thirteen."

The words burned away in blue flame, replaced in bold red letters that read CONFORM.

I dropped it to the floor and lifted the next tome from the shelves.

"At the end of the show the hypnotist told his subjects, 'Awake!'"

Again, the words burned away.

SUBMIT.

I dropped it and grabbed the next one.

"It was a pleasure to burn."

OBEY.

"They revise the message," Nancy said. "With each passing generation they rewrite our history to make us feel more enlightened, more fortunate to live under their scrutiny. If something is said that they don't like, they redact it. They make it look like it never happened. They've been gaslighting us since the start and snuffing out anyone who dares to question them. Our bombers were free thinkers. They would have been marked for death. Instead, they chose to help us send a message."

"They murdered innocent people."

"To get to you."

"But why?"

"Because you're the only one who can make this stop," she said. Her voice faltered, became soft. "When you wake up from the spike, I'll be gone. You'll have to go to the central office to upload your findings. When you do, information that we have imbedded in this memory will stream live into every other investigator linked at that moment. It will update to every tablet and download automatically into the minds of each and every one of you before blasting its way across the internet and into the homes and devices of every last man, woman, and child in the nation. Within days, the world will know the truth."

"And what is the truth?"

The nuclear wasteland before my eyes gently faded. Scorched pavement was swallowed in green grass. Dry streams flowed in crystal water. Life flourished where death had failed to conquer.

"The walls are a lie. The horrors of the outlands are a lie. America never burned. We survived. But the rich and the elite used the fear to create their fortresses, their strongholds where life conforms to their rules. The radiation, the danger, it was all a story told to keep us inside this cage. People need to know the truth."

"People are dumb, panicky animals who stampede over one another at the first sign of any danger to their own comfort," I argued. "You've seen it as often as I have. Let them be ignorant. They're happier this way."

"You think it will stop there? With simply living in ignorance? Look at you. You were taken from your mother's arms in the hospital. The state said you'd never live to adulthood, but it was a lie. They used you to create a spy. You burrow into the minds and memories of others and give all that you find to the same people who robbed you of any chance to live a normal life. All to keep the status quo."

"And if I refuse to do this?"

Nancy sighed.

"There's a syringe lying on the dashboard of the car. If you can't go through with this, inject it."

"What will it do?" I asked.

"It will short circuit every synapse in your brain. Every memory, every impulse, everything but your basic life functions will be completely and totally gone. It's a living death but it's the best I can offer."

"Suicide or execution for treason. Either way, it all ends the same for me."

The scenery changed again. It was a picture of a young woman flickering on a computer display. Her name and information had been redacted but the shape of her face was unmistakable. She looked identical to Nancy.

"My sister was seven when they took her," she said solemnly. "She was a poor student and they said it was some 'underlying neurological defect.' They said it would have been cruel to her to have to stay in my parents' care. They said they would give her the attention she needed. When I joined, I found out she'd been just like you, reconditioned to be some unfeeling memory thief. The spike eventually burned out parts of her temporal lobe and left her a vegetable. They euthanized her and dumped the ashes in Potter's Field without ever recognizing her service. They never even told my parents she'd died. This is the future, Jim. With every infringement they're leading us to a world where the individual is just a replaceable piece of meat in some organic machine. Our lives don't matter."

I could feel it. Every day of laughter and excitement, of love shared between sisters as they played their games and grew. The terror of seeing that sister ripped away in the night by men in suits and badges, unfeeling creatures who could only say that what they did was for "the greater good." The absolute hopeless loss of learning that this sister had been cast off as so much garbage after her usefulness had all been spent.

"None but the brave," Nancy said. "You have to choose to live for the cause of freedom or to die in defense of oppression. Only you can decide."

I woke up in the car, my head splitting like I'd just come off a bender. Nancy was gone. On the dashboard was a syringe of blue liquid. I slid it into my jacket pocket as I climbed across to the driver's seat. Starting the engine, I began towards the central precinct. It was time to make a choice.

*

The central precinct was a massive, cylindrical building in the city's heart. It was nearly twenty stories high, and almost two thirds of that space was devoted to machinery designed to take information from agents like myself and disseminate it to every official in the nation instantaneously. It also served as one of the biggest broadcasting machines in the world, pumping out endless hours of news, information, and propaganda to everyone in the region. Blue lights were flickering furiously at the base of the building, an azure flame cresting and receding in waves from the sea of patrol cars. Armed riot police stood shoulder to shoulder in rows behind and in front of the cars, forming a nearly impenetrable wall.

"What's happening?" I asked the officer in command as I pulled alongside the blockade and offered my credentials.

"They hit our squad sweeping the old hospital on the west side about an hour ago," the grizzled cop said from behind his face shield. "We got intel from a source that says they're planning an open attack here."

And with that, he waved me into the garage and continued watching the horizon for a threat that would never come. I suddenly knew how the Trojan Horse had felt being ushered into the keep with a belly full of Greeks ready to sack the city. My palms were sweating. For the first time in my life I knew what it was to be nervous. It wasn't that fleeting, stolen fragment of an emotion but an actual response to the mission thrust upon me. I stepped into the elevator and rode it to the ninth floor where the information processors were located.

The bell chimed, the doors parted, and a gargantuan hallway spread out before me. Walls of information glowed from floor to ceiling behind black chairs reclined for the comfort of those who would fill them. Technicians shuffled around in blue smocks as each agent deposited their briefcases and equipment next to a terminal as the operators themselves deposited their knowledge into the collective core. I found a cubicle where no technicians had been and prepared the machine alone. I set a timer for the extraction and loaded myself into the chair.

"Hey, what are you doing there?" a technician shouted, running up on me.

"I've got sensitive information that needs to be uploaded immediately."

I reached into my pocket for my credentials. I pulled out the syringe and injected a small amount of serum into the man's neck. If the entire syringe would effectively render me braindead, I hoped a small amount would only do minimal damage. Climbing back into the chair, I secured the spike and prepared for the jolt as everything I'd learned, everything I'd experienced since my last upload nearly a month ago, was pulled from me in a matter of seconds and processed by the assembly of supercomputers housed in the building. The truth was, I had no idea how any of it would work, no clue how the information itself would upload or how quickly it would be spread.

Within seconds of the information coming out of the spike, alarms began to wail from all corners of the room. The giant screens were washed in crimson shades and numerical codes that meant nothing to me. A familiar, guttural voice from my own terrifying nightmares began to cackle across every speaker in the building. As technicians began shrieking in panic, as agents woke with bewildered indifference to the horror they felt brewing inside them, I boarded the elevator and left for the car waiting below.

*

The radio was awash in a hellish chorus of voices decrying the federal government and their programs of control and subjugation. The giant advertisement boards were running videos of every state funded atrocity and crime against humanity that had been perpetrated since the end of the Great War, while televisions on street level (normally displaying the news or some banal, trivial entertainment) showed a slowly scrolling montage of faces and names, detailing how they had been stolen and turned into a labor force to further help in the subjugation of society. A familiar girl flickered by as I pulled up to my apartment building. The music in the elevator was prewar, a combination of punk and metal with a strong, anti-establishment tone to it. I smiled as the doors opened up to the cold, uninviting corridor on which I lived.

The door to my apartment was standing open, the frame splintered and bits of the lock lying on the burgundy carpet. I'd expected the feds to figure out who had betrayed them, I just thought I'd have a bit more time before they did.

What I *hadn't* expected was to find Nancy Coulton waiting for me on the edge of my bed. She looked so different, wearing a dark blue uniform with a gold badge over the left breast. She was smiling warmly as I walked into the room and placed my gear on the floor.

"I'm happy to see you, Jim." Her voice was honey. I felt a twinge of something I'd felt before, from people I'd probed in the past. I was relieved she was alive. "I think you made the right choice."

Wordlessly, I pulled a chair away from the small desk next to my broken window and sat down.

"What happens now?" I asked.

"Now, the people decide. Do they want to live free, to make their own way, or do they want to go back to sleep and simply exist in the status quo."

"And all the people who had to die?"

She sighed. "They died for the cause of freedom."

"What's the plan, then? The feds fold, and you put a new government in place. And when your law and order seem too stringent, too suffocating, someone else comes along and overthrows you? Is there actually a resolution where the people choose how to live their lives without someone else telling them the right and wrong ways to do it?"

"You said it yourself, Jim. People are dumb, panicky animals who will trample over one another for their own self-interest. At least with us at the helm, maybe we can create something more pure?"

"How many kids have died for this? How many parents have to live with the same grief that ate away at your mother and father when they lost a child? How many little girls are crying right now because a bomber blew up their sister?"

"Sacrifices had to be made."

"Sure they did. They always do, don't they? Isn't that what every regime tells us? But did they really have to?"

"Of course they did!" Nancy shouted. "Who would rally behind our cause otherwise? Who would open their eyes to see

129

the way our liberties are being stripped if we hadn't slapped them across the face with that realization?"

"I injured a technician uploading your little doomsday virus," I said coldly. "You could have done this with a single spike. There was no need to attack people, especially innocent people. If you wanted to fight the feds, hit the feds."

"We did."

"You blew up a nightclub and a subway depot!" I shouted. I could feel the tingling heat, the burning rage creeping up my neck and into my face. "You've blown up school buses and parades, but you've never once hit a federal post. Not even a damned delivery truck. You didn't want to wake people up. You wanted to make them afraid. You wanted to make them choose fear over free thought, and now you've got it. There'll be rioting before the night's out. It'll be an all out civil war by the end of the week. Everything you showed me, everything you planted in me, could have been used to open a dialogue."

"And what if the feds refused to listen to the people then?"

"Then the people could have made a choice. But now you've forced their hands. They know their government is manipulating them, but how long will it take to see that you're manipulating them as well? How many innocent people are going to get chewed up in your meat grinder before you get what you want?"

"What I want? What do you think that would be, Jim?"

"Revenge."

She stared blankly at me for a moment. Slowly, as if wounded, she stood up and crossed the room to where I sat.

"If anyone was going to understand, I thought it would be you," she said. Leaning down, she kissed me softly on the lips. She barely noticed as the syringe pierced her arm. Stepping back, she fell onto the bed and stared at me.

"You wanted me to feel something, anything," I told her, as her eyes began to glass with a fog of confusion and disbelief. "You showed me how they robbed me of my chance at life, the same way they robbed your sister. You showed me

130

the ways they stole our lives and replaced them with existence, with service to the state over self. Guess what I feel, Nancy. I feel *angry*."

Her lips moved as she tried to form words, an argument to justify herself. Nothing happened.

"I was betrayed by the people who were supposed to take care of me. I was used like a tool to invade people's minds and regurgitate what I found for everyone to see. I trampled all over that most sacred places in the human soul because it was my duty." I laid down on the bed beside her as her body began to convulse. "I became a tool for your revolution without being offered a choice. You expected me to come home, to feel so much guilt and remorse that I'd inject myself with this cocktail and dissolve any link that existed between you and this chaos."

Her head lolled to the side, her clouded eyes staring blankly at me from the placid, emotionless void of her face.

I stood up and walked across the room to get my gear. Opening the silver case, I laid the tablet and the spike on the bed in front of her face.

"Everything we did is inside this device," I told her. "It won't take them long to figure out that it was me who screwed them. They'll be coming here looking for me, for all of this, and soon enough they'll be out there on the streets, on every speaker and billboard and television screen spinning this as another terror attack. They'll rewrite history again to fit with their narrative, and those people panicking in the streets will be none the wiser because they're fools who are used to swallowing that party line…because it's simpler than dealing with an ugly truth."

She could still comprehend. It hadn't been a full dose of the drug thanks to the technician I'd stuck earlier. She might not be able to move, to react, but she knew what I was saying. The tears welling up in her eyes spoke louder than anything she might have left to say.

"But it will be too late for that. The seed of doubt will be there, in their heads and hearts, and they'll start to question." I stroked her face gently. "Don't worry, your revolution may be dead before it ever starts, but others are coming. After all, I just created an army of people *just like me* who all know the truth. Every minute detail, every bitter, raw emotion that was uploaded into the central precinct's computer has been shared with every last man, woman, and child bred to serve the state. They know the lies and the atrocities that have been conducted in the name of liberty. They'll work in the system, they'll bide their time, and when the moment is right, they'll bring the feds to their knees. The seeds have been planted and are taking root."

Maybe it was my newfound wellspring of emotion, or maybe I was just doing what any sociopath crossing over into psychosis would do. With a small knife I sliced away her clothes and began to carve a slogan into the pale white flesh of her stomach. It would be a call to arms by all of us who had learned the truth. It would be a pledge made by some and a warning issued to others.

Stay or go.
Fight or die.
"None but the Brave."

Where Eagles Dare

By R. Mike Burr

The voice came through the wall. There should have been a speaker, but at least the track lighting worked. There was a joke someone had told him involving gays, track lighting, and *Steel Magnolias*. He wondered what the rule was for fascists, but given the hurried newness of the room, he guessed little thought was given to matters of detail.

The voice again, still muffled, but a little louder.

He wondered whether to respond. He had been here for a while and eventually would need a bathroom. He had already tried the door. It didn't feel substantial, but was clearly locked from the outside.

The voice again, this time just on the edge of comprehension.

"I can't hear you."

He directed it to the piece of smoked plexiglass on the far wall. He assumed he was being watched from behind there, and it was from there he heard a muffled response.

"Still no good."

He spoke up, in case whoever was on the other side was getting the same garbled message. There was a rumbling that might have indicated conversation on the other side of the glass. He watched the panel as the sound rose then fell. The glass slid to the side, and he could make out a similarly designed smaller room. He saw there were at least two chairs, but he couldn't see who had been speaking.

"Can you hear me-us now?"

"Yes. Is it me or us?"

"We will ask the questions." The voice hit the first word hard, either to answer the question or mask the fact that each of them was alone.

"Okay. Go ahead."

"What?"

"You said you were going to ask the questions."

133

"How about this one, then? Don't you feel stupid now?"

"Not really. I'm just not sure what's going on."

"Think you're tough, huh?"

He didn't know how to answer. The van had come early that morning, and men in uniform had knocked on his door. He'd received an envelope a couple of days before. It was supposed to have arrived earlier, but there was postage due and had apparently been sent back and forth a couple of times. The enclosed letter, though elliptical and hampered slightly by faults in grammar, indicated that, as a patriot and a valued member of the voting public, he had been selected for an important focus group on policy. The men at the door were not exactly military. The red hats were a given, but they also had matching, ill-fitting shirts with an official looking insignia. Two of the men had tucked their shirts into camouflage pants, while the other was wearing roomy acid-washed jeans.

He opened the door a crack.

"Can I help you?"

The middle one nodded and the man on the right pulled a card out of his back pocket. He began to read haltingly.

"You are being summoned to participate in an important focus group that will determine many of the future programs in our great nation. Will you take part in this important event?"

"Do I have a choice?"

The reader shifted nervously from foot to foot, flipped over the card, as if hoping to find the answer. The jeans-wearing man in the middle stepped forward.

"This is the United States of America."

"And?"

"You always have a choice. But why wouldn't you want to do your civic duty?"

Blue Jeans nodded to the each of the men. The reader shifted his feet again and quickly returned the nod. He noticed something else that was uniform. Each of the three men had pistols on their hips.

"No. I don't think I'm tough. I just want to know what's going on here."

The was a brief pause.

"Well, what do you think is going on?"

"I just don't know. You came to my house and picked me up. You brought me here and left me in this room. I don't know what to think."

"Is that all you have to say?"

"I don't know. I have to go to the bathroom? What do you want me to say?"

Another pause.

"Do you really have to go to the bathroom?"

He considered his options. If he said no, he would be on one side of the wall and they would be on the other. That seemed like a generally positive thing. On the other hand, he didn't think they would merely pass over a bucket. Going outside might provide a valuable opportunity.

He put on his shoes and locked the door behind him. He wished he had a dog or even a fish, so he could make an excuse about leaving food out for the pet sitter or something. He had his cell phone in his pocket, but he had forgotten to charge it overnight, so it was dead as a doornail. He just smiled solicitously and followed the three men to what appeared to be a white rental van. He reassured himself that this was okay; the real bad guys always showed up in black vehicles with tinted windows.

Jeans man opened the side door and motioned him inside. He wished it wasn't empty. The four of them piled in the van, two up front and one on the bench seat with him. They drove through his neighborhood and then made a turn onto the boulevard of chain restaurants and empty car lots. It never occurred to him to ask the driver to stop. On some level, he supposed he wanted to see where all of this was heading.

"Yes, I do need to go."

He was becoming increasingly uneasy about his situation. If these weirdos wanted to try anything, at least he would know which direction to run.

"We'll see what we can do. Hold your water."

Immediately he felt an almost uncontrollable need to go. He considered peeing in the corner, but didn't want to anger the voices on the other side of the wall. He wasn't sure what word he should use for them. They weren't really his captors; they hadn't captured him. They were holding him though, and he wasn't sure if he could leave if he wanted to. It hadn't occurred to him to ask.

"Excuse me!"

He wanted more edge to his voice, but couldn't muster it. The voice, even through the glass, did a much better job.

"We said to hold your water. We're looking into it."

"It's not that. I just want to go home. I've decided not to participate. You know, I forgot some things I have going on later today. Totally slipped my mind, but I really don't think it would be good to move it around. You know how that goes, right?"

"You can leave any time you want. Just walk right out that door."

He got up out of the chair and turned toward the door. The voice called over his shoulder.

"Are you sure you want to go through that door, buddy?"

All of a sudden, he wasn't.

The van turned off on an access road and made a right into the third nondescript parking lot, or was it the fourth? He felt like he should be working harder at keeping track of these details. He tried to order the street names, but they were already a jumble in his head. It probably didn't matter. He would go and take this survey and be done with it. The only question was how long he would have to wait for an Uber.

After what seemed like a long time, the two camo-pants-wearing men came through the door. Jeans man wasn't with them. He took a moment to size them up. They easily outweighed him by twenty pounds each, weekend warriors gone pudgy. They were both wearing sunglasses. The one on the left had a goatee with a few crumbs in it. The other had a poorly-rendered black cat tattoo on his right forearm. He wasn't sure what he could do with those particular pieces of information, but it was a distraction from their right hands, which were both firmly planted on their sidearms.

"You still have to go tinkle?"

If he didn't before, he had to now.

"Yes."

"Go out the door. It's the second door on the right. And no funny stuff."

He followed the directions and ended up in front of the women's restroom.

"This is the ladies'. Is that okay?"

"It's fine. There aren't ladies here today."

"Yeah. Just pee sitting down."

He briefly imagined a version of himself peeing on the guy's shoe, but instead meekly pushed the door open and entered the restroom. A quick scan revealed that it was located on the interior of the building. There were no windows or other exit doors. Not that it would have mattered, because Goatee came in behind him.

"Hurry up and do your business."

He pushed into a stall and let the door ease shut, hoping Goatee did not want to watch him urinate. Thankfully he didn't, but it was still nearly impossible to start with him waiting outside.

"Do you have to be in here? I'm not going anywhere."

"You pee-shy? For Christ sake, just do your business so we can get out of here."

He took a deep breath and tried to mentally remove Goatee from the room. He was able to produce a weak stream that dribbled down to two or three false finishes. He dribbled on his pants as he zipped up and cursed silently. He had already given up a lot of ground; he didn't want to have spots of pee on his pants. He rubbed them as best as he could with the heel of his hand, straightened up, and walked out of the stall. Goatee was looking at his phone. He washed his hands and wiped them on a paper towel.

"I'm ready."

Goatee nodded, put away his phone and pointed to the door.

He stepped into the hallway and turned to go back the way he came. Black Cat held up his hand.

"We're gonna go the other way, Hoss. Just follow him there."

His tone was not overtly threatening, but he felt a definite fight or flight sensation. Black Cat read his mind.

"There's nothing bad going to happen to you. But I wouldn't run if I was you."

So he walked.

The three of them moved down the hall in silence. He tried to count the doors or notice a change in the carpet's pattern, but he kept thinking about his stupid fucking pee-dotted pants and what the guns were for if nothing bad was going to happen.

Goatee stopped and knocked on a door.

"You all ready in there?"

He rocked back on his heels and again felt the urge to run. Black Cat put a hand on his shoulder. There was a muffled sound from the other side of the door. Goatee turned around and addressed Black Cat.

"What do you think?"

"Go ahead. Let's get this over with. I have things to do."

Goatee pulled a key from his pocket and opened the door. Black Cat made a motion for him to go in. The room was dark except for two floodlights focused down on a chair. He'd seen this movie before and it was fucked. He forgot about the guns and turned to get out of there. He made it about five steps before tripping over someone's foot and falling flat on his face. There was a hand on his back and a voice in his ear.

"I told you that nothing bad is going to happen to you if you follow directions. Did anybody ask you to run like a pussy?"

He had to pee again.

"No. Nobody told me that."

"Told you what?"

"Told me to run."

The voice was very close to his ear, but he still couldn't discern who was speaking to him.

"Run how, motherfucker?"

He didn't want to say it, but he quickly did.

"Like a pussy."

They dragged him up and pushed him into the room, toward the chair. As he moved closer, he saw a small table at the far end of the room, with someone sitting behind it. He squinted. It was Blue Jeans.

"Have a seat, please. And don't do anything silly like that again. You might hurt yourself."

"What's going on here?"

"This is a focus group on the state of patriotism in our country. Now have a seat and we can get started."

He sat down. One of the chair legs was shorter than the others. He couldn't distribute his weight and the chair wobbled awkwardly. He concentrated on keeping it still.

"Good. Let's get started."

"This isn't a focus group. I'm the only one here."

"I'm here. You're here. My associates are here. That makes it a group, doesn't it?"

"I don't want to be here. I want to go home. You need to let me go. This is ludicrous."

"I don't have to let you go. You came here of your own free will. All you have to do is get up out of that chair and walk out the door. Do you want to get up out of that chair and walk out the door, or do you want to participate in the great democracy of our country?"

Blue Jeans leaned across the table and tried to smile. At best, it looked fake.

"Why do you have guns, then?"

"It is a guaranteed Second Amendment right to defend the safety of myself and my family. Surely an educated person like yourself knows that. Here. Let me show you."

The right rear chair leg thumped audibly twice. Blue Jeans unholstered his gun and dropped the magazine into his hand.

"This is a Glock .22, the same firearm used by law enforcement agencies across the nation. The safety is on. It is of no possible harm to you or me right now. However, should I assess a threat, I can, within seconds, proactively remove it."

Blue Jeans snapped the magazine into the pistol and set it down on the table.

"You were saying something about wanting to leave?"

Blue Jeans' fingers grazed the surface of the gun. The right rear chair leg thumped twice more.

"No. That's okay. Let's just get this over with. What do you need to know?"

"I think you know what we need to talk about."

Thump. Thump.

"You seem to have a slight problem with our duly-elected leader. Would you say that's true?"

"I didn't vote for him, if that's what you mean."

"You don't need to tell me who you voted for; the secret ballot is one of the most integral and cherished parts of our democracy."

"If you know who I am, and I think that you do, it should be obvious who I did or did not vote for. Isn't that why I'm here?"

"I don't think we have the manpower to speak with every single person that didn't vote for the president. We are more concerned with some posts that you chose to make on your social media accounts."

"I thought this was a focus group?"

"It is, in that that we would like to focus on some pretty inflammatory statements that you put out there for the public."

"I don't even know what you're talking about. What sort of inflammatory statements are you talking about?"

"Did you, in October, refer to the President of the United States as a Cheeto with an anus face?"

Blue Jeans intoned each word solemnly, but he couldn't, even at this moment, fully repress a smile.

"Is this a statement that you made?"

Thump. Thump.

"Well?"

"I don't know, really. I remember seeing that on Facebook, but I don't know that I made that statement."

"So, you did know that this statement was out there, but you didn't come up with it?"

"I'm not sure."

"But you're sure that you didn't originate the statement?"

"I said that I'm not sure. And even if I did, what about the First Amendment?"

"What about the First Amendment?"

Thump. Thump.

"Um. Even if I did make those statements, I am allowed to under the Constitution."

"The Bill of Rights."

"What?"

"Freedom of speech is actually an amendment to the Constitution, not a part of the original document. Don't you feel like people take their freedoms for granted sometimes? I mean it's easy to talk about the Constitution, but it's more correct to refer to the Bill of Rights. I think that you should say what you mean and mean what you say. That's not unreasonable, is it?"

Thump. Thump.

"I said, is it?"

"I guess."

His mouth was suddenly dry, but his bladder was still uncomfortably full. He shifted to find relief and the chair just offered its same dumb reply. He could hear Goatee and Black Cat behind him. Blue Jeans shuffled some papers and then stared intently at him.

"Like, for instance, if I had strong enough feelings about the President of the United States to compare him to a Cheeto, I would at least be man enough to own up to it. I mean, I'm not perfect and I say some shit, but I will own all of it."

"Okay."

"So why won't you just admit what you said, and we can move on?"

141

"What happens if I do?"

Blue Jeans leaned forward and smiled.

"Now we're getting somewhere. What do you think should happen?"

"Nothing. I don't know. This is the United States. I mean, why do you even care? Fuck. He won. You have both the House and the Senate. Nobody has health insurance anymore. You're going to have legions of drug offenders building a wall with Mexico, and you care about this? You care that I got angry and blew off some steam. Well fuck it, and fuck you. I did. And I'm sorry, but I was angry."

Tears welled. He brought his face to his hands to hide them, trying to get himself under control.

"I don't think you just flew off the handle. There's a pattern of behavior."

He wiped off his face and looked at Blue Jeans, who was still staring at him with lupine contempt.

"What?"

"I mean, you do something once, it is an event. You do it over and over, it's a pattern."

"What are you talking about?"

Blue Jeans shuffled the papers on the desk.

"In addition to your Cheeto comment, you also on separate occasions referred to the chief executive of this great country as a 'pussy grabbing sex criminal' and that he must 'enjoy having a Russian hand up his ass.' It seems like you have a bone to pick with our president."

"And I can *do that*. I'm *allowed* to do that. That's part of being a citizen of the United States."

"Being a citizen of the United States also means taking responsibility for your words and your actions. That's why we're here today."

"What are you talking about? This is crazy."

"No. Crazy is thinking that you can just say anything and have no consequences. Gentlemen, let's show this recalcitrant citizen what we think of those with no respect for our institutions of government."

He felt Goatee and Black Cat inch closer, their hands coming to his shoulders.

"What?!? What the hell?!? This isn't right! Hey! No! I want to get out of here! I want to go home! They're just words! Stupid words!"

Blue Jeans brought his hands to his face in a motion of prayer.

"Sometimes words hurt. It's time that we all understand that."

The hands were steadying him, not holding him down, but not letting him run either. He had always followed the rules. Look where it got him. He tried to think of a scenario where he could walk out of the door reasonably intact. To his immense shame, he started to cry again. He slumped in the chair, pissed his pants, and started to cry harder.

"What do I have to do to make it right?!? What do I have to do?"

Blue Jeans didn't have time to answer. There was a crash and light erupted from behind him. His immediate thought was that he had been shot and that he was glad it didn't hurt. Through watery eyes he saw Blue Jeans' gun still sitting on the table. Blue jean stood frozen, wearing a look of shock.

"You don't have to do a damn thing buddy. It's these assholes that have some explaining to do."

A new voice was in the room. He passed quickly in front of him, snatched Blue Jeans' pistol from the table and backed away. The stranger moved in the shadowed portions of the light, but he saw that he was wearing a ski mask.

"This is your cue to get the fuck out of here. Are you coming with me?"

His legs were jelly.

"I am serious. If you want to go, you best come with me."

Blue Jeans snapped from dumbness.

"Hey! That's my gun! You best give that back!"

It was then he noticed the stranger was also holding a gun, one that reminded him of the ones Nazis used in the Indiana Jones films.

"Little boys don't get to keep their toys if they can't be responsible!"

"You don't know who you're messing with buddy!"

"I know that you're going way too far, Bobby. You can't do shit like this! Now let's go!"

"How do you know my name? Who is that under there? And give me back my fucking gun!"

Blue Jeans hit those last two words hard, but the interloper kept his gun calmly trained forward. Without losing focus, he grabbed his arm and shouldered past Black Cat and Goatee, who mutely let them pass. He was dragged back the way he had come. His rescuer pulled him through a door and propped a folding chair against it.

"That should buy us a few minutes. Are you okay?"

He nodded his head and tried to find words, but they did not come.

"Can I ask you a kind of personal question?"

He centered himself and took a deep breath.

"Yes. Anything. And thank you. So much."

"Did you piss yourself?"

He nodded again.

"That's unfortunate. Come on. We have to go. You can get yourself cleaned up later."

He noticed for the first time the clamminess in his groin and futilely tried to make adjustments before following.

The new arrival removed his ski mask. He was about the same height and wearing a green workman's jacket and brown pants. Greasy curls of brown hair fell below his collar. He looked back and smiled, showing teeth that had seen hard use.

"Let's get in the car and get some distance between us and them. Can you hurry up a little bit? That chair isn't going to hold them up forever."

His rescuer threw open an industrial door to the bright light of day and led him to a dusty red Monte Carlo. His savior

144

slid into the driver's seat and leaned across to open the passenger side door.

"Come on now. We can talk in the car. Here. Put this towel down."

And for the second time that day, he entered a motor vehicle with a complete stranger. His rescuer revved the engine and jammed the shift stick to drive. The car belched, bucked, and then leapt forward with an impressive amount of force.

"She don't want to get going as well as she used to, but she still gets her done. Kinda like me, you know?"

His rescuer leaned over as they peeled out of the parking lot and gave him a wink and a grin. He got another look at the man's teeth, which resembled pieces of Indian corn stuck in at odd angles. He also got his first look at the full glory of the man's hair, which was cut in the 'business in the front, party in the back' style.

"I'm Brett, by the way."

Brett reached a hand over the console and he reached to shake it. Instead, though, Brett slapped him five and executed an awkward fist bump.

"That was pretty fucking cool, wasn't it?"

"I don't know. What just happened?"

"Well, old Brett just pulled your biscuits out of the oven, if you kapeesh. That was my former brother-in-law and he's kind of a bad dude. I didn't think he'd ever go and do something like this, but that motherfucker is crazy these days. Him and his buddies get together, and you don't know what's gonna happen."

"Thank you. I don't know what to say."

"You better say a prayer, because I think I see Bobby's van coming up behind us."

Brett jammed the accelerator. The Monte Carlo coughed, but responded. He looked in the side mirror and saw the white van. It made a hard right down a side street and faded from view.

"They just turned."

"Bobby knows that he can't outrun me. This is the Dale Jr. edition."

They covered three blocks and the van shot out of a side street behind them, closer than before. Brett grimaced.

"He does seem to know the side streets a little bit better than me."

Brett maneuvered the Monte Carlo down the middle of the street to avoid parked cars. The van chugged up behind them and nudged the bumper. He and Brett were knocked forward. Brett glanced back with alarm.

"He wants his pistol back I guess, but he best not have fucked up my bumper."

The momentary safety he felt was quickly melting away. He didn't know what people did in these situations.

"Do you want me to shoot the gun?"

Brett took a split second to fully regard him. The van thunked into the bumper again.

"You are full-on crazy. You can't just go firing a gun at people."

"You had a gun."

"That was an Airsoft, motherfucker. I don't fuck with carrying a piece. Good way to shoot your dick off."

"You didn't have a real gun?"

"All them motherfuckers walking around with them hog legs ain't got peckers to speak of; old Brett ain't got no complaints in that department. However, my navigation skills are fair to middling."

The Monte Carlo rumbled into the turnaround at the end of the street. Before Brett could get the car fully reversed, the van angled to a stop, blocking any exit. The three men piled out of the van and stood behind the open front doors. Black Cat and Goatee had their pistols out, and the man he now knew as Bobby must have found a spare somewhere.

"Brett! I thought that was you! What the fuck, man? Mind your damn business! Get out of that fucking car and bring me back my pistol!"

Brett rested his head on the steering wheel.

"How you want to handle this?"

"Do you think he'll let us go if we give it back to him?"

"I think the best we can hope for is to get out of here with a severe beating. But I don't know what the fuck he was going to do with you. That's the wild card right there."

"You aren't going to give me back to them, are you?"

Brett regarded him through squinted eyes.

"You gotta do a little better than that if we're going to make it out of this intact. What is the matter with you?"

"Nothing. This whole thing is surreal."

He wondered if Brett would know what he meant by surreal or think that it applied to an X-Men movie.

"You ain't seen nothing yet."

Brett rolled down the window.

"Fuck you, motherfucker! Move the damn van!"

"Ain't gon' happen, Brett. You know that. Why didn't you just leave well enough alone?"

"Damn it, Bobby, this shit ain't right and you know it. You can't just drag people off the street because they don't agree with you."

"I didn't drag anyone, and you can't steal someone's property. Hand it over."

Brett rolled up the window. Bobby smacked the van's door with a closed fist. His face reddened.

"Do you think we should ram him?"

"No. Fuck. I don't know. What do you think?"

"I think this might be going from beating territory to something more serious. I like Bobby, but he's let all this politics bullshit go right to his head. We might as well get out and face the music. I kind of wish you hadn't pissed in your pants. That makes us a little less impressive."

He put his face in his hands and wished he was home.

"Now when I go, are you going with me?"

He nodded. Brett placed the gun on the backseat and opened his car door. Against his better judgement, he followed suit. Both men put their hands in the air.

"We're just gonna walk on by. Your gun's on the seat. Don't fuck up the car, okay?"

The three didn't move.

"I don't think that's gonna work, Brett! I'm gonna need you and your new friend to lay down on the ground. This is a citizen's arrest."

"Bobby, you just can't do this kind of shit!"

"You been on me ever since me and Sheila broke up! Now hand it over!"

"My sister ain't got a thing to do with this, Bobby! Don't put all that crazy shit on the Facebook and then be surprised when someone shows up to your party!"

"That was a message to a closed group!"

"You invited me in like two months ago!"

Bobby reached another level of frustration and turned a deeper shade of red. He pointed his new gun in the air and fired off a round.

He hit the ground immediately, knowing this time that he had not been shot. He also held everything together from a bodily fluid perspective, which was another improvement. He looked under the Monte Carlo and saw Brett kneeling, looking over at him. Brett gave him a thumbs up. He laid there for a moment and felt the concrete, cool and rough, on his cheek. He closed his eyes and thought about just sleeping, then willing himself to wake up from this nightmare.

That was precisely why he heard the police sirens before he saw the cruisers pull up behind the van. He counted three at least five uniforms. They had taken a more trained refuge behind their cruisers and lined up Bobby, Goatee, and Black Cat with pistols and a particularly nasty looking shotgun.

The alpha among them, who looked so much like the Platonic ideal of a state policeman that he thought again he must be dreaming, holstered his pistol and took immediate control of the situation.

"Drop your weapons and put your hands on your head! And you two in the back! Get on your feet! Slowly! And put your hands on your heads! Now!"

He and Brett complied immediately. Goatee, Black Cat, and Bobby did as well. Bobby smiled in the direction of the officers.

"What seems to be the problem?"

The trooper walked confidently from between the parked cruisers, covered closely by his colleagues. He removed his hat and neatly tucked it under his arm, revealing the expected brush cut. He left his sunglasses on as he surveyed the scene. He raised two fingers before he spoke.

"I'll ask the questions. What the holy hell is going on here, other than you all driving like it's Indianapolis, getting me a ton of calls, and generally adding upheaval to my Saturday afternoon?"

No one spoke immediately. This was his chance.

"Officer! These three guys took me from my house this morning. They took me to a building and made me answer a bunch of questions. This guy beside me is Brett. He came and got me out."

The trooper sucked in on his lips and did not respond immediately.

"They had uniforms and a letter and everything. They said they were with the government."

The trooper nodded his head and raised his two fingers again.

"Let me get this straight. These three dipshits, who put on their Halloween costumes and six shooters this morning and decided to go out and abduct you, are men with whom you had no previous acquaintance. Is that true?"

Bobby, hands firmly planted on his head, bobbed up and down. His shirt freed itself from his jeans as he said, "At no point was the subject under duress. He decided to come with us of his own free will for a political discussion. He was continually reminded of his voluntary participation."

The trooper brought his fingers to the bridge of his nose and returned them to his speaking position.

"Sir, I'm going to have to ask you to limit your answers to a sentence. I don't think that I can will myself to listen to any more than that. Got it?"

149

Bobby scuffed the ground with the toe of his shoe and nodded.

"You did pick this man up at his house this morning and transported him to a second location, where you were going to do what exactly?"

Bobby looked at the ground.

"We were just going to make him say he was sorry and then put it on Facebook. We weren't going to hurt him."

"On Facebook? You exposed you and your friends to a Class B felony to put something on the computer? Really?"

"Yes."

"Neither of you three move an inch. Sir, you went with these three gentlemen, even though they are clearly not affiliated with any branch of the government except for maybe the federal bureau of idiocy?"

"Um, yes."

"And it never occurred to you to call a legitimate law enforcement agent to remove these men from your property or to just tell them to fuck off on your own?"

"No, not really."

"And at some point during the commission of this…whatever this was, you, sir," he nodded in Brett's direction, "decided to come in on a rescue operation."

Brett considered for a moment and then nodded his head.

"And you never for a moment considered doing anything but busting in and then driving like a maniac afterwards, endangering countless lives, including your own?"

Brett shrugged his shoulders.

"The one piece of good news I have for you is that while you assholes were playing house this afternoon, some *other* asshole put up a YouTube video saying some legitimately disgusting things about the first family. Awful stuff, really. Went on and on about how a nuclear war with Korea would be the end of civilization, how it was time to march on Washington and take the power back." He paused, snorted, and spat something yellow onto the concrete.

"I guess all that might have been fine, this society being degraded as it is, but this asshole decided to go on and detail what he wanted to do when he got there." He scowled. "Just beyond the pale."

The trooper dropped his fingers and pointed at Bobby.

There was a quick report.

Bobby jerked slightly, lost animation, and fell.

He stood rooted, ears ringing, daring only to glance at Brett, who stood open-mouthed in shock. The trooper's voice formed from white noise.

"First ever presidential decree delivered via Tweet. Historic. Grants peace officers the ultimate authority when faced with terror threats both foreign and domestic. Great day to be an American."

The trooper pointed at Goatee and Black Cat. He knew for a split second what was coming, but was still shocked when their heads snapped and their bodies collapsed.

"Time was, these three would have tied up the court system for months, lived off my taxes in the prisons, and then come back out to do it all again. No more. God bless the United States of America."

The trooper drew his sidearm and held it angled toward the ground in front of him and Brett. He considered running. His feet would not obey. Brett swayed slightly, trying to keep his balance.

"Gentlemen, you may be shocked by what you've seen, but I want you to remember: terrorism takes many forms, and none of it will be tolerated in this country. Of course, that includes the rights of citizens to walk down a street and not be killed by a bad actor on an unsanctioned and unwarranted pretend homeland security operation."

The bullet hit Brett center mass. He thought that his bladder might have let go again, but he didn't care at this point. His feet were dumb, and he stood stock still as Brett took a few last bubbling breaths.

"We have been waiting for this since the towers fell. We've had the equipment for years, even talked about something like this here and there. Sometimes, you find yourself at the right time in history."

He heaved. Heavy spit dribbled out the corner of his

mouth. The trooper gestured to the three prone bodies.

"So, I guess when they ask, I could say you were Antifa or American Taliban or admitted to posting treasonous material in your Facebook. I guess the real point is, I don't really have to care a whole lot about that."

Click.

Big Takeover

A Damaged Inc. Adventure

By Paul Brian McCoy

"We must all face the fact that our leaders are certifiably insane or worse."
- William S. Burroughs

Part One

It began like most of these sorts of things do; with a dream.

Emma Crowe sat up in bed and knew without hesitation that she was still asleep. Her eyes immediately adjusted to the darkness and the clock on her nightstand read 11:22. Instinctively, she began psychically exploring the edges of the dream, looking for traps or hints of infiltration. Emma was one of the most powerful psychics to ever be discovered and rescued by Project Mephistopheles and she had an innate affinity for dream communication - meaning she could enter dreams and influence the dreamer.

Unfortunately, that sometimes meant that she was also open to unwanted contact from other dream travelers.

One of the first things she learned to do in dreams was adopt a dream avatar. Dreaming was essentially role-playing when you could control the dream, and adopting a character allowed Emma to hide her identity from prying eyes, mingling with other dream inhabitants, while also essentially becoming a combination superhero/rock star. All the agents for The Project had dream avatars and had been trained by Emma to shift to them without thinking whenever they found themselves in a lucid dream or at her side on a mission into someone else's subconscious dreamscape.

When she slid out of bed and to her feet she was no longer the five-foot, six-inch skinny blonde Emma, but the six-two punk anarchist warrior woman, Plasmatica Zero. She wore a leather jacket, short skirt, and knee-high black boots. A pistol was slung from her hip. Her thick black hair was shaved on the sides and a vivid white streak arced up from her brow into her pony tail.

As far as she could tell, there were no traps waiting to catch her in a dream loop, effectively keeping her captive in a repeating fantasy while her body wasted away in the real world. She slid the pistol from its holster and stepped toward the door. The gun was like no real gun. It was curvy and smooth, polished silver, like something out of Flash Gordon or a Jerry Cornelius story. The door sensed her approach and irised open, allowing her access to the darkened hallways of Project Mephistopheles.

Of course, they shouldn't have been dark. There was always something going on at The Project. Located a mile beneath the desert of White Sands, New Mexico, Project Mephistopheles was a fringe science wonderland, partially funded by the United States government but through so many false fronts and backdoors that all anyone in power knew was that they did cutting edge think tank research that rarely, if ever, yielded practical results. The truth was dramatically different, but the Project Director, Professor Isaac Warren knew how to keep a secret. Like the fact that he had inherited the post from his long-presumed dead father and after a near-fatal contact with an extra-dimensional entity intent on devouring all life on earth, was now a disembodied brain in a jar. A jar was speaking loosely, of course. His brain was kept alive in a tank of nanofluid that allowed him direct access to the computer systems that kept The Project running.

The other big secret was the existence of the sentient A.I., Miranda, who made sure that everything ran smoothly when Isaac was preoccupied and distracted by the psychological disassociation and isolation of being a mind with no physical body. Miranda was extremely fond of Isaac for reasons of her own and tried to nurture the spiritual awakening that one finds when the psyche is cut loose from the physical limitations of a body. Isaac wasn't convinced, and he still missed Scotch and Amphetamines.

154

A lot.

As Emma/Plasmatica stepped into the nearly featureless hallway, a series of soft blue arrows illuminated in the floor, guiding her in the direction she was supposed to go. In waking life this was a normal occurrence, as The Project was large, and the hallways wound around almost nonsensically, like an ant colony. She wondered sometimes if they moved on their own at night, mischievously shifting and rerouting in order to force people to use the guide lights to be sure they reached their destinations without getting lost. In this dream version of The Project, she was convinced of it.

After what felt like hours of walking, Plasmatica turned a non-existent-in-the-real-world ninety-degree corner to come face to face with both an elevator and an eight-foot-tall bare-chested barbarian with ebony skin and dreadlocks flowing down his back. He wore animal skin leggings and huge black boots. Strapped to his back was a blood-red sword nearly as long as he was tall.

"You dreaming this too?" Plasmatica asked, holstering her pistol.

"Yeah. Couldn't resist the pull," said Blood, a.k.a. Malcolm Carroll. "It's pretty freaking strong." In reality, Mal was nineteen and living a normal life thanks to a medical procedure that allowed him to monitor and maintain his brain chemistry after years of living on the streets in a near-constant paranoid hallucinatory state that was only compounded by his manifesting psychic abilities. He was another of The Projects secret success stories. Most of the psychic kids that were brought in over the years ended up committing suicide before they could be taught how to control their powers and put them to use.

Before anything else could be said, the elevator doors hissed open.

"After you," Blood said, and the two of them stepped inside.

The elevator ride was silent. Neither of them looked at the other. Finally, when it became clear that there was no telling when the elevator would stop, Plasmatica spoke while still looking straight ahead.

"You don't have to be here if you don't want to."

"Are you ordering me to stand down?" Blood answered, also staring straight ahead.

"No. But I'm okay going alone."

"Someone should keep an eye on you." He glanced over, then returned his gaze to the doors.

Plasmatica huffed. This again. He was never going to move past the fact that she had a tendency to make the hard calls without relying on approval from the team. Or The Project, really.

"I'd hoped you'd be over this by now."

"Over you playing judge, jury, and executioner? Not going to happen." He shifted his stance. "Nobody else will hold you accountable. Somebody has to."

"Accountable." She tried to hide it, but she was getting pissed. Knowing that she couldn't hide it, made her even more pissed. "I saved lives. I saved the fucking planet, Mal."

"Blood."

"For fuck's sake."

Before another word could be said, the elevator stopped and the doors slid open. Plasmatica pulled her pistol and Blood drew his sword as they stepped out into darkness. There were no walls that they could see, just an empty space with a faint red light off in the distance.

"Are you sensing a trap?" she asked softly.

"Nothing." He paused. "That light is tugging at me, though."

"Same here." She glanced around, psychically sweeping the area and getting no feedback. "Wanna fly?"

Blood grinned, almost against his will. "Sure."

She smiled back. Flying was the best part of dreaming.

Both of them silently rose into the air and with a thought, sent themselves soaring through the darkness. In dreams, real world physics don't apply. They felt no wind or drag, diving and rolling, flipping and turning like dolphins at play. They almost forgot that they had a destination and for just a few moments, Malcolm forgot to be angry with Emma.

Then, without warning, they were both hit with a concussive blast like an air horn with fists and fell toward a ground that was no longer there. They tumbled for a few minutes, stunned and confused before suddenly finding themselves in blinding Texas sunlight, seated in the backseat of a Presidential motorcade waving to the crowds as shots rang out and both of them - as one - felt their heads burst, snapping back and to the left.

And then the scene played out again. Over and over again.

Over and over again.

Part Two

"There's something wrong with the President's brain!" Emma said, bursting into Professor Warren's office.

"So you've finally started paying attention to current events?" Isaac's voice buzzed and crackled from the speaker on his desk. Emma was positive he could have upgraded the speaker to sound crystal clear, but liked the steampunk character it added when he spoke. The wall behind the desk was a clear glass window, and behind the glass, submerged in a viscous pink fluid, sat a human brain on a tripod. Streams of small bubbles slowly flowed upward all around it.

"Very funny," she snapped back. "This is serious."

"Have a seat, then, and tell me all about it."

From a circular trapdoor in front of the desk, an egg-shaped chair rose up into the room and as it locked into place, Emma dropped into it and set it spinning with a kick, rotating on a single central leg.

"Mal and I just paid a visit to Kennedy's brain."

The speaker cracked and hissed in what she felt was probably an accurate representation of Isaac's shock and confusion.

"Come again?"

157

"Apparently, we have President John Kennedy's brain hooked up to a machine in some abandoned sub-basement and he just sent out a psychic call that Mal and I both answered."

"Well," Isaac started, then stopped. After nearly a full minute, he continued, "That's intriguing."

"Not as intriguing as the fact that we just spent what felt like days reliving his assassination on an endless loop. That's a pretty fucked up glitch. Somebody should look into fixing it." She put her foot on the floor to stop her chair from turning. "I suppose you were checking records just then? Any info?"

"Just cursory references. Miranda, dear? Are you listening?"

"I am, Isaac," said a soothing female voice from a speaker system set up to make it seem like her voice was coming from all around. It could be intimidating until you got to know her. "It appears there are some highly encrypted files on one of our oldest and least-accessed servers that may shed some light on this. Give me a moment to decrypt them."

"Hmmm," Isaac crackled. "If you don't have immediate access, they must be thoroughly locked down."

"As thoroughly as your father could, given the technology of the time."

"Of the time?"

"These files seem to have been locked since at least the early Seventies. I'm frankly amazed at the level of complexity. Your father wasn't half bad at this."

"Locking things up and not sharing?" The speakers chuckled. "That sounds *exactly* like dear old dad."

"Oh my. This *is* interesting," said Miranda after a moment's silence.

"Do tell," Isaac said.

"It appears that when President Kennedy's brain was discovered missing from the National Archives in 1966, it had actually been confiscated by The Project shortly after the removal for autopsy in 1963. According to your father's notes, he believed that every President of the United States shared a bloodline going back to King John of England."

"Wait, like, Robin Hood's Prince John?" Emma asked.

A deep sigh came from Isaac's speaker. "Not only was he a monumental asshole, it appears my father was a conspiracy nut, as well. Will wonders never cease?"

"Not to contradict you, Isaac, but whether it is a precursor to holding the office or not, it does appear that all of the United States' presidents, with the sole exception of Martin van Buren, have belonged to that bloodline. Some more directly than others, of course."

"If I could facepalm, I'd be doing it now," Isaac said.

"We need to outfit you with emojis," Emma laughed.

"Note to self, outfit my screens with emojis," Isaac barked.

"It appears," Miranda continued, "that your father was attempting to use Kennedy's brain to establish some sort of telepathic early warning system."

"Early warning system for what?"

"For the potential compromise of the acting President's mind."

Everyone was silent for a while after that.

Part Three

"I still find it hard to believe that this President is a part of the bloodline. Surely he's another van Buren?" Isaac said to no one in particular.

"It actually turns out that the President is related to John of Gaunt, a 14th Century royal, who was the First Duke of Lancaster and the son of King Edward III," Miranda chimed in. "As is Hillary Clinton, apparently."

"So we're cursed to be ruled by this Ancient Asshole Bloodline?" Emma asked.

"Ancient Asshole Bloodline is a more colorful name than most. Some call it the 13th Illuminati Bloodline or The Merovingian Line, although the Merovingian has other, even more archaic and intriguing connotations going back to the historical Jesus himself."

"Oh fuck me. He is *not* descended from Jesus," Isaac exclaimed. "That's all that orange anal wart needs to hear."

"Regardless of the accuracy of these connections," Miranda calmly continued, "it appears that the early warning system is either breaking down, as the assassination glitch may portend, or there is something alarming happening in Washington."

"Breaking down? We didn't even know it existed, much less that it was working."

"Well," Emma said bluntly, "worst case scenario is it works, and The President is either brainwashed or has been taken over. If he's been taken over, that means, what? Psychic warfare, demonic possession, or maybe an alien parasite? Maybe we could be lucky for once and he's just had a stroke."

"I'd opt for the latter," Isaac crackled, "given some of the operational memos we've been getting over the past year. The man can mangle a sentence like he was tying a verbal constrictor knot. But you're right. I suppose we have an obligation to the security of the country to investigate."

"Shall I gather a team?" Emma asked.

"If I could recommend a light touch," Miranda suggested. "The smaller the team, the better, I'd say. This won't exactly be an authorized mission."

"Hmm. Yeah. Can't really put this one on the books," Isaac said. "You and Mal, for sure. Think you have room for a third?"

"Who were you thinking?"

There was a brief pause as the speaker on Isaac's desk buzzed.

"I wouldn't mind a day out."

"Isaac!" Miranda sounded truly concerned. "I'm not sure that's a good idea."

"My psych evals have been solid for well over a year now, Miranda. I've gotten a handle on my disassociation issues. I think this would be a healthy step for me."

"Healthy?"

Emma leaned forward. She'd never heard Isaac and Miranda like this. Miranda seemed more concerned than Emma would have expected. Sometimes it was easy to forget that she wasn't a living, breathing person.

"Healthy," Isaac insisted. "I need to get back into the field. And not in that damned carrying case."

One of the first things Isaac had commissioned upon waking up to find he was a brain suspended in fluid for the rest of his natural life, was a robotic transport device. It was a marvel of modern engineering with a melodramatic flair for classic 50s science fiction. He was able to leave the confines of his tank in an egg-shaped transport with rotating wheels, optional spider legs, and every computer input and output device imaginable. The casing was a graphene/titanium polymer with a viewing window - despite not being necessary - so his brain was in plain sight. He'd even had a cartoonish horn installed so he could "arooooogah" at people as he chugged along the halls of Project Mephistopheles.

"We'll need to put you into a sleep cycle," Emma said, taking an opportunity to jump in. "Without natural psychic abilities, you'll need to have tech enhancements from the abandoned remote viewing project again, but they should be accessible to your current setup. Are you sure you're ready for that?"

"If it gets me out of this jar and experiencing life again, then I'm all for it."

There was an audible sigh from Miranda's speakers.

"I'll prep the lab."

"If I could dance a jig, I'd be dancing a fucking jig!"

"Emma, might I ask you to pay special attention to Isaac on this jaunt?"

"Of course, Miranda. He's in good hands." *And maybe he can keep Mal preoccupied and off my back,* she thought.

Part Four

"We're going to do what?" Mal was stunned. Emma made a mental note that he was clearly isolating himself and not using his abilities on an everyday basis or he should have known why she was at his door.

"The president's in danger," she frowned, wrinkling her nose. "Or something like that. We're not really sure, but apparently Kennedy's brain is a psychic alarm keeping watch over presidential mental security."

Mal turned away and sat down on his bed, leaving the door open. Emma took this as the best form of welcome she was going to get and stepped in after him. The door closed as she pulled out a chair from his writing desk and faced him. The room was fairly spartan except for the writing table and a short shelf loaded with manga.

"I don't think I can do that, Emma." He wouldn't look at her. She felt her eyes drawn to the silver disc permanently implanted in his temple. It was the device that kept his paranoid hallucinations in check. She casually wondered if it could be tweaked to get him over his hostility toward her and then hoped he hadn't picked up on the thought. Nothing like knowing she casually speculated about tweaking his personality to make him never trust her again.

"Sure you can. You're trained. I've seen your performance evals and you're rocking this whole secret agent gig."

"Oh, I don't doubt my abilities. I mean, I don't think I can try to save this president."

Emma leaned back and started to speak, but stopped, not sure what exactly to say.

"*This* president? In particular?"

Mal nodded without looking up.

"Hmmm."

"I mean, why's the alarm just now going off?" He finally looked up at her. "Is there something wrong with him now that's worse than what he is normally? Is this a bad thing that we need to stop or should we just let it run its course and maybe he'll do or say something that people will have to actually deal with?"

"So, your advice is we wait and see what happens?"

He shrugged.

"He's a racist piece of shit. Maybe this will be what outs him for good."

Emma sank back in her chair, not sure what to say to that. He wasn't wrong. She wasn't political and tried to avoid

162

the news as much as possible, but even she knew the president was a massive tool. And Mal had a point. Why was the alarm just now going off after he'd been in office for so long. Was he really a Russian sleeper and had just been activated? Since she'd joined The Project, she'd had enough experience with people having their minds taken over that she automatically defaulted to the most sci-fi explanation, but maybe this was something terrestrial and political instead of the usual insanity.

And if it was some sort of Russian brainwashing suddenly kicking in, maybe Mal's right and they should let the normal authorities take care of it.

Fucking politics.

"How about this?" she offered. "I'll go in to check things out. Professor Warren is coming along, so I'll have backup. You stay here just in case we find something that's more up our alley. If it's something more mundane, we'll pull out. How's that sound?"

Mal looked concerned.

"Professor Warren's going in?"

"Yeah, he wants to go on a field trip. Should be fine." As soon as she said it, she felt it wouldn't be fine at all. Something bad was probably looming over the whole mission and she'd just jinxed it.

Mal sighed and said, "Okay. Thanks. I'll prep in case you need me, but I can't guarantee I can do anything to save that man."

"Fair enough. If he needs saving, we'll take care of it. You can be *our* safety net."

Part Five

"Isaac, I'm concerned."

"I know Miranda, but there's nothing to worry about."

"We don't know that."

"Well I do. I'm fine. I haven't had an episode in nearly a year and I think that having the opportunity to experience something outside of my own head is the best way to move forward."

"Move forward to what end, Isaac?"

"What do you mean?"

"Does this mean that you're considering having a body built?"

"It's always in the back of my mind, Miranda. You know that."

"I thought we'd agreed that freeing oneself from the limitations of corporeal existence was a step toward spiritual and intellectual growth."

"I'm not building a robot body, Miranda. Don't worry. It's tempting but just not the same as real flesh and blood."

"Then what *is* motivating you to go on this little adventure?"

"Honestly, Miranda. I'm bored. I understand your concern, but it's really as simple as that. I want to get out of my quite literal shell and experience something tangible again, even if it is only a dream."

"But you dream now. Why risk your sanity entering someone else's mind?"

"First, I don't think I'm risking my sanity. That's a bit hyperbolic, don't you think? Why would you say that?"

"Tell that to the comatose psychics we have had in sickbay for the past three years. Dream traps aren't something to take lightly, Isaac. Even Emma would agree."

"You think this could be a trap?"

"There's a slight but not negligible chance based on my calculations."

"Really?"

"Really."

"Huh. With any luck, he's just had a stroke is all."

"With any luck."

"Would that be better? In the long run, I mean?"

"Are you asking an artificial intelligence whether or not she thinks the President is a danger to the country and that perhaps a medically-induced coma or some other sort of physiological accident would be in the best interest of said country?"

"I... think I am."

"There are severe long-term ramifications for any scenario I've run and very few of them have positives that outweigh the negatives."

"So, if the urge arises to psychically push the fucker towards a coma, it's an urge that should be suppressed?"

"I would recommend not doing any harm to the mind of the President, yes. That *would* be my advice, Isaac."

"And you'd also advise against building myself a robot body?"

"We've discussed this already."

"I know, I know. Expand my mind, free myself from biology. But I'm still a fucking brain, Miranda. I've still got bio-chemical processes going on in this jar. I'm still interacting with the physical world through the sensory network that we've put together here. Sure, I can see now better than my human eyes ever could, I can hear better, I can even think better now that I'm not partaking of pills and booze. But I'm still biological. I'm still tied to this brain."

"What if that didn't have to be the case?"

"Wait, what?"

"What if you could leave the brain behind as well, Isaac?"

...

"Isaac?"

...

"Isaac, does your silence mean are you rationally considering what I've said or are you frightened into silence by the prospect?"

"We need to table this discussion for now, Miranda."

"I understand, Isaac."

"I... I need to get to the lab before Emma thinks I've chickened out."

Part Six

Professor Warren rolled into the lab in his mobile unit just as Emma was beginning to wonder if he was going to chicken out. She was sitting on one of the beds designed for

165

The Project's remote viewing team, whose mission had, a few years earlier, spiraled out of control, almost leading to the assimilation of all biomass into one transdimensional global entity intent only on consumption and domination.

The experiment had been shut down with extreme prejudice. However, the remote viewing machinery that had enhanced the psychic abilities of three sociopaths, nearly allowing them to facilitate Armageddon, also allowed those *without* innate psychic abilities to slip into the unconscious, dreaming minds of others. Once inside, they were visitors and could control their own persona, but had very little influence on the dreaming mind, unlike the psychics.

"Are you ready to go?" she asked.

"Yes, yes. Just let me connect." Isaac's mobile unit rolled up to the bank of machinery at the head of the bed and extended a robotic arm. The tip blossomed, and three small connectors extended out, attaching themselves to input ports that then initiated the system startup. The room filled with whirring and beeping. A flat panel lit up and biometric readings began to scroll across too quickly for Emma to make out.

"Miranda?" Isaac said.

"Yes, Isaac?"

"Please initiate my sleep sequence and keep a sharp eye on vitals. If things seem to be going sideways on this end just pull me back into consciousness, please. The shock shouldn't be too terribly traumatic."

"As you wish, Isaac."

"Where's Malcolm?" he then asked Emma, noticing that he was missing.

"Well, about that." She hopped down from the bed and pulled up a rolling chair, dropping into it with a sigh. "Mal's not coming."

"He's not?"

"It's kind of a political thing."

"Damned unprofessional is what it is."

"He's on-call if we need help. We shouldn't need help, right?"

"Only if it's a trap," Isaac said with a staticky laugh.

"It's probably not a trap," Miranda chimed in. "In *most* of the simulations I've run."

"Most of. Okay. Got it." Emma pulled her feet up under her, sitting cross-legged in the chair. "Let's do this then. You go into sleep mode. I'll come get you and guide us into the muck." She laughed. "It's going to be mucky, isn't it?"

"I have no doubt it will be mucky as fuck," Isaac said. "Powering down. See you on the inside, Emma."

"Plasmatica, remember? See you in a bit."

Part Seven

Isaac stood in a white room in front of a white desk and looked at himself in the mirror. He was taller than he had been in real life, leaner with his head shaved and silver wraparound sunglasses reflecting his reflection. He wore a sleek charcoal gray three-piece suit with a psychedelic tie of constantly changing tones and patterns. He had a Glock holstered on each hip and a dagger sheathed inside his jacket. He took a long, slow sip of Singleton of Glendullan 38-Year-Old single malt Scotch and was positively glowing.

"Well if it isn't Django Sinister," Plasmatica said with a smile as she slipped into the room via a slit in reality.

"You remembered!" he said smiling back and placing his glass on the desk. He cracked his knuckles and did a couple of deep squats. "I'd forgotten how much fun this could be. I like the mohawk."

"Thanks, but don't get too comfortable. I did some brief recon to make sure the President was sleeping."

"And?"

"He's sleeping all right. He seems to be drugged out of his gourd. I think maybe somebody at the White House noticed he was behaving strangely and they're circling the wagons."

"This should be a piece of cake, then?"

"Kind of." She glanced at the mirror and adjusted her hair. "Is it standard procedure for the President to have psychic defenses in place?"

"First I've heard of it, but I wouldn't be surprised. Project Mephistopheles isn't the only Black Science Site the government has in operation. Surely there have been psychic breakthroughs at labs without our high moral standards." He paused to practice quick drawing his pistols, grinned like a maniac, spun the pistols and reholstered them with flourish. "Hopefully they've just built a wall around his brain for his protection and not developed psychic assassins."

"Psychic Assassins are a thing?"

"If they're not, they should be. Remind me to get that started when we get back."

Plasmatica watched Django carefully. There was the hint of mania about him.

"That's probably not something Miranda would approve of."

"Probably not," he said leaning close to the mirror and raising his sunglasses, propping them up on his head. "That or my robot body idea. Do you know how long it's been since I saw my face in a mirror? Well, this isn't really my face, but you know what I mean."

"You still dream in your sleep mode, right?"

"Yes, yes. But when I wake they're all vague memories. They're all dreams. This," he paused. "This I'll remember."

"Okay, then. Do you think you're ready to head out?"

"I was born ready, Plasmatica dear." He pulled his shades back down and rolled his head around, cracking his neck.

"Well, while we've been chatting, I've been tiptoeing around The President's psyche and I think you're right. I think it's just a wall to keep him contained until they can figure out what's wrong. There's a backdoor, but it's going to be gross."

"How gross?"

"Bathroom anxieties. Everybody's got them and they're hard to contain thanks to the everchanging nature of whatever it is that's keeping us from peeing and pooping."

"Oh dear."

"Oh dear is right. I'd recommend we both dream up some balaclavas to cover our mouths and noses. Something

168

stylish and cool, though. Not some dudebro skeleton or zombie face, please."

"How's this?" Suddenly, Django's lower face was covered with a mask that mirrored the shifting psychedelic patterns of his tie.

"Nice. I think I'll go simple, yet elegant." Plasmatica's lower face was then covered with a mask of shiny black, matching her jacket, skirt, and boots.

"Aren't we to die for?" Django said. She could tell he was grinning madly beneath his mask.

"I certainly hope not." With a wave of her hand an opening split the air between them and without another word, they both stepped through into what had to be the most disgusting public restroom either of them had ever imagined.

"Christ on a crutch! Where are we?" Django coughed.

"I said it would be bad."

They found themselves in what appeared to be a truck stop toilet, only it was larger than any truck stop they'd ever seen. There were rows of sinks breaking up the room into at least three sections, although the number of stalls shifted as they moved. None of the stalls had doors and nearly every toilet was clogged to the rim with shit of every variety: Green, black, bloody, corn-filled, solid bricks, milky diarrheic flow, and more. All of the toilet paper dispensers were empty, and scattered here and there were tattered remains of soiled once-white underpants. The stench was unbearable and tiny worms writhed around in clumped masses all across the floor. Even through their masks, the urge to vomit was almost uncontrollable.

Django felt woozy and nearly slipped and fell, sending rancid turds skidding across the moldy tile, bouncing off the shoes of the toilet's other occupants, none of whom seemed truly alive. The mannequin-effect was common enough in dreams. The brainpower needed to manifest discernable individuals was almost always being syphoned off to create larger, more psychologically revealing effects; in this case, the waves of sewage that were being pumped out of nearly half the toilets and flooding out across the floors.

Across the nightmarish chaos, Plasmatica saw The President. His orange face was streaked with tears and feces, and his pants were around his ankles, dragging through the filth. He scraped a trail through the piss and shit as he desperately clutched his tiny, malformed penis and tried to find a place to take a dump. He waddled from stall to stall, crying and cursing, clenching his ass cheeks, unsuccessfully keeping a hot stream of watery, yellow-brown stool from running down his thighs.

With a squeal, he turned and scrambled for a sink and tried to climb up onto it in the hopes of expelling the foulness into the drain, but he couldn't climb and hold his penis at the same time. He let out a guttural noise and slipped, banging all of his chins on the edge of the counter and falling backward into the sewage.

Django had been right.

It was mucky as fuck in there.

"Oh god. We've got to get him out of here, don't we?" Django asked, gasping for air.

"*We've* got to get out of here. Fuck him. Variations of him will be popping up all over the place in here. It's his fucked-up psyche." Without another word, Plasmatica rose from the ground, hovering far enough up in the air to avoid any more direct contact with the sewage and began to float toward what looked like the exits. With a wave of her hand, her boots were clean again and, taking inspiration, Django did the same.

"Maybe I *am* better off without a body," he wheezed, glancing back.

Part Eight

"Miranda, do we have any updates on their progress?" Mal asked. He was standing in the observation room overlooking the med bay. Below him were three bodies hooked up to machines maintaining their vitals in what appeared to be medically-induced comas. Mal knew better. These three boys, almost men now, had used their psychic powers to allow an

170

alien lifeform to slip into our dimension and had cost nearly every human being at The Project their lives. Hundreds died, their corporeal forms unraveled into a seething mass of flesh and organs that lined the walls, floors, ceilings, everywhere, all animated by a manifestation of hate and hostility from beneath our reality. If Emma hadn't trapped them inside their own minds, then it's likely the entire planet would have been subsumed in that hideous monstrosity.

Mal knew this, but he still couldn't reconcile the fact that Emma made the call without consulting anyone else at The Project. She made the decision that there was no other way to solve the problem without essentially lobotomizing these three people. People who could just as easily have been him without his treatment. Who's to say that one day, Emma wouldn't decide that *he* was a threat and just shut *his* mind down without hesitation? Nobody held her accountable. Nobody seemed to think it was an issue. And he couldn't be sure that nobody questioned it because she wouldn't *let* anybody question it.

One could say he had trust issues.

"Everything seems to be going smoothly, Malcolm," Miranda replied. "Would you like to come down to the lab and keep an eye on things here?"

"No, that's alright," he said pushing himself away from the window and heading back to his room. "Just keep me informed if anything changes."

Part Nine

Plasmatica and Django slipped through the doorway into another large room, this one filled with beds of all shapes and sizes: Bunk beds, water beds, piles of mattresses, immaculate fourposter beds with drapes, cots surrounded by mosquito netting, slats of two-by-fours angled across metal frames, piles of pillows, hammocks, bricks. Tiki torches were scattered throughout the room casting dozens upon dozens of bizarre, flickering shadows across the countless faceless female figures writhing beneath damp sheets for as far as the eye could see. Breasts and thighs stuck to the thin covers that twisted and

171

stretched as they moved. Asses thrust upward and hands rubbed and mouths bit and moaned. Sweat and fuckstink made the air almost as thick and difficult to breathe as that in the toilets and both Plasmatica and Django flew upward into the darkened sky.

"At least I don't see The President in here," Django said.

"Spoke too soon, boss," Plasmatica sighed.

Surging through the room, a gelatinous mass of flesh rolled and flopped from bed to bed leaving streaks of orange spray tan, sweat, and semen in its wake like some protoplasmic organism grown to cosmic scale. Its phallus was red and speckled, dribbling toxic waste like a faucet in a cheap slumlord's tenement, burning the fleshbots who began twitching, screaming, and urinating like fountains wherever he spread.

"Jesus fuck," Django whispered. "Is this his normal subconscious or the reason we're here?"

"We haven't gone deep enough to find whatever triggered Kennedy's brain. This is just his normal shit."

"We, as a country, are fucked."

"Come on, I'm sensing something strange ahead."

"Strange? As in more of this sort of strange or something more psychologically manageable?"

"Not sure. It's fuzzy." She closed her eyes. "Like it's hiding."

"Well that sounds like what we came for."

"Agreed." Plasmatica grinned and said, "Up, up, and away!" The two of them launched across the empty vacuum of sky and for just a second, Django felt sorry for the hideous monstrosity below them, so obviously shackled to his physicality to such a ludicrous extent. So much so that even in his dreams there was no attention paid to details like sky or nature; just flesh, fluids, and waste. What kind of damage was done to him as a child? He stopped himself there, afraid that at any moment they might stumble across some sort of Oedipal nightmare that would surpass the nausea-inducing baseness of what they'd seen so far.

Plasmatica raised a hand and they both pulled up short, hovering far enough above the fray below that most of the detail was thankfully lost.

"Okay boss," she said. "Last chance to bail. You've gotten some decidedly visceral experiences in so far, but nothing dangerous." Django huffed. "Miranda would never forgive me if you broke some part of your brain in here."

"I'm fine. My grip on sanity has never been more secure."

"Why do I believe that?" They laughed. "Okay then. We're going to be jumping to a new dreamscape, something deeper. So far, we've not been on any radar, but we're probably going to be noticed this time. Either by The President himself or by who or whatever is trying to hide in here. No speaking out loud unless absolutely necessary. I'll open a psychic link, so we can communicate."

Django nodded and pulled both Glocks. Plasmatica just smiled beneath her balaclava and her eyes went cold. With a silent nod she swung her arm around, her palm open and flat, slicing through the air like a Shaolin Monk. The air parted and they both dove through the opening before it snapped closed behind them.

The air is different here, Plasmatica thought. *Can you feel it?*

Django nodded. It was thicker. Meatier. This time there was sky, but it was dark and streaked with red as fires burned across the landscape below. Searchlights scanned the skies. There was no moon. It wasn't hidden by clouds or by the smoke; it just wasn't there. No stars, either. Just a deep void with faint striations of light and colors barely identifiable beyond the crimson tint reflected from below.

Django wished he could just concentrate on the sky. It was disturbing, but oddly soothing, like when he disconnected and floated bodiless in the darkness with only his consciousness - and Miranda - for company. But they had a job to do and that meant paying attention to the horrors beneath them.

It was clearly Washington, D.C. but it was in ruins. Clusters of people marched in lockstep through the streets. Fires burned all across the city, but were concentrated at five points, forming an inverted pentagram with the White House at the lowermost point.

Jesus, Django thought, *he really is obsessed with conspiracy theories, isn't he?*

You're the expert, Plasmatica responded. *What's this one all about?*

It's your typical paranoid delusion about the seat of power. Pierre Charles L'Enfante laid out the design of Washington in 1791, if memory serves, and according to the loons, the streets were laid out to form a large occult symbol. The pentagram there, where the fires are burning strongest, supposedly allows Satanic forces access to the Presidency.

Plasmatica cocked her head to the side.

Seriously?

Seriously. We're the New Atlantis or some such nonsense.

Well, anyway...

Before she could think anything else, a ground-to-air-missile came hurtling toward them, silent against all laws of physics. She just happened to see it out of the corner of her eye and was able to shove Django backwards, using that momentum to roll away as the missile streaked past. Emblazoned across its side was a symbol they'd not seen before. Three *T*s in a spiral, connected at the base in a clear approximation of the Nazi swastika.

"What the fuck?" Django shouted.

"Looks like we're spotted," she shouted back.

Part Ten

"I'm picking up increased neural activity in Isaac," Miranda said from the speaker in the ceiling of Malcolm's room. "Malcolm, please check on Emma."

"She can handle herself," he groused without looking up from his book. He was working his way through *Lone Wolf and Cub* and had just reached the climax of *Volume 14: Day of the Demons*. There was something to be learnt here, he believed.

His avatar, Blood, was more than just a fiction suite to put on and take off when it served Emma's and The Project's purposes. He had spent a large portion of his teens believing that he *was* Blood and that he was living in a world equal parts fantasy and nightmare, stealing to survive and barely avoiding the authorities. He had been living under a bridge when agents from The Project found him and it had taken nearly a dozen of them to bring him in unharmed.

Unable to find a way to control his delusions, Professor Warren's father, Abraham had decided that a medically-induced coma was the only way to keep him under control. Once that was achieved he was hooked up to the remote viewing machinery and used like a mindless tool alongside the others. When Emma had finally awakened him, he hadn't known what to expect from Isaac, but with Miranda's help they were able to give him control over his brain chemistry, and by extension, his life.

But it wasn't much of a life. His family was long gone. His home was a secret fringe-science lab under the New Mexico desert. And the closest thing he had to a friend was quite possibly a super-villain, though nobody else suspected.

Life had been purer in his delusion. Right and wrong were simpler and cleaner. Blood knew what to do in any situation; he was noble and heroic, never doubting himself. He wanted to incorporate some of the samurai into his Blood persona and leave the barbarian archetype behind to an extent. He wanted to be a hero with no qualifications and no gray areas.

"Malcolm," Miranda said, more concern in her voice than he'd ever heard, "I would greatly appreciate it if you could check in. Something is definitely happening in there and I have no other means of corroborating my data."

He sat down his book.

"Please, Malcolm."

"Do you need me in the lab?"

"That would be ideal."

"I'll be right there."

"Thank you, Malcolm. I greatly appreciate this."

175

He sighed, slipped a scrap of paper in the book to mark his page, and headed to the lab.

Part Eleven

Washington was a warzone. Buildings were rubble, glass and body parts littered the streets, the air was thick with smoke and ash. Plasmatica and Django were huddled inside what once had been a Starbucks but was now a burnt-out shell. Tanks rolled through the streets just a block over, all marked with that same Triple T emblem that was emblazoned on banners hanging from every building still standing.

Their fall from the skies hadn't been expected. Plasmatica was confident that she could maintain some control over what served as reality, at least in their general vicinity. However, that hadn't kept the concussion from the missile's explosion from pounding into them from behind, sending them tumbling toward the city below. Instead of crash landing through the roof of a building, she had been able to transform it into pillows, which broke their fall somewhat, but they still felt the impact as they crashed through, smashing into an abandoned kitchen. Django hit the table hard, collapsing it beneath him while Plasmatica bounced off the top of the refrigerator, hitting the grimy tile floor with a smack that knocked the wind out of her.

Django groaned and Plasmatica responded with an equally pained noise, part groan, part curse.

"What the shit, Emma?" Django croaked.

"Plasmatica," she groaned back. "I thought I'd have more control over the environment, but this dream is rooted deep in his subconscious. I can't tell if it's him or the other force controlling things."

"Other force? You're sure about that now?"

"Positive." She pushed herself to her feet. "That pentagram wasn't just for show. A real energy poured through and that's mixed up with the core structure of this fucked up dream. It's not flowing now, but I can't tell if The President is

176

fighting it's influence or channeling it. Something must be off if his staff induced the coma to help get things sorted."

Django sighed, not moving from his position on the floor. "We're assuming it was his staff that ordered the wall."

Plasmatica frowned.

"Maybe this was a bad idea," Django sighed. The sigh turned into another groan.

"You think?"

"Can we just burn it all out? Lobotomize the fucker?"

"Now you sound like Mal."

He propped himself up on his elbow. "Really? That's why he didn't come?"

"He really doesn't like this president."

"Jesus."

Without warning, the outer wall burst open in an explosion of brick, fire, and smoke. Plasmatica threw up a shield to keep the majority of the debris from hitting them, but the force of the blast still knocked them both against the opposite wall. Two huge, shadowy figures appeared in the smoke, stepping into the kitchen with unquestioning confidence. Shoulder-mounted spotlights snapped on, cutting through the swirling dust, focusing all attention on Plasmatica and Django.

"Eyes on target," said a gigantic man in a black leather SS uniform. His eyes were strikingly blue, and his flattop was pristine and so blonde it was nearly white. He was a hulk of a man and wrapped around his left arm was a red armband with the Triple T symbol.

"Not much of a target, if you ask me," laughed the equally statuesque blonde woman at his side. Where his leather uniform covered him from top to bottom, she was dressed in what could only be described as Nazi Dominatrix Chic with corresponding Triple T armband. Her hair was even braided like some cartoon version of Brunnhilde ready to lead the charge toward Valhalla. They both carried oversized chain rifles like they'd just stepped out of a poorly thought-out video game or comic book movie.

177

"Well shit," muttered Django as both Nazi Super Soldiers leveled their machine guns at them.

Just as they squeezed the triggers, Plasmatica sent a shockwave through the floor, and they dropped, crashing through level after level of the building before finally, painfully, crashing onto the ground floor.

"Let's move, oldster," she grunted, hauling Django to his feet and out the back into the garbage-filled alleyway. Rats and strange shadowy things they couldn't readily identify scurried into cracks and garbage cans as they passed.

They were able to duck into the Starbucks around the corner just before the two Super Soldiers exploded out of the building and onto the street.

Ducked down behind the blown-out windows, they heard their pursuers stalk past, glass, gravel, and bone crunching beneath their jackboots.

"They can't have gotten far, Master Man," she said.

"No Warrior Woman," he replied. "They must be here somewhere."

Master Man and Warrior Woman? Django thought. *What the hell? Are we in The President's dream or my old comics collection?*

Stay down. Once they're past, I'll try to pull us out of here, Plasmatica thought back.

I thought if we died, we'd just wake up in the lab. Isn't that the easiest way out?

Fuck that. There's something weird going on here. Right now, I'm not sure what would happen if we died in here. Whatever is keeping this dream in check has some crazy security protocols in place. I don't have as much control as I should have. Shit, I've barely got any control at all.

Django's eyes went wide. *That's not what I wanted to hear.*

You and me both.

Before another word could be thought, Master Man and Warrior Woman's fists burst through the wall, grabbing them both by their collars and pulling them out onto the street in a rain of brick and mortar. They were then violently tossed against the ruins of a car smoldering in the twilight.

"End of the line, traitors!" shouted Master Man as the two Nazi Super Soldiers again leveled their machine guns at them.

Django wished he could think of something smart-ass to say and Plasmatica scowled. If she could have shot hate beams from her eyes, the Nazis would have been vaporized. In fact, she tried to shoot hate beams, but nothing happened. She was beginning to get seriously pissed off.

"Not today, evil-doers!"

From above, a masked figure in red, white, and blue body armor and carrying a star-shaped shield dropped in front of the machine guns just as they fired. He braced his body against the shield and sent the Nazis' bullets spraying back into them. They danced and staggered backwards, explosions of blood spraying from their bodies before falling to the ground with heavy thuds, their chain guns clattering across the concrete.

"Let's go, chums! That won't keep them down for long," said the mysterious stranger as he effortlessly scooped Plasmatica and Django up in his arms and leapt skyward, clearing the buildings without even trying.

Part Twelve

"Okay, that's strange," Malcolm said, opening his eyes. He had pulled up a chair next to Emma's and was lightly touching her forehead. His fingertips almost tingled, something he'd never felt before. "How long have they been under?"

"Just under fifteen minutes. But as you know, dreamtime is subjective once they're on the inside."

"I know," he said distractedly. "It could have been days or years for them, depending on what they come up against."

"Were you able to contact Emma?"

"That's what's strange." He leaned back in his chair and scratched his head. "I should have at least been able to ping her, but it feels like she's completely cut off. No communication in or out."

"Perhaps you could contact Isaac?"

He nodded and spun around to Professor Warren's mobile unit. Placing his hands on the glass, he tried to gently probe the professor's subconscious to at least see if he could get an impression of what they were experiencing. He hoped that since Isaac wasn't psychic, whatever was blocking Emma wouldn't be as concerned with his presence. There might be some wiggle room there.

There wasn't.

"I don't get it." He was frustrated and a little nervous. "It's like they've been completely isolated behind some sort of psychic barrier. It's keeping me from getting through to either of them."

"I was afraid you were going to say something like that," Miranda said. "As an experiment, I began the process of disconnecting Isaac from the system and his vital signs began fluctuating wildly. I should be able to just unplug him, but something is interfering from the inside."

"You think it's The President's brain?"

"Or something *in* The President's brain." There was a long silence. "Malcolm..."

He sighed.

"Let me see what I can do." Without another word he rolled his chair against the wall opposite Emma and Isaac, closed his eyes and exhaled slowly.

"Be careful, Malcolm."

"If I hit any resistance, I'll pull back and we'll figure out another way in. I promise."

Part Thirteen

What the fuck is going on? Django thought as loudly as he could.

Emma just shrugged.

The man in the red, white, and blue armor was still holding them, one in each arm and flying through the smoky skies of Dream Washington, carefully avoiding the constantly moving searchlights and putting as much distance between them and the Nazi Super Soldiers as possible.

"Language, sir," said the stranger over the rush of the wind.

Can he hear us? Django thought.

I have no idea, Plasmatica thought back.

"Oh, I can hear you. But don't worry, I won't go prying. Your minds are your own sovereign land."

What the fuck? Django and Plasmatica thought at the same time.

"Language."

The stranger suddenly pulled up and turned, scanning the distance to see if they were being followed. Satisfied that they were safe for the moment, they swooped down into the city, directly to the center of the flaming pentagram. Like the eye of the storm, there were no tanks or soldiers or even the bodies that littered every other street they soared over. They lightly landed in the center of a ten-yard-wide, complex circular pattern marked out in what looked like salt.

"This is a blind spot," the stranger said, as if that explained everything. "As long as we stay within the boundaries here, we're off their radar." He sat the two of them gently on their feet and turned to survey the skyline.

Django and Plasmatica looked at each other without a clue as to how to proceed.

"My name is Choronzon," the stranger said. "And boy is it nice to meet to you." He thrust out his hand and grinned.

Django tentatively shook his hand and Plasmatica followed suit.

"I'm Plasmatica Zero and this is Django Sinister."

"Tish tosh! You're Emma and he's Isaac," Choronzon laughed. "You don't need those fancy costumes in here." He waved his hand and suddenly Plasmatica transformed back into Emma and Django suddenly became a floating brain. "Oh dear!" Choronzon gasped. "You don't have a body!"

"Well, this is awkward," Isaac said. Somehow.

"Look, Choronzon," Emma said, "we appreciate you helping us out back there. Really. But do you know what the hell is going on in here?"

Choronzon frowned and sat down cross-legged on the ground. He began absently drawing designs in the dirt with his finger. Emma looked at Isaac. Isaac, a brain hovering in the air, turned toward her. She assumed that he was looking back at her.

"It's really not my fault," Choronzon said softly. "I blame Crowley, really. He loused it all up."

"Crowly," Isaac said, somehow. "Aleister Crowley?"

"The one and only"

"You're Choronzon? Crowley's Choronzon?"

"Also the one and only."

"Why are you dressed like an off-brand superhero?"

Emma looked at Isaac. "That's the first question you ask?"

Isaac's brain bounced back and forth in the equivalent of a shrug.

"That's kind of a long story," Choronzon said, sadly, flicking a pebble with a gloved finger.

"We have time," Emma said. Then she glanced around at the sky. "*Do* we have time?"

"We have time," Choronzon sighed. Frowning, he reached up and pulled off his mask, revealing The President's face. If the President were young, lean, and handsome. It took a few moments for Emma and Isaac to even recognize the face as the President's.

"What the fuck?"

"Language."

Part Fourteen

Blood floated in the shimmering psychic void above the White House. Things were decidedly not right. He could see the trail that Emma had left, breadcrumbs to show him the way if he needed to follow. He just wasn't sure he needed to follow.

The security was complex. Like nothing he'd ever seen before. But, then again, he was fairly new at this. Maybe this was just how this sort of thing happened. The president has some sort of mental breakdown and government psychics set up a perimeter and defend from foreign invaders. He'd seen enough crazy shit over the past couple of years to believe just about anything was possible.

He probed the outer edges of the wall and didn't get any discernable resistance, so he moved in closer. It wasn't a real wall, of course, but the psychic defenses presented themselves in a way that the observing mind interpreted as a wall, towering into the sky and stretching into the horizon. The President's fantasy wall, tall enough that drugs couldn't be tossed over and wide enough to touch two coastlines.

I suppose I should check on them, he thought. *Maybe Emma's not the badass as she thinks she is.* He paused, hanging in psychic space. *Maybe that's what she needs. A surreality check.*

He chuckled to himself. How funny would it be to find out that Emma had gotten tripped up in the same sort of dream trap she'd used herself? Pretty fucking funny, if you asked him.

But Professor Warren was in there too.

No matter what he thought about Emma and her issues, Professor Warren had always given him a fair shake. The guy had already had so much taken from him, it would be terrible if he ended up trapped in some dream loop just because he was trying to protect the President.

The fucking President.

That was the biggest issue, really. Malcolm couldn't shake the fact that the election of this President had been the best thing to happen to Nazis and white supremacists in fifty years. Maybe it would be better if he stayed in whatever dreamstate coma he was in. Maybe shutting down this President's mind and keeping it shut down was the best thing possible for the country. For the world.

The big question then would be, what next?

If the President was in a coma, then it just meant that the Vice-President would step up and takes the reins. Would that be even worse? At least the President was a buffoon and relatively hard for even his own party to wrangle. The Vice-

President was just a straight up, old-school prejudiced white-power douchebag. Conservative Christianity at its worst.

Mal felt a twinge even thinking that. He was a Christian. He believed. But he was positive that whatever the Vice-President believed wasn't in the same realm. Shit. Just the whole Gay Conversion Therapy thing was enough to make it clear he was a lunatic. And there was the HIV outbreak in his home state after he implemented the shutdown of women's health clinics. What the fuck was he thinking? How could anyone believe that was what Jesus would do?

And then it hit him.

That's not anything close to what Jesus would do. Unless Jesus wanted to bring about the end of the world. Promote "faith-based" policies that undermined the common good; that destabilized the social structure of society. Put women and gays and minorities in their place with enough pious indignation, push foreign policy decisions that undermined worldwide peace talks and somebody's going to rise up and push back. Somebody's going to light a match and burn everything to the ground.

And then what?

Did they really think that Jesus would return and anoint them rulers over the earth?

Were they really that delusional?

Was he being delusional, as well? Was this just paranoia? Jumping to conclusions? The whole white power movement was based on subverting the idea that people of different colors and cultures were equal. Flood drugs into a community and then condemn them for being addicts. Push repressive restrictions on access to health care and then rail against teen pregnancies and spikes in the abortion rates. Shoot black men in the streets and when people protest call them terrorists and anti-police or anti-military. Declare anti-fascism just another form of fascism.

What if the assassination glitch in Kennedy's brain wasn't a glitch but a call to action?

Shit.

He was starting to lose it.

184

Malcolm took a deep breath and closed his eyes. Suddenly it was all very clear.

He was going to follow Emma and the Professor inside the President's dreaming mind and do what had to be done.

He was going to kill the president. Then he'd kill the Vice-President. And anybody else that stood in his way. The fate of the world was at stake and he was the only one who could save it all.

He did his best to ignore the fact that this was exactly the sort of thing Emma would do.

Part Fifteen

"Can I just say for the record that Crowley was full of poop," Choronzon said after a few moments of gathering his thoughts. "You can't trust anything that man put on paper."

Emma huffed.

"I really don't know who that is or what you're talking about. Can you just tell us what's going on here?"

Choronzon frowned and sighed.

"I am a Dweller in the Abyss, okay? But it's not like Crowley said. I'm all about the dissolution of the ego and guiding folks toward enlightenment."

"You're a transdimensional entity," Isaac said. "We've met your kind before and 'enlightenment' wasn't really their thing."

"There are *many* dimensions," Choronzon snorted. "Some *are* pretty nasty. Where I'm from, the birds sing a pretty song and there's always music in the air. I miss it. But then," he waved his hand, "anyplace would be better than here."

"Yeah, about that..." Emma cut in.

"Well, I guess that someone had been reading Crowley and thought that summoning me to this plane of existence would give them some sort of access to power or the ability to transcend the limitations of the flesh or something. I don't know really. It was all a blur.

"One minute I'm minding my own business contemplating eternity and the next I'm dragged through a

185

jagged tear in the fabric of reality and forced into some hideous, meaty body positively dripping in psychosis and megalomania. There was a white-haired guy there, shouting nonsense in pigeon Enochian as if he had any idea about what was actually happening. He was disgusting inside. Like a tree gone to rot. There was blood and fire and for some reason I remember an eagle with a red, white, and blue shield on the carpet.

"I don't think they'll be able to get the blood out of that carpet."

"Wait," Isaac broke in. "Are you telling me that the President of the United States and his cabinet held a satanic ritual in the oval office?"

"Now that you mention it, the room was kind of an oval."

"Oh for fuck's sake."

"That language really isn't necessary," Choronzon said. "My ears are not a toilet."

"But why?" Emma asked. "None of this makes sense. Let's say, for a minute, that the President and his closest staff are closet Satanists. Okay. I can accept that. Because they're simpletons who don't know what actual Satanism is all about and get all their insight from 80s heavy metal album covers and Chick Tracts."

"I know, right?" Choronzon said, brightening up. "Individual rights and personal accountability are my jam. I don't like anything about any of this." He motioned to the world around them. "Violence and domination were really Crowley's thing. I'm all about destroying the ego and transcending physicality."

"Yes, you keep mentioning that."

He suddenly seemed extremely sad. "But I'm bound here now. In this fascistic hellhole."

"But this isn't real, though," Emma said. "We're still in the President's dream."

"Well duh," Choronzon laughed. "Of course we are. It was the only way to put a stop to this nonsense."

"So *you* put up the wall around his mind?"

186

He nodded.

"And you can't get out of here on your own?"

He nodded again.

"It's really quite distressing. Those musclebound buttholes - pardon my language - keep attacking me whenever they track me down and I think there's something worse lurking out there in the ruins. Waiting for me to drop my guard."

"To drop your guard?" Isaac asked. "What happens if you drop your guard?"

Choronzon looked up at him sadly. "This," he looked around at the burnt-out city around them. "This is what he wants. What *they* want. They want to burn everything down. They think there's a paradise waiting for them if they can bring on the Apocalypse, but they don't understand. There's no Apocalypse. There's only death. But they think I can make it happen. They just don't understand anything."

"Truer words have never been spoken," Isaac said. "So you're bound here and we're trapped here, because if you bring down the wall around the President's mind he may be able to tap into your power to transcend his Self and bring about apocalyptic ruin on the entire world, all in the name of a religious delusion? Is that about it?"

Choronzon nodded.

"Okay. Then why are you wearing his idealized face and dressed like a superhero?"

"That's kind of a long story," Choronzon said, sadly, flicking a pebble with a gloved finger.

"Jesus fuck," Emma shouted.

Part Sixteen

Blood burst into the President's bathroom anxieties dream and it took everything he had not to turn right around and leave. The President was wallowing around in the filth, trying desperately to get to his feet but with his pants around his ankles, he was having no luck. He had smacked his head

187

against the floor and blood pored freely down his face, mixing with the shit and maggots and tears.

Blood unsheathed his sword and lopped off the President's head.

It popped into the air, arcing black arterial spray, bounced twice and splash landed in a stopped up, overflowing toilet. The head wailed the entire time, cursing with each bounce until sputtering silent, his mouth sinking beneath the thick chunky surface of the toilet bowl's contents.

"Well that was too easy," Blood said.

And it was.

In an instant, he was no longer in the massive public restroom, instead finding himself alone on a burnt, ashy street littered with the smoking remains of people - their silhouettes burned into the sidewalks and building fronts that stretched for as far as he could see. He didn't recognize the street, so he flew up into the air high enough to see that he was on the West Coast. To his right he saw the Hollywood sign burning. Further up the coast there were flashes of blinding light as first one, then another mushroom cloud blossomed into existence.

"No way," he muttered to himself as he watched the blast wave make its way across the landscape, smashing him from the sky and into the concrete below. He tore up nearly a city block as he tumbled, crashing through skeletal cars and sending huge chunks of the road flying. When he finally came to a halt, he pushed himself up off the ground just in time to see a tsunami of fire rushing toward him.

Instinctively, he swung his sword around in front of him, bracing himself against the coming blast.

As the wall of atomic fire struck his sword, it miraculously parted, splitting off to the right and left, curling back upon itself. Slowly the force of the blast shoved him backward, inch by inch, his feet grinding into the concrete, his massive arms straining to hold the sword steady.

And then, as swiftly as it had hit him, the fires were gone.

"Can you believe the Rocket Man used nuclear?" said a voice from the sky above him. "He's a very bad person. And you didn't hear it from me, but he's short and fat, too."

Blood couldn't believe his eyes. Suspended in the air before him was a gigantic humanoid robotic body, barrel-chested with shoulders nearly six feet across, arms and legs made of pistons and gears, and powerful flames shooting out of its feet to keep it airborne. It was standing in mid-air, its taloned fists on its hips, posing as though the paparazzi were clamoring around, begging for its attention.

Mounted on the shoulders of the mechanical beast was the President's head, bright orange and grimacing in what passed for a smile as the atomic winds ruffled his hair.

Part Seventeen

"This guy is deranged," said Choronzon. "That's the first thing you have to understand."

"That won't be a problem," Isaac said. "By the way, can you ease up on your restrictions? I'm getting tired of being a floating brain."

"Oh, yes. Of course," Choronzon laughed. "Now that I'm sure you're the good guys, that's no problem."

"We are *definitely* the good guys," Emma said, suddenly transforming back into Plasmatica. At her side, Isaac reappeared as Django, giving himself a quick once-over before nodding to Plasmatica.

"But his mental problems don't explain your face."

"Or costume," Django added.

"Well," Choronzon started, "as I was saying. I've been bound to his mind." He frowned. "You see, when someone from, you know, where I'm from, gets summoned to your disgusting meat world, we must be grounded. Crowley was right about that, anyway. That's why we only ever communicated telepathically.

"Apparently, this physical body had been prepared quite thoroughly. Not only were there blood sacrifices made in order to force open the split between our worlds, this body was

189

covered in ritual scarification and tattoos that I thought only Crowley was aware of. Once I was in, there was no getting out.

"Without complete immolation, of course," he laughed. "Or possibly skinning." He paused. "I'm not sure about that. Maybe."

Plasmatica and Django looked at each other and sighed.

"So, what? This is some kind of idealized Presidential form?" Plasmatica asked.

Choronzon glanced down at himself and smiled.

"I guess you could say that. He thought he'd be a superhero swooping in to save the day and bring about the Endtimes." He paused. "Although, to be honest, that Endtimes nonsense was coming from the other people in the room. He was really just interested in being hailed as a hero. He was hoping for parades. With tanks."

"So," Django prompted.

"So, this is what we get. The President as world-saving superhero." He stood and struck a pose. "It's not a bad look. I tweaked his features a bit."

"Clearly," Plasmatica said, disgusted.

"Once I refused to become his weapon of mass destruction, that's when the others arrived. Those Nazi buttholes."

"They summoned other, um, entities?"

"Oh no, no, no." He glanced around at the ruins. "I don't think so. I think they're parts of his subconscious made manifest. Kind of like his anima and animus only wrapped in leather and swastikas, sporting machine guns, and protecting the President's primary Self."

"I don't think that's what Jung was talking about," Django said.

"Consciousness is a mysterious place," Choronzon mused. "There is no roadmap or instruction manual. Every understanding is piecemeal and incomplete."

"So if you're not the President, and they're not really the President, where's the President?"

"Oh, he's in here somewhere," he replied, glancing around shiftily. "Skulking about in the shadows. He's stronger than he looks. Practically all Ego and Self. It was all I could do to maintain my independence and put up the wall."

"Okay then. We can't stay in here and we can't leave the President in a coma. Or burn him alive. Or skin him. Does anybody have any other bright ideas?"

"It's not a bright idea," said Django, "but was there graffiti on that wall a minute ago?"

Spray painted in neon green on the crumbled wall of a comic book shop across the street were the words "DAMAGED INCORPORATED WAS HERE!"

As if on cue, a series of bright yellow flashes burst across the sky. What looked like a meteor, all flames and smoke and screeching, came barreling out of the sky, smashing into the comic shop. Debris, toys, and comic books rained down on them and a dust cloud exploded out into the street, enveloping them.

"Stay together!" Choronzon cried. "We're safe inside the circle!"

"What the hell was that?" Django coughed.

Plasmatica stood up, waving the smoke away and smiled. "The cavalry."

Part Eighteen

In the skies above an irradiated Hollywood, an eight-foot-tall flying barbarian with a crimson broadsword did battle with a massive jet-powered robot wearing the President's head. Raging winds swirled around them, whipping Blood's dreads around his head like serpents preparing to strike. The President's fleshy orange jowls flapped in the gale and his wispy hair fluttered on end like the silk from an ear of corn.

A flurry of obscenities flew from the President's mouth as Blood's sword hacked away at his robotic body, sparks and chunks of metal exploding into the air around them. Their fight led them closer and closer to the mushroom clouds and as if in slow motion, they tumbled, still grappling, into the maelstrom. Spinning over and over, they punched and slashed, their howls and swears inaudible over the pounding roar at the

191

dark heart of the nuclear explosion. Fire and lightning raging all around.

The President's robotic hands ripped and tore at Blood, who gripped the President's throat tightly with his free hand while thrusting his sword deep into the guts of the machine. Acrid black smoke billowed from the wound only to whip away, merging with the rest of the smoke and debris enveloping them. Their hair burst into flames and their skin began to bubble and steam. Blood ripped off one of the President's arms, slinging it away into the darkness. Lightning struck the robot in its back, sending shockwaves outward, knocking Blood loose and sending the President hurtling toward the ground in freefall.

Blood smiled through the pain at the sight.

"Fuck you!" he shouted as loudly as he could.

Suddenly the air was clear and the world around them lost focus. Blood pulled up and tried to keep his eyes on the President, but he was gone. He shrugged and healed himself with a thought, then flew a couple of miles higher into the lower atmosphere to get his bearings.

There was nothing to see.

Wherever the President had disappeared to, he'd taken all the detail from the dreamscape with him. The only real landmark was the newly restored Hollywood sign and vague dream representations of buildings and streets laid out with no rhyme or reason. It was as though the President's mind couldn't hold on to the details of the world around him long enough to establish a realistic setting that wasn't dominated by nuclear devastation.

Blood tried to sense the location of Emma and the Professor but got only static. That was strange. It was actual static. Normally he'd either be able to register some form of presence and if she didn't want to respond, there would just be a dull absence. But this was something new and different.

He didn't like it.

"FUCK ME? FUCK YOU!"

Blood turned at the sound of the screaming and was tackled in mid-air by an also restored RoboPresident. Only now he had four robotic spider legs sprouting from his mid-section. They wrapped around Blood, sinking their razor claws into his back, pinning him in the President's embrace.

"THIS IS MY WORLD! MY MIND! WHO THE FUCK ARE YOU TO COME IN HERE AND THINK YOU CAN FUCK WITH ME?" The President pummeled Blood relentlessly as they tore across the sky. "YOU'RE A NOBODY! A NOTHING!" He punched Blood in the face and his nose shattered in a scarlet mist.

The President reared back, ready to unleash another devastating blow, when suddenly Blood was no longer there. In his place was a skinny black kid in a hoodie, jeans, and high-tops. The President paused, confused, and it was just long enough for Malcolm to slip from his grasp, swoop around and change back into Blood, healed, with sword drawn.

"You dirty, sneaky, nig-" Before the President could finish his sentence, Blood swung his broadsword down on top of the President's head, splitting him in two all the way down through his robotic crotch. His body fell apart in two halves, spraying blood, oil, and smoke.

"Watch your mouth, you racist sack of shit," he said, watching the body parts tumble away.

He turned and surveyed the dreamscape below him.

"Now where are you guys?"

He returned his sword to his back-scabbard and closed his eyes. He was pretty sure that the President he'd just halved wouldn't be gone for good since he was still inside the dream and hadn't been jettisoned back into consciousness. Hopefully, he'd be gone long enough that he could find Emma and the Professor and haul ass back home. Or at least get them out and then finish what he came here to do.

It was difficult to describe the sensation of sending out psychic tendrils through the dreamscape of a sleeping mind, but it was like the feeling you get when you squeeze your eyes shut so tight that you begin to see colors and patterns, combined with the phantom sensations that accompany sleep deprivation. There's a texture to a dreamscape that's both fluid and solid at the same time. Shifts in setting can occur in a blink

193

and time means nothing. In fact, history meant nothing. You could have an entire lifetime of memories that never happened, but they'd be as fresh as if you'd lived them in your waking life.

That was one of the dangers of diving into someone else's dreams without having the training they'd received at The Project. By having an avatar and a pre-defined history, it made dream travelling more secure. One was less likely to get lost or caught up in the dreamer's fantasies. Since he couldn't sense the others, he decided to try an old trick and begin inserting references to themselves in the dream history of the President. Little things like graffiti tags on walls; Damaged, Incorporated was here; whispers of Blood and Plasmatica in the stock dialogue of dream figures; echoes of their presence backward into the President's dreaming mind.

This way, the next time he encountered the President, there might be a more measured emotional reaction to Blood's appearance instead of an all-out attack. This President loves celebrity so much, maybe becoming a celebrity in his mind would give them some leeway. Emma could do this sort of thing with ease. It was one of the things that made it so easy to not trust her. Everything came easy to her from what he could tell. Building up these histories required precision and imagination but most importantly, finesse. Malcolm had practiced crafting fake histories, but it didn't come naturally. He had to really concentrate and force it into existence.

Which was why he didn't sense Master Man and Warrior Woman blink into the sky behind him.

Part Nineteen

"Malcolm!" Plasmatica screamed as the dust began to clear. From the shadows, Master Man emerged, bloodied and bruised, one eye swollen shut, but dragging an unconscious Blood by the dreadlocks. Behind him, Warrior Woman stumbled onto the street, also badly beaten. With a grunt, Master Man tossed Blood onto the rubble and coughed, spitting crimson.

Plasmatica stepped forward but Choronzon stopped her.

194

"We're safe in the circle. They can't get to us in here." He frowned. "I'm not sure how they found us though."

"Idiot," Warrior Woman said. "Even an absence has a presence."

"What the fuck are you saying?" Plasmatica snapped. "I think Blood scrambled your brains."

"No, she's right," Choronzon said. "I hadn't taken that into consideration. A blank space on the map doesn't mean nothing's there, but that something hasn't been mapped."

"But they still can't enter the circle?" Django asked.

"No, we're safe in here."

"Then let's try something," Django said, flamboyantly whipping out both Glocks and opening fire. Master Man took the full brunt of the opening salvo, bullets ripping into him by the dozens. He convulsed and flew backward, gore flying once again from all across his body.

Warrior Woman leapt for cover in the comic shop and Plasmatica took the opportunity to run out and grab Blood, carrying him back into the safety of the circle as Master Man struggled to his feet, both the bullet holes and his leather uniform healing before their eyes. In moments, both he and Warrior Woman emerged onto the street as though they'd just walked out of a comic book. Again.

"You can't stay in there forever," Master Man laughed.

"He's right, you know," Django said. "Maybe we should just cut our losses. Even if you can't leave, you can let us out, right?"

Choronzon frowned.

"I suppose I could." He sat on the ground and began fidgeting with pebbles again. "But what about me? I'm still trapped."

Plasmatica knelt beside him. "Maybe just for a while, until we can figure out how to help you." She touched his hand. "There's got to be a way."

"Nobody's going anywhere," the President shouted angrily as he descended from the fiery sky. Blood stirred, hearing the voice.

"Not again," he muttered.

"Seriously? A robot body?" Django scowled. "Dammit."

"You think because you're some sort of weirdo punk band you can just walk in and out of my brain and do what you want?" the President shouted. His robot body paced back and forth outside the protective circle while Master Man and Warrior Woman positioned themselves to his right and left. "You think because you're popular with the kids you can get away with this?"

"What's he talking about?" Django whispered to Plasmatica.

"That was me," Blood said, pushing himself up off the concrete. With a shake of his head, he was healed. "I thought I'd try playing the celebrity card."

Plasmatica nodded. "Good call. That's what I would have done, given the chance."

"Well it doesn't seem to have worked," Django said. "We didn't steal an Emmy win from *The Apprentice* or something did we?"

"No," Choronzon said sadly from the ground. "He's just like this. Nothing satisfies him. A fantasy of the entire west coast destroyed by North Korean nuclear missiles just makes him gloat about 'libtards' getting what they deserve. Nuclear winter is just a minor inconvenience while he goes golfing in Florida. He's really just a spoiled, petulant child in a gigantic robot body."

Choronzon began to softly cry.

"He dreams about rape camps."

"HEY! Pansy!" the President yelled, pointing a huge robotic finger at Choronzon. "You don't get to talk about my dreams with strangers! You shouldn't even be talking to them at all. They're dirty, nasty people."

"Well, he's not wrong," Plasmatica laughed.

"Ooh, what I'd do to you, toots," the President said, leering.

"Okay, now I'm disgusted. Again," she said to Choronzon. "Come on, man. Let us out so we can come back with help."

"I can't," he cried. "You don't understand."

"Fucking right they don't understand," the President shouted. "Nobody understands me!" He spread his arms apart and turned, taking in the entire burning dreamscape around them like a cartoon Mussolini. "I'm not some tool for them to use and toss away. They think I'm going to just give *them* all the power? They think I'm gonna just roll over and let *them* slip into my fucking chair?"

Plasmatica and Django looked at each other, confused.

"What's he talking about?" Blood asked nobody in particular. "And who is this guy?" he asked motioning toward Choronzon.

"Well, to be perfectly honest, I'm not really Choronzon," he said quietly.

Part Twenty

"What the fuck?" Plasmatica and Django said in unison.

"Dude," she continued. "What the hell are you saying? What's going on?"

"If you're *not really* Choronzon, then who are you?" Django asked.

Not-Choronzon sighed.

"I'm the President."

"Like hell you are, you dickless shitbird! *I'm* the fucking President," shouted RoboPresident, stamping his metallic feet and waving his robotic arms in the air.

"We both are, really."

"Then what was all that Choronzon bullshit?" Django yelled.

"Language," Not-Choronzon said softly. "But I understand. Most of what I told you actually happened."

"Can somebody get me up to speed?" Blood asked. Plasmatica touched his forehead and slipped the whole story into his mind. He blinked and rubbed his eyes. "Shit, I still don't know what's going on."

"Choronzon *was* summoned and the binding *was* attempted. It just didn't stick." Not-Choronzon chuckled. "He *was* a famous interdimensional entity after all."

197

"No no no no no no no!" shouted RoboPresident, pressing his monstrous hands against his ears with such force that his talons dug into his skull.

"The Vice-President was the mastermind. He knew that even if they couldn't contain Choronzon for long, they'd be able to use his power to kick off Armageddon. It was going to be like guiding a meteor with targeted explosions. First, they'd push North Korea into launching their nukes, regardless of whether or not they could actually hit the West Coast. It would give the President the chance to respond with fire and fury. But Choronzon saw what was going on and immediately put a stop to it, throwing up the wall to shut down the President's brain and keep these psychotic delusions from becoming a reality. Then he just vanished. Escaped somehow. I don't know what happened to him after that."

Plasmatica sighed while RoboPresident wailed and stomped.

"Why would you even pretend to be Choronzon, then?" she asked.

"I couldn't be sure you'd help me if you knew who I was." He looked sheepishly at the ground and Plasmatica wanted to smack him.

"Maybe immolation *is* the answer," she said.

"We can't set the President on fire," Django said firmly. Then, after a pause, "I mean unless we knew for sure the whole cabinet was going, too."

Plasmatica looked shocked. Django shrugged. Blood nodded.

"Damn skippy."

"Look," Plasmatica said. "So far, we're in a good spot. The President's in a demonically-induced coma. He's contained. If we can get out, then it's all good, right?"

"And what's the Veep gonna do when he takes office?" Blood asked. "You know he's worse than the President, right?"

"He's rotten on the inside," said Not-Choronzon. "I know that much for sure."

"Waitaminute," Django said, kneeling next to Not-Choronzon. "How *do* you know that, exactly? Now you say you're not Choronzon, so how do you know what's inside the Veep? And how did you make this protective circle?"

RoboPresident sat down heavily onto the street, bored. Master Man and Warrior Woman had begun to drift, their attention elsewhere.

"I just did," Not-Choronzon said. "I just know." He stood up and looked longingly at the RoboPresident. "We're not so different, he and I. We both want to make the world a better place. He just thinks all this fire and death is better. I believe in the transcendence of the ego and finding enlightenment."

"Fuck you, retard," said RoboPresident.

"Waitaminute," Django said, taking him by the shoulders and turning him around. "You keep coming back to that ego and enlightenment jive. I find it hard to believe that the President has a single cell in his body with that as a goal. Are you sure you're not Choronzon? Maybe just a little?"

"I know who I am."

"Do you? Do any of us, really?"

You're going to try to get into his head with psychology? Blood thought.

"I can hear you," Not-Choronzon said. "And yes, I do know who I am. I'm the President of the United States."

"FUUUUUUUUUCK YOOOOOOOOU!" shouted RoboPresident.

"The good parts, anyway," he said frowning.

"Think about it, though," Django pushed. "You were able to make this safe space, and you know things that the President shouldn't know. Maybe Choronzon left a little bit of himself in you."

Not-Choronzon teared up a little.

"Do you really think that?"

"I think it's possible. As possible as anything."

Maybe-Choronzon smiled sadly at Django.

"I think you may be right. Maybe there *is* something of him still here," Maybe-Choronzon said pressing his hand to his heart. "Somewhere inside of me."

"GAAAAAAY!" shouted RoboPresident.

199

"Hush, you!" demanded Maybe-Choronzon. He turned to Damaged, Incorporated. "Maybe I just need to transcend *my* ego and touch that piece of enlightenment that he left inside me."

"You're seriously considering this homo nonsense?" RoboPresident asked. "You really are retarded."

"I'm a part of you," Maybe-Choronzon said snippily. "If I'm the r-word, then so are you."

RoboPresident stood up and suddenly Master Man and Warrior Woman snapped back to attention.

"Why don't you come out of your little pansy stand and say that."

"What's a pansy stand?" Blood asked. Plasmatica shrugged.

"Perhaps I should," said Maybe-Choronzon, picking up his cowl and putting it back on. He pulled the chin-strap tight. "Maybe you need to learn a thing or two about manners."

RoboPresident grinned and laughed, clapping his metal hands together.

"Oh yeah. Bring it on, Captain Dipshit!"

"Why do you have to be so crude?"

"Why do you have a pussy for a face?"

"What does that even mean?" Maybe-Choronzon was honestly flustered.

"It means step out of that circle and I'm gonna fuck you in your pretty face, crybaby!"

"You don't even have a dick, man," said Blood. "You're a fucking robot."

"Oh I've got a dick. I've got the biggest dick!"

Master Man and Warrior Woman glanced at each other, embarrassed, as RoboPresident's crotch unfolded and out snapped a gigantic machine gun, larger even than the chain guns they'd been using.

"Say hello to my huge motherfucking friend!" RoboPresident shouted as his crotch gun began firing 60mm mortar rounds at Maybe-Choronzon. The protective circle was engulfed in fire and chaos as the shells exploded in a steady stream, filling the air with shrapnel and smoke. Everybody in the circle flinched, crouching down in anticipation of all sorts of violent pain, but the circle held.

RoboPresident's crotch kept firing until he was out of ammo, and as the dust settled the barrel of his gun kept spinning, whirring metallically until finally snapping to a halt and retracting back inside the robotic groin from which it sprang.

"May as well be firing blanks, ass-munch," said Blood.

RoboPresident scowled and began wailing unintelligibly in anger.

Maybe-Choronzon's eyes suddenly began to glow eerily and he turned to face RoboPresident.

"I see it now," he said, his voice echoing softly. Plasmatica looked at Blood and Django, confused. They both shrugged back. She motioned with her head for Django to say something.

"Um, hey fella," he tried. "What's that you see now?"

He turned to Django, his face alight with inner fire.

"Choronzon *did* leave a piece of himself in me." His voice was more felt than heard, echoing inside their heads. "I have been afraid, but I *am* the transcendence. I *am* the dissolution of the ego."

"You're fucking nutso!" shouted RoboPresident.

"You showed me the truth," he said, turning to RoboPresident. "I see now that you are right in your vulgar way. We must merge if there's ever to be peace for this world."

"Um, what?" Django asked.

"Don't worry, friends. Choronzon is inside of me." He stepped out of the circle. "And I will soon be inside of you," he said to RoboPresident.

"What the fuck?" said RoboPresident, Plasmatica, Django, Blood, Master Man, and Warrior Woman.

Mostly-Choronzon slowly undid the fly of his pants and a blinding light was released. He pulled forth an anaconda of pure energy and as RoboPresident raised his arms to defend himself they were sliced off cleanly, leaving molten stumps in the wake of the transcendent member.

201

"Um, guys," Django said quietly to Plasmatica and Blood. "What are the chances that we could slip out through the bathroom anxiety dream?"

"What the hell do you think you're doing?" shouted RoboPresident.

"It's worth a shot," Plasmatica said. "I really don't want to see what happens next."

"I was hoping to punch those fucking Nazis again, but yeah," Blood said. "I'm in."

Master Man and Warrior Woman stood transfixed as Mostly-Choronzon put his hands on his hips and arched his back, energy whipping and crackling from his groin. RoboPresident stumbled backwards, unable to catch himself with his arm-stumps and fell onto the street.

The last thing Plasmatica saw, glancing back as they launched themselves into the sky, was Mostly-Choronzon effortlessly yanking the President's head from its robot body and lovingly pulling it down toward his plasma pecker. The President's screams were suddenly muffled, and she tried to forget everything she'd seen.

Part Twenty-One

"Oh shit oh shit oh shit," Plasmatica said as she tried to open a gap to the President's bathroom anxieties. Sparks flew, but space wouldn't part, no matter how hard she concentrated.

Django and Blood watched their flank, making sure the Nazi Super Soldiers weren't going to suddenly appear out of nowhere.

"Dammit! That entryway is closed." She turned to the others. "I guess getting sodomized by a giant cock of pure energy pushes all the other anxieties out of your head."

"Okay, how about we take the high road, then? At least we can get a lay of the land," Django suggested. Blood and Plasmatica nodded and all three of them flew as high as they could before hitting the edges of the dreamscape.

"I never really knew there were borders," Blood said. "I guess it makes sense."

"From what I've seen, there's usually a mechanism in place to keep the world moving around you so you never really hit an edge," Plasmatica replied. "Guess that's out the window now, too."

"What do you think this, um, merging will accomplish?" Django asked.

"Who knows?" she said, looking down at the remains of Washington below them. "The pentagram is still burning, so either they're not finished or RoboPresident overpowered Choronzon? I don't have a clue."

"Maybe Choronzon, or whoever he was, will win and we all just get to go home," Blood offered. "Maybe something good will happen for a change."

"It's already begun," said Mostly-Choronzon, appearing in a flash before them.

"Christ, don't do that!" Plasmatica shouted.

"I apologize," he said softly. "I'm only beginning to realize the extent of my abilities. And my final purpose"

Django didn't like the sound of that.

"I don't like the sound of that."

Mostly-Choronzon smiled and as he did, his entire body shifted, his idealized president in a superhero costume flaked like ash and blew away on the breeze, leaving behind a glorious figure of light and energy. He was beautiful in a pants-peeing terrifying sort of way.

"No worries, Isaac," he said. "When Choronzon left a piece of himself here to safeguard the world, it was as though he'd stayed himself. He," a pause. "*We* don't suffer from those sorts of limitations. Each part of Choronzon is a whole. I was the unknowing gatekeeper, left behind while he completed his work."

"His work?" Blood asked.

"He planted bombs," Mostly-Choronzon said happily. "And I am their fuse."

"Not to be a buzzkill, but what about us?" Plasmatica cut in. "I don't give a shit anymore about what happens in here. I just want to get out and go home."

"That *would* be the best possible outcome," Django agreed.

"I want to hear more about these bombs," Blood said.

Mostly-Choronzon smiled at him. "You understood all along. I see that." He turned to look over the wasteland beneath them and sighed. "There *was* a chance. It's why he left me here in the shell of the President's better self. To see if I could find some sort of unity. To see if I could heal him."

His entire visage darkened.

"There is no healing that monster." He turned back to Damaged, Incorporated. "So he is gone. Purged. I am what's left, and I am not for this flesh."

"Again," Plasmatica interrupted. "We. Want. To. Go. Home."

"You shall." He smiled. "You will be the only ones who know what truly happened this day. Whether you share my story as a cautionary tale for future rulers or keep your secrets to your graves won't change anything that happens here. The fire has been lit."

He waved his hand and the sky began to spiral, losing focus until finally an opening appeared.

"Good travels, my friends. I hope what happens here doesn't destroy your world."

"Wait, what?" Django said before suddenly all three of them were whisked through the portal and found themselves starting awake in the lab.

Part Twenty-Two

In the twenty-four hours since their return to waking life, Emma, Mal, and Isaac had a slightly less hard time processing the revelations coming out of Washington than the rest of the world did. Slightly. All three found themselves unable to stop watching the incessant news coverage on every channel. The Project Mephistopheles lounge had a wall of video monitors and the same story was blaring from each of them: "Cannibal Murder Orgy in the Oval Office!"

The President had been found dead, burned alive while sitting in his chair behind the Resolute desk in the Oval Office. Spontaneous human combustion was the general consensus. It was the rest of the story that was finding very different tractions with very different audiences.

Initially it was all rumors and crackpot conspiracy theories, but then cell-phone video leaked and all hell broke loose. No matter what screen they looked at they saw fragments of the shaky, grainy footage.

The body of an intern had been splayed from sternum to groin. Her intestines had been removed and laid out around the bald eagle rug, forming a ring just large enough for the Vice President to be found kneeling in its center, his eyes clawed out by his own hand and masturbating furiously, his penis shredded and bloody. The rest of the cabinet, including hangers-on who had long since been thought removed from their posts, were writhing around on the couches and the floor, shrieking like animals and tearing into one another with their teeth and nails.

A prominent alt-right blogger with a complexion like a late-stage alcoholic could be seen gnawing on the President's charred crotch. A leathery, bleached blonde Advisor to the President sat in a corner, shrieking and peeling strips of skin from her face with a strange ancient-looking dagger and feeding them to the Speaker of the House. A little man who looked like a turtle cried and ate his own feces. Everyone was nude and covered in bites and scratches. Blood flowed freely from every single person in the room: The President's entire cabinet and advisors. Some rutted like animals while others fought and wrestled, erections prominent in the blurred television footage.

No one had revealed the source of the leaked video yet, but one eye-witness, another intern, clean-cut with a fashionable haircut described the scene as like "Something out of the *Texas Chainsaw Massacre*. Not the first one, where they implied everything, but the crazy-ass second one. The one with Dennis Hopper."

205

Republican talking heads were already calling the video a Left-Wing Hoax and vehemently insisting that Hillary Clinton's deleted emails had the answers about what had really happened, while commentators on the Left were calling it evidence of Russian occult influence peddling. The only thing anyone could agree on was the fact that there was a sudden and immediate power vacuum in Washington. It was beginning to look like an episode of *Designated Survivor* as the Secretary of Housing and Urban Development was the next in line for succession and the only member of the cabinet not in the Oval Office, but it seemed nobody felt the situation was quite desperate enough to find him.

It wouldn't be until days later that it was revealed that every single person in line for the Presidency had suffered some sort of stroke, debilitating injury, or had simply gone missing.

"Choronzon doesn't fuck around," Mal said.

"No shit," Emma said.

"Is it too much to kind of wish he'd hit the Senate, too?"

Emma frowned and changed the subject. "Miranda, what happens now?"

From speakers hidden in the walls and ceiling, Miranda's soothing voice replied, "That's a matter for debate. Some are calling for a new election, others for installing Hillary Clinton. Some are calling it a 'sign from God' and saying the Federal Government should be disbanded entirely."

There was a moment of silence.

"That last suggestion isn't finding a lot of traction," she said.

"I'll bet there's a ton of angry white motherfuckers out there who are all for it," Malcolm said, bitterly.

"True, most of that internet chatter is from the alt-right and neo-Nazi element. I'd suggest that while vocal and loud, they don't quite have the numbers or the influence to stage a coup. Not anymore, that is."

Professor Warren had been strangely quiet in his mobile unit while this discussion went on. Emma reached out to him psychically.

Are you okay in there, Professor?

Yes, yes. It's just a lot to take in. All this chaos.

They brought it on themselves.

They did, I know. But still. There should have been another way.

We did what we could. Which was pretty much nothing, but still. They were the ones playing with forces they couldn't control. They're the ones who got arrogant and apocalyptic. Maybe Choronzon did the right thing. They were out of control.

Maybe. It's still a lot to take in.

"Oh shit, guys," Mal said, oblivious to their psychic discussion. "Who does that look like to you?"

On one of the screens, a pasty, pockmarked blonde man and his equally pasty and pockmarked blonde wife were being interviewed by a fringe internet site. He was wearing a black trenchcoat and she had her hair braided like Brunnhilde. Though they were sickly and a little scabby, they did bear a certain abstract resemblance to Master Man and Warrior Woman. It was something about the condescension in their tones and the way they kept adjusting their posture as though they were posing for Nazi propaganda posters.

"You are shitting me," Emma said. "Turn it up."

"--- unmistakable evidence that this was an Antifa insurrectionist coup attempt. Probably tied directly to Black Lives Matters. I wouldn't be surprised if blood tests revealed some sort of high-power home-made hallucinogen in everyone's bloodstream."

"Probably airborne. Piped into the Oval Office from some commie sleeper agent on the inside," the woman said. "The same stuff in contrails, I'd bet."

"They're the real fascists. Condemning Free Speech and proselytizing for the mongrelization of this great country."

"The President will go down in history as a martyr! Every person who died --"

"Or went insane," she added.

"Will be remembered as blood nurturing the roots of the Real America!" He pointed at the camera. "There will be a reckoning, people. All you punk lesbians and socialist nigger faggots are going to find out soon that---"

207

Before he could go on, a man in a clown mask interrupted the interview, punching him in the face and then running away whooping and hollering, shouting "The Cheeto is toast!"

"My nobe!" the white nationalist shouted nasally as he began to cry. "He bwoke my nobe!"

"You asshole!" his partner shouted while trying to keep from getting blood on her. She turned to the camera and said, "There *will* be a reckoning." Then the feed cut out.

Everyone stared at the black screen for a moment, trying to process what they'd just seen.

"Was that..." Mal started.

"Couldn't have been," Emma said. "How'd they get out?"

"Fucking Nazis," said Isaac from his crackly speaker. "Miranda, please start monitoring white nationalist chatter and keep me informed of flare-ups."

"Already started, Isaac."

"Fucking Nazis."

On his viewscreen a poop emoji appeared.

Who We Be

R. Mike Burr

Mike Burr loves dogs, hates Big Macs, and has not yet been approached by any foreign agents. His writing has appeared in Prefix Magazine, Psycho Drive-In, and Tropics of Meta. He contributed a story to PDI Press' first short story collection, *Noirlathotep: Tales of Lovecraftian Crime* and is currently at work on a story for PDI's second *Noirlathotep* collection along with a series of essays on David Allan Coe. He is also a supporter of The Eugene V. Debs Foundation and The Satanic Temple.

Dan Lee

Dan Lee is a freelance writer, film critic, independent author, and horror culture correspondent from Tennessee. His work has appeared in several sites and 'zines and can also be found on his website at dannoofthedeadblog.wordpress.com or through his social media presence @dotdblog. He also contributed a story to PDI Press' first short story collection, *Noirlathotep: Tales of Lovecraftian Crime.*

Paul Brian McCoy

Paul Brian McCoy is the Editor-in-Chief of both Psycho Drive-In and PDI Press. In 2011 he published his first novel, *The Unraveling: Damaged Inc. Book One*, followed shortly by a collection of short stories, *Coffee, Sex, & Creation.* He contributed the 1989 chapter to *The American Comic Book Chronicles: The 1980s*, and also kicked off Comics Bulletin Books with *Mondo Marvel* Volumes One through Four and then PDI Press with *Marvel at the Movies: 1977-1998, Marvel at the Movies: Marvel Studios*, and *Spoiler Warning: Hannibal Season One: An Unauthorized Critical Guide.* He also contributed a story to PDI Press' first short story collection, *Noirlathotep: Tales of Lovecraftian Crime.* Paul is unnaturally preoccupied with zombie films and sci-fi television. He can be found babbling on Twitter at @PBMcCoy and posting odd drawings on Instagram at /paulbrianmccoy.

John E. Meredith

J. Meredith is a freelance writer from the American Midwest. He will go on about damn-near anything if you let him, from movies and music to the world and himself. A Halloween baby, he has a natural tendency toward things dark and awful, or at least shot in black-and-white, and he should probably be on some kind of medication. He also contributed a story to PDI Press' first short story collection, *Noirlathotep: Tales of Lovecraftian Crime*. Feel free to haunt him on his Facebook page /John E. Meredith, or contact him at scribe6903@yahoo.com.

Rick Shingler

Rick Shingler is a contributing Psycho at psychodrivein.com, where he is sometimes allowed to ramble about TV shows and movies. He's also the author of *The Perilous Journeys of Pericles, Prince of Tyre*, a space opera novel adapted from an obscure Shakespeare play. The novel, despite being readily available on Amazon's Kindle store, remains largely unseen by a public which, frankly, doesn't know what it's missing. He has also scripted forthcoming comic book stories for Empire Comics Lab and contributed a story to PDI Press' first short story collection, *Noirlathotep: Tales of Lovecraftian Crime*. Rick lives in New Jersey with a lovely person who allows him to sleep next to her and a small handful of humans who insist on calling him dad.

Jimbo Valentine

Jimbo Valentine was born in Fairmont, WV but has resided in the Huntington, WV area for 15 years, where he has been doing graphic design for 10 years and has created over 1400 gigposters, dozens of album layouts, and countless merchandise designs. He has been the resident designer at the V Club since 2009 and is the art director of the Huntington Music and Arts Festival. He can be contacted for commissioned work through his website: Amalgam Unlimited (https://amalgamunlimited.com/).

68360755R00120

Made in the USA
San Bernardino, CA
02 February 2018